Enchanted Notions

Barry Bonnell

Valetis
Publishing

Enchanted Notions

A Valetis Publishing Original

Valetis Publishing
2102 179th Ct NE
Redmond, WA 98052
Valetispublishing.com

ISBN: 0996912800
ISBN-13:978-0-9969128-0-8

DEDICATION

To all those sensitive souls in the world who would like to use their power for good, and not be misunderstood. To romance, action, and urban fantasy fans in all the worlds temporal and spiritual. To the Goddess...

Blessed be...

Valetis
Publishing

Contents

ACKNOWLEDGMENTS

This book would not be possible without the support and encouragement of the real people who appear as characters herein… Yes, some of them are real people, and they are the sweetest, most dedicated practitioners anyone could hope to know.

Also, this effort would not be possible without the support and understanding of the lovely Stefnie, my wife of 42 years as of this writing, who is known among the aficionados, owners, and operators at Enchanted Moments gift and metaphysical shop, as the Sewing Goddess.

And I can't forget my good friends and proof readers, Valli Eichstedt, and Oliver "Chip" Batcheller. Their input has been invaluable.

Valetis
Publishing

Jason - 1

Jason cruised down Main Street in his little red '67 Corvette with a white top, not too worried about traffic, not since the bypass passed. Most traffic ran into the valley around the East Fork of the Little Miami River where there used to be farms. The big-box stores were out there now and Main had suffered the consequences.

Where is this place? Jason thought. *I know it's in the middle of this block, on the west side, and I heard they like purple.*

At 6'4" his rough styled but parted short blond hair brushed the inside of the convertible top, but he was comfortable enough as he drove north on what people used to call 50. The first U.S. route to span the entire country had crossed the Little Miami at the ford, where the gristmill used to be, hence, the name Milford. Nobody paid attention to the route number anymore, now it was just Main Street, pretty much the same street in every other mid-west town like Milford, Ohio. All the main streets were populated by hundred-year-old two story red brick buildings with store fronts on the sidewalk and apartments or office space or storage above. Clapboard constructions were mixed in here and there, but as they had burned up in days past, the wood buildings were replaced with brick.

The old stores had failed one-by-one when the US routes turned into interstates that passed them by. Sad really, but nostalgia still attracted a smattering of customers to the quaint old storefronts.

Maybe the old Woolworth's had become an antique mall, the former hardware store--another antique mall. Maybe the renovated old bank on the corner had struggled through four different restaurants in turn and is now a pizza parlor or a fancy cupcake shop, or an antique mall. The same thing had happened on all the old main streets where stores evolved into the assorted mix required to lure curious, sentimental shoppers. The new stores relied on charming, historic ambiance to pull clientele away from Wal-Mart and Target.

Prices on Main are high out of necessity, due to the low foot traffic, and products must be different enough to attract a more discerning crowd.

Only the historical society senior citizens remember the original stores and the new owners don't really care, all they want is more customers, updated plumbing, updated wiring, a non-leaky roof and a fresh coat of paint. The buildings have remained the same for more than a century; only the use of them has changed.

Jason craned his neck to peek under the leafy pear trees, Cleveland Select pear trees to be exact, that lined the street and he checked his mirrors often, to make sure he didn't block another motorist, but there were no other cars on a Thursday morning. Trees obscured the sign, but he noticed a flash of purple in the display windows and the purple awnings of a store as he passed.

Enchanted Notions is a gift store, but a very special kind that sells an eclectic mix of items that range from crystal healing stones to porcelain fairies through books, essential oils, decorated hats and other unique clothing. In addition to the myriad products, a patron might enjoy services that include Tarot reading, Palmistry, Reiki, tuning fork healing, Astrology, or Chakra balancing, as well as every other metaphysical technique practiced since ageless time.

Jason knew one of the owners, Robin, from high school, but hadn't seen her since their ten year reunion a couple of years before. After graduation he had entered Ohio State University and popped out as a brand new veterinarian eight years later. He had married a girl from Loveland and made his home there, close to the in-laws, and built his business in an up-scale strip mall just a couple miles down the street. His new bride took only three years to trade up to a real doctor; her own 45 year-old Gynecologist on his third try at matrimony.

Jason didn't suffer from guilt; the breakup was no fault of his own. Perhaps he claimed a bit of responsibility when he searched hard enough, because he was too generous when it came to employees or anybody who approached him with a sob story. His wife turned out to be a simple gold digger, and she figured he'd never afford the kind of lifestyle she envisioned. The divorce hit him hard, in terms of personal failure and a setback to his ego, but he was happy with the settlement because she left with her clothes, makeup, a Mercedes SUV, iPhone, her Shih Tzu, and that was it. He was free and clear in a material sense, and with his rugged good looks, he felt like his prospects were pretty good if he wanted to find somebody new.

Loveland had become a progressive community with lots of upward moving professionals, the perfect place for a vet, since the mini-dog toting, Barbie doll wives could afford a $250 fee every time Snuggles got the sniffles. Jason had been unattached for a year and his ex still expected him to tend to her little dog for free. He thought the ex looked ridiculous, horribly off balance, with her new double d's. Perhaps she'd leave the Gynecologist for the younger Plastic Surgeon? Nothing would surprise him less.

Jason drove around the block and retraced Main back to Enchanted Notions where he parallel parked in the first open spot a couple of spaces past the entrance. He wanted a good luck charm for his 'baby' sister, Honore, now in her late-twenties, for her trip to Mount Everest where she intended to scale the highest peak on the planet.

There was a bit more method to his madness, but he couldn't really put his finger on why. He was just drawn to the shop from the moment he'd first heard about it from classmates that he'd kept in touch with. A magnetic pull had tugged at him to investigate the strange shop, but he never could put together a reasonable excuse to drop in, not until he thought of the idea of a good luck charm for his sister.

Jason noticed a calico cat in the left side display window and thought the animal was stuffed, a child's doll, until the tail twitched and the head turned with his passing while the eyes pierced him as if he were a sparrow, or a mouse. He reached for the doorknob and read a hand written sign at eye level, "Don't let the cats out!"

The cat in the window still stared and he figured that particular one was no factor but the sign was plural, and a black one sat on the floor just inside the full-length glassed door. This cat stared just as hard as the calico and Jason wasn't sure how to enter, or sure he wanted to, not with the cats making eyes at him like he was lunch.

Have I worked on these cats, he wondered? *Maybe they didn't have too good an experience and they're after some payback.*

He peered around the sign and tapped on the glass. Somewhere within he heard a muffled voice, "Come on Pye, here kitty, kitty, kitty," and the black trotted away. Jason opened the door and stepped in while he transferred the knob behind his back to shut it before any unnoticed cats darted out between his legs.

He looked up and saw two women behind a counter dead ahead that extended out into the middle of the store from the left side wall. One woman sported short-dishwater blond hair piled on top with chopsticks to hold it together, and the other was a taller, chestnut brunette with a French bob. The women stopped what they were doing and stared at him, just like the cats had. The hair on his neck stood up and he hesitated, a decision worked inside his brain, and just before he stepped back out he heard a sultry voice call his name.

"Jason, my old friend, I'm so glad you stopped by," Robin said as she slipped with feline grace out from an aisle of goods to stand at the end of the checkout counter. Jason studied his friend, not recognizing her for a second because his attention snapped to her black top hat adorned with a silver buckle medallion on a field of pheasant feathers. Her blond hair was up, probably under the hat, Jason reasoned, since he remembered longish hair. She was already tall at five nine, and the hat made her look seven feet, *Stunning*, he thought. His eyes slid down to take in the whole picture and he was shocked that Robin appeared so young and trim. She wore a full length slinky black dress with long sleeves that ended in multi-tipped tapers that extended beyond her long fingers, fingers that were adorned with blood colored nails. She sported an earthy stone necklace that drew his eye down to a subtle curve of breast that peeked out of the v-shaped neckline. Not too much, not too deep, just enough to be spicy but not slutty, not off balance at all, not like his ex-wife's new breasts. The hem of the dress tickled her ankles in the same way her sleeves were cut, but the dress sported multiple layers that overlapped at the hem in long tapered points, or was the layering an illusion because of the way the dress hugged her figure and spilled around her feet that modeled spiked heels the color of her fingernails? Jason didn't know about the layers, but wanted to find out. *Stop that*, he said in his mind.

Her waist was belted in black felt with a silver buckle that matched the medallion on her hat. The dress hung smooth on her curves, which were evident, but tasteful. She placed one hand on the counter and one hand at her slender waist and waited until Jason had finished his gawk.

She was used to it and enjoyed it if the man wasn't too obvious, and this one was just right.

She beckoned with a wave and Jason somnambulated in her direction. He stuck out his hand to shake but she wrapped him up in a big hug, "I don't shake with my old classmates, I hug. I hope you don't mind?"

"No, no, it's fine," he said and returned the hug. "I'm so glad to see you Robin, you look great. I love the hat," he said, and withdrew to arm's length.

"Monica, this is my old friend and high school classmate, Jason," Robin nodded to the chestnut with the bob.

Monica owned the shop with Robin and she continued to stare like one of the cats. She smiled and stuck out her hand, "We'll have to get to know each other a little better before we exchange hugs, but don't worry, it won't take too long, I imagine."

Jason took her hand; she sucked in a breath and gripped his hand tighter and stared wide eyed into his eyes, her mouth turned to an O shape while her left hand rose to cover her chest just below her throat. A chill shivered down his spine before he said, "Pleased to meet you Monica," and she continued to hold his hand.

Monica's eyes relaxed, a smile stretched across her face, "A seventh son," she said, and let go.

"What?"

"Jason, you naughty boy, you never mentioned you were a seventh son," Robin said as three other women converged on them, unseen by Jason.

"I knew it when he walked in the door," startled him from behind. "Hi, I'm Sara," she said as Jason turned to greet her. She was the dishwater blond that he'd spied when he first entered, now she stood on his side of the counter. Short and stout, she took his hand in both of hers and stared up into his eyes, "We could set the circle now."

"Hey Jason, it's good to see you," came from behind him again. He unclamped his hands from Sara and turned to meet this new voice that seemed familiar, as she wedged in next to Robin.

He recognized her immediately, "Oh, hello Susan," he said. "I didn't know you worked here, or maybe you're a customer."

"No, no, I work here. I'm a Reiki Master, and Robin's cousin. I bet you didn't know that either."

"Cousins, wow, what a small world," he said. Susan had been a classmate as well. "You're right, I never knew that."

"Aren't you going to introduce me," sideswiped him again as another woman entered from Sara's side in the now crowded aisle in front of the counter. He turned again, *where are they all coming from*? This one was tall, like Robin, with long, straight blond hair that reached to her slender waist.

"Of course I'll introduce you. Jason, this is Francine, she's Tarot, Palms, and Reiki," Robin said.

Francine took his hand in both of hers, just like Sara had done, and stared into his eyes. "Yes, I see, a seventh son. I'm so pleased to meet you."

Nothing happened for a few pregnant seconds while Francine gazed into Jason's eyes like she was searching for something inside his skull.

"Let him go Francy," Robin chided.

"Sorry."

"No problem, I'm happy to be surrounded by beautiful women, but what's the big deal about me being a seventh son?"

"Where are all your big brothers, Jason? I don't remember them at school," Robin asked and Jason spun like a top to address her.

"We moved here just before our junior year and my brothers were gone by then, in college or married with their own families all around the country."

"Mind if I ask about your father's family?" Monica inquired.

"Ok, I guess, what do you want to know?" He answered as he revolved.

"How many brothers did he have?" Robin jumped in.

"Same as me, six."

"And where was he in the mix?" Susan asked as Jason swiveled to face each question.

"Same as me, tail-end-Charlie; well, as far as brothers go, I have a younger sister, so I guess she's really the tail end."

"A seventh son of a seventh son, excellent!" Monica added and Jason swirled.

"I've heard something about old wives tales and seventh sons but what does it mean? I'm no different from anybody else."

"Oh, you're different all right. You have healing powers, among other things, probably," Monica answered. "What do you do for a living?"

"He's a vet," Robin answered for him.

"See," Sara said. "You're a healer."

"Cats and dogs, and there's nothing mystical about it. They come in sick or hurt and I give 'em shots and pills and casts, nothing too inspirational about that." Just then, Jason noticed three cats sitting erect and attentive on the counter between him and Monica; the black in the middle, and the calico from before on the right with a big fluffy gray to the left. All three stared at him and all three cocked their heads. The black raised a paw as if to shake and Jason took the paw between his thumb and forefinger, shook it a couple times and let it go, as if it were the most natural thing in the world to shake hands with a cat.

"Excellent," Monica said again. "This is Pyewhacket. The cats like you, Jason, and as a rule they don't like strangers. Do you realize that you just shook hands with a cat?"

"Um, yeah, I guess. Seemed like the right thing to do at the time."

"Oh, believe me, that was the right thing to do," Francine said.

"See? Seventh son of a seventh son; you have power you don't even know about," Sara added.

"Let's not get ahead of ourselves ladies," Robin said. "What can we do for you Jason?" Susan asked.

"Well, you know my little sister Honore, right?"

"Yes, she was a class or two behind us," Robin answered.

"That's right. She's been living in the Seattle area since college and she's gaga about mountain climbing. She works as a guide for a group up there that takes fat cats on climbs up Mount Rainier, and all over the west really, all the way up to McKinley in Alaska, and some in Europe too."

"Wow, sounds scary," Francine interrupted.

"Right, I know, that's why I wanted to get her a good luck charm. She's headed off to Mount Everest in a couple weeks for her first try at that one. She wants to summit so she can use that experience to get into the big money guide business. Did you know it costs something like eighty thousand bucks to do a guided climb on Everest?"

"You're kidding?" Monica asked.

"Honest to God," Jason added.

"Is she tall and blond and beautiful too, like you?" Sara asked.

"Yes! Oh, my, gosh is she ever," Susan answered for him as he turned a light shade of scarlet. "She's blue-eyed and over six feet tall. She was a star volleyball player and a track star too. Set the state record in the pole vault, high jump, and long jump, if you can believe that. She earned herself a scholarship to UCLA for volleyball, if I remember correctly. She could have been a movie star for sure."

"Yep, you got it. That's my little sister," Jason affirmed and tapped the tip of his nose.

"Ok, Jason, we're gonna' fix you right up," Robin assured him.

"First we need to take him next door," Monica added.

". . .and?" Robin asked, wondering where her partner was headed with this.

"Jason, are you up for an adventure, something you never dreamed of doing?" Monica asked.

"As long as it's not dangerous, illegal, immoral, or unethical, I guess."

"It's none of those things, well, depending on your definition of moral, but certainly not something to be afraid of, and you'll have an amulet like none in the world, because you'll be making it yourself," Monica continued.

"You mean like a craft project or something?"

"Yes, something like that," Monica answered. "Sara, would you go out first and provide security for us please?"

"My pleasure," Sara replied and moved to the front door.

Robin knew exactly where they were headed now and took the bewildered man by the elbow before he could ask the obvious question about the need for security. They followed Sara to the door where Robin hesitated until Sara looked around and then nodded her head toward the door. Francine and Susan turned the other way and strode deeper into the store.

The cats all jumped down but Monica admonished them, "Not you three. You can wait in the window if you want." The cats meowed and jumped into the display window where Jason had seen the calico when he first entered the shop.

Monica followed the others out where Jason watched Sara turn over a rock in the grass verge that served as a planter around one of the pear trees in front of the store. Robin turned him left and guided him to a storefront that was actually the third door to the north, where the windows were painted over with a starry night scene that incorporated a big silver crescent moon.

A vertical banner hung on the door:

Enchanted Notions

Spiritual
Wellness
and
Healing
Studio

Robin produced a key from somewhere that made Jason wonder, . . .*did she get that from a pocket or up her sleeve, or where?*

Robin led him in, flipped a light switch and held the door for Monica. Jason noticed that there was nothing in the room but a long folding-leg table surrounded by chairs, also the folding kind, and next to the wall another table that looked like one of those portable massage platforms he'd seen set up in malls occasionally.

"I expected a display of charms," Jason started, but he was interrupted by Robin.

"Don't worry sweetie, you're not in any danger. We're just gonna' make the very best good luck charm in the whole world. Sit down, please."

Jason sat at the end of the table but before he asked how he could make a charm when there were no supplies in sight, the door opened and Francine entered with Susan.

"We picked these out, you can choose the one you want," Francine said as she laid more than a dozen pendant necklaces on the table. All of them were carved out of stone with leather thongs or hempen rope either tied directly through holes in the stone for the larger ones, or affixed with a wrapping and small ring of silver. They ranged from donut shaped, to a naked, well endowed, headless female body.

"Francy, this is a fertility charm," Robin said and held up the naked woman.

"Well, it could be a strong woman charm when he gets done with it. You know, the unconquerable feminine divine, he could cast to that, or something," she replied.

"No, I don't think so," Monica admonished and Robin disappeared the trinket into an invisible pocket.

"What do you mean, 'when he's done with it'?" Jason asked. "These all look like they're finished already."

"Don't worry honey," Francine comforted. "All will be made clear in a minute. The less you know now, the better."

The door opened again and Sara entered, "All clear, and I have a worm." She held her hand out to Jason, "Here, hold this worm in your left hand, the heart hand."

"What! I will do no such thing."

"You want a charm that will be guaranteed to protect your sister, don't you?" Susan asked.

"Guaranteed? What do you mean? If she dies on the mountain I get my money back?"

"No, of course not, she'll be guaranteed to come back perfectly healthy, having suffered no ill effects at all," Monica replied. "And we're not gonna' charge you for the charm, so you won't get your money back. It's not that kind of guarantee."

"Listen, I. . ."

"Oh hold the worm you pansy," Sara chided. "It won't bite and we'll let you wash your hands after. What've you got to lose?"

No man likes to be called a pansy, so Jason took the worm between thumb and forefinger as he wondered; *what the hell have I gotten into?*

"Not like that. It has to be in your palm," Sara directed and shook her head.

"Wait a minute," Robin said, "Let's think about this for a second. We don't want to take this dark. We have a seventh son. There's no need to use a worm. Besides, we only use a worm for protection if it's needed, and we've never actually needed one, not even during the attack last Hallows Eve."

"Robin, she's going to climb Mount Everest. Ev-er-rest!" Sara argued.

Monica jumped in, "Robin's right. We don't do that unless absolutely necessary, and since there are five of us, plus Jason, the cost will be negligible spread over all of us. I don't think we'll need it. We'll cast without it and see what happens. We can always do it again and add the worm--how's that?"

"Fine, so we're takin' the cost, no problem," Sara repeated and carried the worm back out to its rock.

"I don't understand any of this," Jason said. "What do you mean 'cost,' and what about the worm, and what about me making an amulet when they're done already, and what kind of attack, and you said it would be free, but now you're talking about cost for cryin' out loud. I just wanted a good luck charm like you get in one of those bubble gum prize machines, that's all."

"Jason, you didn't come to us for a bubble gum charm, I'm pretty sure. It's all right honey. Please trust me and it will all be perfectly evident when we're done. You are in no danger at all," Robin's calming voice took effect and Jason relaxed in his chair; waited as Sara re-entered the room.

"Don't worry Jason, we'll accept the cost when we get to that part," Monica added.

Jason started another question about cost, but Robin stopped him mid breath, "We'll all join for the cost, it's not a big deal," she said and the others agreed in turn.

"Don't think about economics right now, Jason," Monica said before he could form another word. "We've got it covered. Just quiet your mind and think about the amulet. Give me your hand."

He did.

Amulets - 2

Monica sat on Jason's right, turned toward him enough
to make the handshake comfortable. With knees
intermeshed, she closed her eyes, and dropped her head as
if she were looking at the ground. She held his hand in
both of hers then bent at the waist, placed her elbows on
her spread legs, and stilled for a few moments.

Jason thought he'd grabbed a heat pack because her
touch was so warm. He inspected their clasped hands and
discovered nothing to explain the excessive heat.

"I want you to focus on your desire to protect your
sister," Monica directed. "Close your eyes, relax, and try to
remember the shapes of the charms on the table--no, not
the naked lady, the ones left on the table. Men! I swear.
Francine, that's your fault."

"Sorry."

"Now we have to fix it, so relax and concentrate. In
your mind, just imagine the naked lady charm, pull a pencil
out of your pocket, perhaps you have an imaginary pocket
keeper and it's full of pencils and pens. Pick out a sharp
pencil with a brand new eraser and imagine a sheet of
paper on the table. Now convert the three dimensional
naked lady into a black and white pencil sketch in two
dimensions, just the outline. You don't have to draw it,

just put it on paper using your imagination, and sink it right onto the paper.

"Good, now use the eraser to rub out the image of the naked lady, all the way, until there is nothing left but white paper.

"Very good, now remember the shapes still on the table. Is there one that stands out? Don't answer; just see it in your mind. You can open your eyes if you need to for a bit."

He did, and studied them all for a full minute.

"Ok, when you're ready, close your eyes again and concentrate on the image of the pendants. The one you're looking for might be brighter, as if it were glowing a little, or it might be more in focus, or it might look a little bigger than the rest, or float above the table, anything that makes it stand out. It could be all of or any combination of those traits, or even something that I haven't mentioned."

He found the one that stood out, it was bright and in sharp focus, a round flattened donut shape in green and brownish pink rock; marble maybe. He'd find out later that it was made of Unakite, which he'd never heard of, a form of granite with inclusions of feldspar and quartz.

"Perfect, you picked the round one with the big hole. Now that you have one in your mind, think about what you want to do with it."

She's getting exactly what I'm thinking. How is she doing that?

"No, don't think about me, concentrate on the pendant, like you did before. You want to protect your sister from the dangers of mountain climbing in the most challenging environment in the world. Think about the highest mountain, Everest, you've seen pictures of it, perhaps a movie of climbers in action. That's better.

"Now, picture Honore in that place, where she could have trouble breathing because of the altitude. Now see her gasping for breath and send air to her, blow fresh air to her like those drawings of clouds with big puffy cheeks blowing the wind across the sky. Not gale force, just gentle and full of life-sustaining oxygen.

"Good, now think about the cold, where she could freeze to death and send her warmth, the sun on her skin on a warm summer day in the country, someplace where she's secure and safe and comfortable. Push these thoughts into the stone, make it brighter, or bigger, or more in focus, or all three. Fill it with air and warmth."

With his imagination Jason blew warm breath into the stone as if it were a balloon and it grew bigger and brighter. Now the size of a volley ball, he handed it to Honore who stood in a field of waving wheat, like the song from Oklahoma, with the sun warm on her shoulders. *The wavin' wheat can sure smell sweet when the wind comes right behind the rain. . .* filled his mind and rain fell.

"No, don't turn on the rain; make it after, all of it after, with the warm sun and sweet smell and waving wheat."

Jason stopped the rain and put Honore waist high in the waving wheat and warm sunlight.

"Good, blow that into your balloon."

Jason took the amulet back from his sister and blew into it more, swelling it with air and warmth and light.

"Now think about steep and treacherous slopes, where there is ice and shale and maybe a big crevasse. Build some nice wooden steps for her, or concrete if you prefer, or stone if that makes more sense.

"Excellent, stone steps right up the mountain. Send her non-slip surfaces; build them into the medallion. Add anything you can think of to protect your sister, like extra strength in her muscles, a strong heart, sound lungs, clear mind, preparation and forethought, oxygen equipment that works and never runs out, even extra batteries for her flashlights. Send her all these things and blow them into the stone of the pendant, and then picture the amulet at its normal size but full of everything you added. Now shrink it back down. See it next to her skin as she treks to the mountain, and up the mountain, and back down the mountain. Send her safe flights and safe passages in all respects. Think of all these things and anything that comes to your mind, but stay away from things that you don't want, like rain and snow, block them when they try to enter, put them on the paper and erase them, and I'll be silent for a while."

Jason floated there in space, as if he were detached from his body. He saw the storms of Tibet and Nepal that crashed over the summit of Everest and called the sun to chase away the clouds, he calmed the winds with a wave of his hand as if he were a God. He remembered the earthquakes of 2015 and calmed the earth so that it was stable and solid. He remembered the avalanches that killed so many over the years and stabilized the ice so that it would not fall. He imagined Honore as she climbed and he calmed her fears, the worry of the unknown, and a thousand other things that flashed into his brain. He blew it all into the glowing pendant that appeared before his eyes, just a simple, earthy donut shape. No beginning and no end to the ring of stone, perfect. Honore stood on the summit of Everest in the crystal blue sky, on top of the world, comfortable and warm in the sunshine.

His mind began to wander, he tried to discern if he'd been hypnotized and thought that he might have been. If he was asleep he didn't want to wake up and he longed for the calm sweet voice of the woman who had directed his thoughts. *What was her name?* 'Monica' she seemed to say in his head, and then aloud she continued.

"Now seal the preparation with a few simple words. Follow along with me, but repeat only in your mind. 'My dear sister Honore, I love you and seek to protect you from all harm, from accident, from ill health, from the evil designs of others who may wish to do you harm, and I seek to protect you from the inadvertent actions of those who are less prepared. I ask for the help of the guardians of earth, air, water, and fire to protect you on your journey and particularly while you are climbing. I bind all of these blessings within the stone that you wear around your neck, to be realized when needed, by the power of the seventh son of a seventh son, sealed and delivered by the spirit of the Goddess.' Ladies, if you will join to accept the cost."

"Wait," Jason said, and pulled his hand away from Monica's. He blinked his eyes open.

"Jason, you broke the link, the line is dropped, and that means the cost is all yours," Monica said.

"It's ok. I think it worked," Jason rattled off, and closed his eyes again. "I heard someone, or something. It wasn't clear but it made me feel everything was ok. I hear it again. I'm being schooled, I see a path and I feel like I'm supposed to walk on it."

"You hear someone's voice apart from mine?" Monica asked.

"You don't hear it?"

"No, not at all."

"Wait please," Jason asked and the women watched with their mouths agape. The seconds ran on and the women fidgeted. Just as Monica was about to speak, Jason opened his eyes and smiled."

"Well slap my ass and call me mamma," Sara said.

"What happened?" Robin asked as the women gathered close.

"I just had the course of a lifetime jammed into my head. Something, or someone, downloaded an encyclopedia into my mind but I can't seem to remember anything more than a few flashes of images. Plants, animals, and scary things like from a horror movie. It all just washed over me like a tsunami. I don't know what it means."

"Don't look at me brother," Monica replied. "I don't have a clue, but it's easy to see if the casting took. Turn off the lights, will you Francine?"

Jason wondered why the lights needed to be off, but rolled with it, which seemed to be the thing to do today. He turned to watch Francine and the room went pitch black when the switch snapped. Now he understood why the windows were painted over. He couldn't see the end of his nose, but the women gasped and when he turned away from Francine at the door, there on the table was a simple donut shaped amulet. It glowed like the numbers on a watch. Jason reached for the pendant but hesitated, worried about it being too hot to touch.

"Go ahead. It's cool," Monica assured him.

Jason picked it up and felt a surge of something close to electricity but not exactly the same. It held a power, an energy that he'd never felt before, warm and buzzing with strength.

"Wow," was all he could say.

"May I?" Francine asked.

Jason handed it over without a word.

"Wonderful. Blessed be," she said and pressed it to her heart the same way she had embraced her favorite childhood teddy bear. She passed it to Sara who did the same thing, "Blessed be," and then Susan and then Robin, who pressed it to her lips tenderly and handed it to Monica with another "Blessed be." Monica cradled it in her open palms like she was holding a pool of iridescent water.

Francine turned the lights back on.

"Did you taste anything, like chocolate, or cotton candy; anything sweet?" Monica asked.

"No, didn't taste anything, but I heard somebody. Sounded like a thousand small voices all saying the same thing at the same time. I couldn't really understand anything, just had this really good feeling while millions of images flashed into my brain. I can't remember more than a couple, but now I have an uncontrollable urge to do something and I don't know what it is," Jason replied.

"Interesting," Monica continued. "Well, anyway, the energy you feel in the amulet is from life force, usually taken from the caster, but I'm thinking something entirely different happened this time. I've heard of it but never seen it."

"What do you mean, Monica?" Susan asked.

"I think the line paid, but I can't be sure," Monica answered and stared at Jason. "I wonder?"

Monica handed the amulet back, "You need to send the charm to your sister before she leaves Seattle and impress upon her the importance of wearing the amulet next to her skin at all times. She is to never take it off for the duration of her trip. Not for the shower, or making love, or anything at all."

"Got it, and thank you, but I have to say that I feel a little bushwhacked and confused and . . . astounded."

"I apologize, but if we'd told you before, then your puritanical sensibilities would have rejected the process before it had a chance. This is very serious business, and we don't perform it lightly, but we know that to have had a chance of working with you in the mix we needed a blank slate."

"Puritanical?" Jason asked with a raised eyebrow.

"Did you come here with the understanding that we could do such things? That you could do such things? Would you have believed if we'd told you?" Robin asked.

"No, I guess I wouldn't have. I see, puritanical in a relative sense. Because, after all, I did come looking for a charm and I'd heard this is the only place on this side of the city to get something like that, plus, I know you Robin, and Susan too."

"Ok," Robin said and waited for more.

"I guess the logical side of me has been at war with the mystical side since I was a kid. I've had, feelings, or maybe impressions, is a better word, for as long as I can remember. I don't understand how any of this can possibly work, but I came here because there is something inside of me that wants it to be true. I want magic to exist, if that's what you call what you do."

"Well, magic is as good a word as any, but we like to think that we simply channel small bits of the life force of the universe, move it from one place to another, and change the form of it if necessary. After all, it's only atoms stuck together in different ways and they can rearrange to form elements or be converted to their constituent energy," Monica instructed.

"The force, huh, like Star Trek," Jason chuckled.

"No, nothing at all like Star Trek," Sara shot back. "Besides, the force was from Star WARS, dummy. That's not what we're talkin' about here; this is real, honest to Goddess life energy. Every living thing is filled with it. And it's like Newton, you know, conservation of energy. It can't be destroyed, but it can be molded, moved, shaped and used, if you know how."

"When you put it that way, the logic side of me grasps it better, I guess."

"Well, we had to show you rather than tell you, and we all knew, except for Robin, because her talents lie in other areas apart from our particular form of sensitivity. We knew that you would be a good subject. That's why we held your hand for so long. We took the measure of you, and we are extremely impressed. Now that the cat's out of the bag, so to speak, we'll teach you whatever you want to know, or you can leave here with your sister's amulet and never see us again."

"Thank you for the option Monica, but I don't see how I can drop this now. I can never go back; I've changed in a fundamental way. I feel a task at hand and a boiling urge to get at it, as I already said. I want to learn everything there is to know about what you do and what I'm supposed to do. How could I not?"

"Yeah, we know," Susan said. "Once you get a taste you can't go back. Well, nobody's minding the store so I better get over there."

"It's ok, we would have felt it if someone had gone in," Monica added.

"Felt it, huh?" Jason was less surprised at such a thought than he would have been just a few moments before.

How it Works - 3

The practitioners looked at each other for several pregnant seconds, waiting for someone to continue the discussion, when Jason burst out, "Ok, I can't stand it anymore, I need some answers," he demanded.

"Fire away," Robin offered.

"Well, first of all, why was your hand so hot, Monica, and why did you need to hold hands in the first place?"

"I needed to draw the line through you."

"What? I don't understand."

"We call a stream of energy a line. A lot of non-practitioners think of the lines as something hard and straight, kind of like a beam of light, but that's not what it is at all. It's more of a mist of energy that's tied to the earth; it follows the lay of the land, usually along the banks of a river, that's why we call them lay lines. They spell it l-e-y in all the books because it's an old English term that describes the paths between historical sites; markers, mountains, piles of rocks and stuff like that, but we think it's more descriptive to spell it l-a-y.

"There's one coursing right through the middle of this row of buildings along Main Street. You're sitting in the middle of it right now, and if you had developed your second sight you could see it passing around you like gauzy blue-green stream of smoke roiling around a post in a gentle breeze, a river of smoky blue-green mist."

"Right here? Right this second?"

"Yes, our lay line has been here since the dawn of time, or at least since the Little Miami cut its way through here. Ours is pretty big for such a small river, and there's a massive one along the Ohio. Cincinnati is famous among practitioners of the craft--the bigger the river, the bigger the line. That's why most main streets parallel the river. Builders seem to know, or they're influenced in some way that brings the line right down Main Street."

"Wouldn't it be just as easy to say that they parallel the river for better access; or for the view?"

"That may be true in places where there are docks or similar kinds of access to the river, but downtown Milford never had any docks that I'm aware of; just stores that needed their produce to stay fresh as long as possible; living places that were cool and inviting to customers. The Little Miami up this far is unnavigable by anything bigger than a canoe, and not even by a canoe, in a practical sense, in the summer.   And the view here isn't all that spectacular. No, the line is what causes it, even if the builders don't realize it."

"Ok, so you had to draw the line through me?"

"Yes, so we could convert the life force from ourselves into your protection thoughts for your sister, after all, you know her and love her; you're the logical person to craft the amulet. Because you don't know how to do it yourself, yet, I drew the line through your body, into mine and back out to the stream. The heat you felt was the energy that jumped across the interface of our hands. I needed to do that for control since you don't know how. Together we added part of our energy to the flow and directed it into the pendant. We blended our energy with the line."

"Is that how you knew what I was thinking?"

"Yes, of course. Seems obvious now, doesn't it."

"Huh," Jason grunted, "and that's how you'd know if somebody entered your shop, because the line flows in our direction from there?"

"Yes, opposite the flow of the river, always. Kind of like heavy smoke, it hugs the landscape but goes up hill."

"What if you had used the worm?"

"Then it would have paid the cost."

"But you didn't have to use the worm?"

"No, because with the two of us linked together, combined with your power as a seventh son, it was enough, but there is always a cost, it's important to remember that, there is *always* a cost. You can't create something from nothing; it has to come from someplace. We wanted to cast energy into the pendant and that energy had to come from life force. We used the line to manipulate it. Since we didn't have the worm, and you stopped the rest of us from paying for it, it should have come from you. It's a serious game, because saving the life of the worm is worthwhile, and taking the cost ourselves is worthy and unselfish, but that can lead to ruin."

Monica continued, "It's easier to use your own life force, and it only takes a little bit, but it's kind of addicting because it's easier and it doesn't taste like a worm, or take the worm's life. It tastes great, in fact, but every time you do it, you spend a little of yourself. That's why the crone is always pictured as an old hag. She may not be that old, but she's used up a lot of her life force and has become drawn, infirm, ugly, feeble, stooped, and angry. In the old days a bunch of people overused their life force with too much casting and they became addicted, and became crones. We don't want to use ourselves up so we take it easy, we don't use too much. The option is to use something else, like a worm, but that takes a life, and it's dark. Some black arts witches are really powerful, because they use something bigger than a worm. Birds, dogs, cats, goats, and other animals have a lot of force to use. Some animals give willingly if the caster loves them, like

Pyewhacket, and we'd never abuse them, and only include them for loving, caring, building type magic, like healing. Black witches are almost always reclusive and shunned by covens, because they spin and cast for their own gain, and they become crones long before their time. They're the junkies of the craft."

"Fascinating," Jason said while he stared into Monica's eyes. He saw nothing but honesty there. "You said a moment ago, you used a term, 'casting' I believe."

Robin interjected, "Yes, Jason, you just cast a spell. Casted, cast, I don't know which is right, anyway, you casted a really good one that took the first time, with more strength than we're capable of combined. You saw how bright the amulet glows. Monica also said a moment ago that the line roiled around you like smoke drifting around a post, but I don't think that's accurate. You're more like a screen door, the line flows right through you and kind of calms along the way. It's nice and smooth downstream from you, or rather upstream."

"And there is where Robin's talents lie," Francine explained. "She's our best caster, and she can see the line much better than the rest of us. She can tap a line in milliseconds, and store the energy for use later on,"

"Wait a minute. It just dawned on me that since I cast a spell, you're saying I'm a witch?"

"A warlock actually, that's what we call a male witch. And you're the most powerful we've ever seen," Monica answered.

"Seventh son of a seventh son," Sara added. "I knew it the second you walked in the door and the cats knew before."

"I get it; the cats are familiars, like in that movie Bell Book and Candle with Jimmy Stewart. Pyewhacket was the cat's name in that movie."

"Bingo," Robin said and touched the tip of her nose in imitation of Jason from a few minutes before. "And don't make it sound like such a big deal, there's a little witch in everybody. It's really just being in touch with nature. And cats are half way on the other side to begin with. I know you've seen cats staring at something only they can see."

"Yeah, everybody knows how weird cats are. Wow, so I'm a warlock. Who knew?"

"When you were born, according to the seventh son myth, your mother might have known. She might have placed a worm in your hand right after they cleaned you up, or within a couple hours anyway, to set your power. If she knew about it maybe she did, because you shine like a lighthouse, your aura, or personal energy. Which takes me to another point, when you leave here, drive across the river as fast as you can. Don't speed or anything but go straight across the bridge," Monica warned.

"Why on Earth would I need to do that?"

"Because, right this minute, just after manipulating the line, you would be really tasty to the Unseelie and they'll try to make a pet of you if they're watching. Pulling a line through you would be nirvana to them. Running water blocks 'em, mostly. Once you get across the river they can't see you or smell you unless they do extraordinary things to cross right after you. That means buying spells and incurring debts that they really don't like. They probably wouldn't risk their lives to pursue you across the river. Not yet anyway," Robin instructed.

"We're talking about what, fairies or something?"

"Exactly," Francine answered. "They're called Bogeys, Boggarts, Butters, Brownies, Lubbers, any of the dark court fairies, or the Unseelie. That's what the whole group of the dark court is called in the old world."

"Wow, sounds like something from a Harry Potter movie."

"Well, it stands to reason that authors use fables that have been around for hundreds of years. All of those things are based on myth and oral tradition that have a rich history and are almost always based a little bit on fact," Susan explained.

"Why aren't the nasty little buggers in here right now?" Jason asked.

"Because we have Robin to protect us," said Sara. "She's the best at wards and protection spells. Our whole block is warded and the shop has several layers of different kinds of protection. If a Lubber tried to get in here, her little fingers would get burned like she'd grabbed a hot griddle if she touched the doorknob. It'd be like the Wicked Witch of the West when she tried to steal the ruby slippers."

"But we didn't want to take a chance of any spies seeing you headed for our special room here, so that's why Sara took up a post as sentry, just in case," Susan added. "If she'd seen one, she would have used the worm to project a protection spell that we could never cast without the life force of the worm to enhance the spell."

"So, Robin, how come you didn't help with the amulet if you're the best caster?"

"Because I don't hear people like Monica does. She's sensitive to live human spirit and I'm more sensitive to the lines and passed spirits. I wouldn't have heard your thoughts the way she did. And that's not the only thing I'm bad at; I can't cook worth a damn, so I stay away from potions too. We actually have a guy that does that for us. Francy's husband, Steve, is a master chef when it comes to potions. Anyway, Monica is the one who can watch what's going on in your brain while she's casting, I'd be working in the dark if I tried. We all have a little different talent."

"Wow! Seems like I say that a lot, doesn't it, but I'm simply overwhelmed. This is such a surprise and so much to take in, for what, twenty minutes of one day? I just remembered that you said something about tasting a worm?"

"Didn't you ever eat a worm as a kid, just to see, or on a dare?" Sara asked.

"I guess, but I don't remember."

"You would, if you ate one now," Francine added. "You didn't taste the worm when you cast to the amulet because we didn't use it, but didn't you taste anything at all?"

"Not that I remember. Did you, Monica?"

"Nothing at all and that's really curious. I'm amazed you didn't taste anything either. Sometimes I taste chocolate the instant I tap a line, but when I pay for a casting, the taste is like the best chocolate I've ever had, every time. You're just full of surprises, Jason. And I have another question for you," Monica said.

"Shoot," Jason replied.

"Do you build things with your hands? Are you handy?"

"Yes, I guess so. I have a workshop that I built myself. It's just a garage, really, and I made our picnic table, and a couple lamps. I like the lathe. And I built a pergola to sit in, back in the trees behind my house, a big one. And I decided to put some ironwork supports in it instead of the usual wooden ones, but I couldn't find anything that I liked. Nothing inexpensive anyway, it seems like all the neat old ironwork costs a million dollars. Just a simple garden gate costs a couple hundred dollars, so I took a blacksmith course and learned to work with iron myself. I made my own supports after a little practice."

"Fantastic! You do real blacksmithing?" Francine asked.

"Hot iron on an anvil with hammer and tongs, just like the old days."

"He's a maker," Sara added.

"Yes, I guessed as much," Monica agreed. "I've never seen anybody cast to an amulet like that, not ever. And on the first try too. He blew it up like a balloon."

"How clever, and novel," Susan added.

"Maker, huh? Sounds like I'm some kind of demigod. I'm not; I'm just regular ol' Jason, the vet from Loveland, nobody special at all."

"Ok, regular ol' Jason from Loveland, give us a few tries and we'll show you how special you really are," Sara challenged. "The Summer Solstice comes up the twenty first of June. You give us one night a week until then-- that's what, surprise, surprise, seven weeks," She added with a giggle. "Sorry honey, you don't have a chance, the planets are lined up and you're caught like a big ol' bass. Regular ol' Jason my ass; Big ol' Jason the bass is what I say."

"I'm caught in the net, huh?"

"Not if you don't want to be," Monica replied. "But I should warn you; sooner or later the other side will make a play for you. It's just a matter of time, and it has nothing to do with you coming here today. Your aura gets stronger as you age, and they'll find you because they're always searching. So it would be better to be prepared for them."

"The other side, meaning the dark court, I guess. I don't understand, really, how bad could they be?"

"Evil, Jason. We're the good guys, and the other side is the bad guys," Robin added.

"Really, the devil, or demons or something like that?"

"Something like that," Sara answered

Jason took in all their faces in turn, "You're not kidding."

"Nope, but it could be years. I doubt it now that you've cast an amulet," Robin said. "Could be months, could be days, could be hours. Depends on how close they're watching the shop. They don't bother us much anymore. They've learned better, but they watch."

"Well that's good I guess. That they don't bother you, I mean. So, what's next? How do I protect myself from these bad guys?"

"You come here every Wednesday night for the next seven weeks and we teach you everything you need to know," Monica answered.

"You think I have enough space from the bad guys to do that? What if they're on me the minute I walk out the door?"

"We'll know as soon as it happens. Monica has a link to you now," Sara replied.

"Because we were connected through the line?"

"Exactly," Sara finished.

"So what happens if they get me?"

"Think Hitler," Francine answered.

"Oh God, was Hitler a seventh son?"

"No, I don't think so," Monica replied. "But you would be just like him, probably worse, if you could be turned. My personal opinion is that Hitler was just a psychopath. And you don't have to be a seventh son to be a maker, and any maker can be turned by the dark forces. That side is all about profit, pleasure, and power, the same old good versus evil story told over and over since the beginning of time. The same ol' white hats against the black hats, the land baron against the farmer, it's the same thing over and over."

"So give me some examples of makers, I've never heard of one."

"Oh, pish tosh. . ." Francine said as Jason interrupted her.

"Pish tosh! Who talks like that?"

"I do, big tall dumb and handsome. Be still for a second and learn. Of course you've heard of makers. You've heard of Henry Ford, haven't you." Jason nodded and Francine continued, "What about Eli Whitney, Ben Franklin, and Steve Jobs for cryin' out loud. Not to mention Leonardo DaVinci, Michelangelo, Beethoven, and Paul McCartney."

Jason knit his eyebrows and wrinkled his nose while Robin continued, "Anybody can be born with a knack, and then turn it into a skill. A maker is somebody who makes things, that's all. But most people are only able to do one thing well, artists do art, musicians make music, goldsmiths do gold, blacksmiths do iron. But a seventh son of a seventh son is born with skills, not knacks that develop into skills. And the folklore says that people like you can just do things right out of the box, so to speak, like Mozart could make music when he was little older than a baby, but he wasn't a seventh son, just gifted. Let's see if we can find an example from your own life. Were your knots the best in Boy Scouts?"

"As a matter of fact, nobody could undo my knots but me."

"But you didn't lord it over the others, did you?" Monica asked.

"No. I just felt sorry for the others and tried to help as much as I could."

"A seventh son is never selfish, so they say," Susan added, "until the dark side gets a hold of them anyway."

"Interesting--it's so much to take in, but I see the logic in it, I guess. I'm a little bit worried about the bad guys though. I wouldn't know what to do if I were accosted. Can't you teach me something now, to protect me after I walk out the door?"

"Yes, we can," Monica answered. "But you have to be sure. You have to commit to it and jump in with both feet. There's nothing more dangerous than a dabbler, but I think it will come easy to you. All you need is a little direction and you can figure out a lot of it on your own. In fact, you probably have the skill sets inside already. You just need a little push, and our experience will keep you on the white path."

"Are you ready to jump in the pool?" Francine asked.

"Let's do it," Jason replied.

$\mathscr{G}host$ - 4

"Francy, will you please turn off the lights again?" Monica directed more than asked.

A second later the lights snapped off and the amulet shone through the spaces between Jason's fingers where he had held it for the entire discussion.

"It'll be easier if you put that in your pocket," Monica suggested. Jason stood up, slipped the amulet nightlight into his pocket, and plunged the room into darkness.

"Sit back down and relax. Give me your hand again but this time keep your eyes open. We'll bring up your second sight and see what we will see. If I'm right, you'll find the line, plus a man in the corner, and I want you to help me move him to the light. Don't speak unless spoken too directly, and then respond honestly, I'll guide you when I can."

"What? Are you talking about a ghost?"

"Yes, I believe he's the original owner of this building and he died in this very room."

"Ok, I'm not sure I can help, but at least it will be interesting."

"First we need to tap the line so guide your thoughts to the energy flowing through the building. Eventually you'll be able to call that energy to you from far away, probably a lot farther than any of us, probably farther than all of us combined. But that's a distraction right now so think about the line; envision it in your mind, a river of smoky blue-green mist boiling from the wall to your left, passing around us, and according to Robin, through you, and out the wall to our right.

"Almost there, give yourself up to it, let go of all control, you must grant the energy access, and stop trying so hard to see, that's why it's dark in here, so you don't have to try so hard. Relax your brow and un-focus your eyes and invite the energy in. That's right, almost there, almost there. Don't speak when you see it or you'll break contact."

Jason gasped because he saw something flicker all around him, like he was inside a jar of fireflies.

"Good, good, that's right, but hold onto it when it flashes, don't let it go. I know it's new and a little bit scary, but when you feel it you won't want to let it go. I think you'll find it very satisfying, warm and inviting, not scary at all. That's it, relax and focus your mind but un-focus your eyes."

The lights flashed all around him and left then flashed again and stayed a bit longer. Jason had seen persistence of vision experiments where a person stares at a black dot on a white screen and looks away or closes their eyes and the dot is still there. The light seemed to act like that so he concentrated to keep it in sight, and each flash lasted a little longer until he relaxed and invited the light in. Suddenly the flashes consolidated into a coherent light and he couldn't help himself, "Fantastic!" he said, and it was gone.

"I told you not to speak, dummy," Monica scolded. "It's ok, everybody does the first time. But after a little practice, you'll be able to call up a line and jabber like a blue jay. For now, don't speak until you are spoken to directly. You might be surprised if what I think will happen, happens. Now try again, and don't speak this time."

Jason struggled through the process again, but this try progressed much faster.   In a few seconds he could see the blue-green light flowing through the room like he'd sat down in the middle of a wispy river.   The experience reminded him of the night vision goggles that the military wore in the movies. He saw everything in the room but all was tinted with the blue-green light. And Robin was right, the smoke flowed around all the women but passed right through him, he could feel it, like static electricity, but he couldn't taste anything and it wasn't all that warm. Except for his right hand where Monica held him. That hand was on fire.

"There, you have it. I'll slip my hand out of yours but you just keep the line for yourself, and don't speak until someone asks you to. It could be anybody so don't be alarmed. As I mentioned, we have a lost spirit in the room and he'll probably see you soon. He sees us sometimes, Robin more than the rest of us, but I suspect he'll see you as if you were real to him since you're a seventh son."

When Monica let go, the light flashed again but held, and everything became ten times brighter. Jason suddenly saw everything in the room as if it were daylight and the blue-green smoke poured through him as if he were a sieve. He felt powerful, the way he imagined superman would feel. A wonderful sense of peace filled him and he thought he could almost hear the real river a couple blocks away, and the rocks, and the grass, and moss, and trees. They seemed to speak to him, and to each other. All of nature flowed into him, through him, and out of him, filled him with strength and an increased understanding of the natural world around him. He felt connected to all of it.

He looked at Monica and saw the line flowing around her exactly like she had described it; she was a post in the river of energy. But he knew she was connected, because he saw the tendrils of energy where they entered her body and flowed through her in a trickle. He turned to the other women in turn and saw that Robin was more like him, the line hugged her, most of the tendrils passed through her, and he could see her heart beating in her chest, and her life energy flowed out to her fingertips like blood flowed in her veins. He concentrated and saw her as she might look in an x-ray machine, one of those old fluoroscopes that showed skeletons in real time. When he focused hard, his sight passed right through her flesh to her bones.

Sara, Susan and Francine looked similar to Monica but a little less connected. And then he saw a man in the corner at a desk. The man worried over a leger and scratched on a paper with a quill pen. The desk and the chair and the man's legs were ankle deep in the floor, as if the ghostly realm existed at a different level than the present reality.

The man looked up suddenly, right at Jason, and shouted, "Boy! Nathaniel! There you are. Where have you been boy? I've called for you. Well, speak up lad, where have you been." The man stood up. He looked and dressed like Benjamin Franklin, but with hair over all his head, not the bald pate of the famous politician and scientist, and he was masked by the same blue-green light of the line. He seemed like the mist made solid, solid enough to see, and solid enough to make out his form and visage, even his period clothes, but Jason could see through him to the wall behind. The desk and even the quill pen were made of the same blue-green mist made solid.

Jason hesitated for a moment and realized that none of the women had heard. Then he took the cue and answered, "I'm sorry sir but I'm not Nathaniel."

"Well who in blazes are you and what are you doing here?" the man demanded.

The girls all turned as intense a focus as they could toward the man, and Jason realized that they were hearing now, Robin in particular was locked on. He didn't know what to do, how to answer, and Robin whispered to him, "Tell him you're here to help with the accounting."

"My name is Jason and I'm here to help with the accounting."

"About bloody time! I've been cheated here boy, someone's been stealing from me, a bloody, infernal embezzler, I suspect. I take in four times my cost and turn it all in a quarter annum, but I can't seem to balance my book. What do you make of it boy?"

Monica whispered, "Ask him if he's seen a light."

"I'm not sure sir, but I wonder if you've seen a light?"

"Light, light, yes that infernal light follows me everywhere. It distracts me boy, I can't do my business with that bloody light pestering me hour upon hour. I keep to my book and it leaves me alone. That's why I've called for Nathaniel. I want him to bring me the counting house master. Are you the bloody accountant who's been stealing from me?"

Jason understood what Monica was trying to do; he'd seen enough of the medium and ghost hunter shows to know what the light was about, "No sir, I'm not that accountant. I represent the light, and I'm here to balance your books."

"The light, what's this about the infernal light? I don't understand you sir."

"You will if you look into the light. Please sir, if you'll just look into the light, all will be made known to you."

"Very well, if you insist, and if it will balance the books, I'll look and be damned or saved, one or the other." The old man turned and looked into the light. "By Jehovah, I see my daughter, no, not my daughter, but my own lovely wife as young and spry as the day I married her. And there I see her sister, no, not her sister, but my own charming daughter. Why, they could be sisters they look so much alike. And there are my own three boys so grown and manly, and the youngest one died when he was seven from the fever, but there he is whole and grown to a man. And my heir, Nathaniel, such a fine young man, my spitting image if can boast and beg your pardon after. Glory be; and lo, there is my own good mother, but as young as my wife, and lo, there is my father in the prime of life. They call to me boy, they beckon; I must go. Thank you my boy, my dear boy, thank you, I must go." And he stepped forward into the light that had grown clear and bright to Jason and all the women, a blazing bright white light that tickled the blue-green mist and drew it up like smoke into a chimney as it pulled the old man in. He left and the light faded.

All the women bawled like babies and gathered in a clutch of hugs and tears. Jason sat incredulous, and the line still flowed through him. He didn't speak but he felt a pull to throw something, not to throw, *to cast*, came into his mind. He reached out and stirred the misty, smoky lay line like he would stir a pool of water before taking a drink. Then he extended his right hand and sent a thought of protection against dark forces and a wisp of the line jumped from his fingers and connected to all the stone pendants left lying on the table.

He concentrated and more mist poured in, he envisioned bullets bouncing off of him like superman, and he used Spiderman's web to catch criminals, and hypodermic needles bent against his skin, and black mists turned back from their attacks with a mere wave of his hand.

The amulets on the table began to glow. Jason poured more energy in and envisioned lightning bolts that blasted out of his fingers to fry monsters on the attack. He switched to flames and blasted more monsters, then he fired silver needles from his fingers like bullets and more monsters died. He launched hurricane wind that killed more monsters and carried them away into churning clouds of thunder and lightning.

The amulets brightened more and more, and as they blazed they caught the attention of the women who broke from their reverie at the passing of the ghost man and Monica grabbed Jason's arm, "No! Jason, stop, stop! Remember, there's a cost."

Suddenly the line dropped from Jason and Francine turned on the lights. Jason apologized, "I'm sorry, was that wrong? I just wanted a protection amulet to keep the bad guys away."

"Jason, wonderful man, no it wasn't wrong, but it was costly. Don't you taste something, something delicious, like the best chocolate in the world, or your favorite ice cream?" Monica asked.

"No, I remember you said I'd taste something but I never tasted a thing. I thought I could hear rocks and grass and trees, animals and stuff talking but I didn't understand what they said, not really, but I seem to know a lot more than I did before."

"No taste at all?"

"Nothing."

"But you heard something, something that you thought were trees and rocks?" Monica grilled.

"Didn't taste anything, but I heard all those things, and moss too I think, and maybe bugs. Trees, leaves, and grass, I'm not sure, that's just what came to me when I heard it."

"Oh my," Susan uttered and put a hand to her mouth to cover the gape of her slack jaw.

"What?"

"Well, Jason, it seems the line paid for you, for sure," Robin answered. "We've heard of it, just in folk tales, but I never believed it was possible. Not until now."

"How is it possible? I don't understand."

Robin continued, "Well, the theory is that every blade of grass is a living thing, and can be used as a casting focus. The grass or any living plant can pay for the casting, but you would normally have to have live grass in your hand and it would be dead when you were done, withered and brown, like the worm would have been if we'd used it."

"But I didn't have anything in my hand."

"Exactly," Sara said. "Seventh son of a seventh son--I told you that you had power. You believe me now I bet."

"Something has power, but somehow I don't think it's really me."

"Very astute," Monica observed. "You're right of course, the power comes from the life force in the plant or the worm or from your own living tissue, but someone needs to direct it, and that's you my dear boy. The difference is that a collective of all the living things that power this line coalesced to grant your wish to cast a protection into the amulets. You didn't kill anything, apparently, because it only takes a little bit and every living thing in the local area bent to your will and everything you heard offered up a little piece of itself to make your cast a reality. It didn't cost you a thing, and the earth seemed happy to do it for you. That's the power of the seventh son. Nothing died; amazing."

"Look at all those pendants," Robin directed. "I can see the glow even with the lights on," and she picked one up. As soon as she touched it she gasped.

"Look at that would ya," Francine added. "He did a dozen amulets in one go, in seconds. That would take us hours with a full coven, and we'd have to do one at a time, and they would never glow in the light."

Robin placed her hat on the table, pulled the amulet's leather thong over her head and the stone rested against her skin between her breasts. She took off the necklace she already had on, placed it on the table, and pressed the new stone into her bare chest. "Oh, I feel something I've never felt before," she said and tapped a line; even Jason could feel the ripple of power that entered Robin.

She turned to face the back wall and stretched out her right arm in front of her and opened her hand with force, like she wanted to flick paint off her fingers, to cast something away, and cast she did. A bolt of lightning blasted out of her extended fingers and scorched a foot wide circle on the wall near the right hand corner, the wallpaper ignited immediately.

They all stood like statues and stared at the round burned spot on the back wall while the wallpaper gathered more flame. "Oh my God," Francine shouted and ran for the obligatory fire extinguisher required in all businesses. She ran to the spot on the wall and activated the extinguisher to put out the growing fire.

They all stood amazed, jaws slack, then the women turned to stare at Jason. He held out his hands, palms up, shrugged his shoulders and said, "Sorry?"

"Seventh son," Sara answered.

"Step away Francy," Robin commanded and turned back to the wall. "But not too far away, and keep the extinguisher ready."

Robin set her feet square to the back wall and extended her arm again, and flashed her hand open again in the same direction. This time fire blazed from her fingertips with the sound of a monstrous blowtorch. A horizontal cylinder of pure flame blasted the wall for a second then Robin closed her hand to stop the flow.

Francine rushed in and put the fire out. "Back up again Francy," Robin said and shot another blast, but this one was needles the size of finish nails accompanied by a buzz like a dozen angry bees flying past. They went right through the burned spot on the wall.

"Oh, my!" Susan exclaimed.

Robin dropped the line and they all inspected the wall, one-by-one, Francine first since she was the closest. "There's barely any drywall left on here, it's down to the studs in the middle. Lucky you didn't burn up the whole building, Robin. And there are little holes where the needles hit, must have gone all the way through." She ran through the central, open door to the adjoining room while the others inspected the burned spot with effusive commentary.

Francine yelled from the other room, "Hey Monica, you know that picture of Grandma Moses hanging on the other side of the wall?" Monica shouted yes and Francine continued, "Well she's face down on the floor and the back of the frame looks like a pin cushion. There's a few of those little nails stuck in the far wall, and they're bright and shiny as silver."

"It's not possible," Monica offered in a quiet voice.

Sara remarked, "Well it surely is, because it just happened. Look at that burn mark. And it's gonna' smell like Hades in here for weeks. Just regular ol' Jason my ass."

"And I didn't even try the wind," Robin added.

"You put wind in too?" Susan asked.

"Well, I tried to do it the way Monica taught me and used everything I could think of. Plus, we need to do an experiment. Are you game Robin?"

"I'm up for anything at this point. I feel invincible."

"Ok. We'll start with something small," Jason said and looked around the room. Nothing convenient came to hand so he approached Francine as she returned from the back room. She still held the fire extinguisher. "May I?" he asked.

"Knock yourself out," she answered.

"No, I'm going to knock Robin out," and he pointed the extinguisher at her.

Robin backed away with her hands up in double stop signs, "Now wait a minute," she said, but as soon as she was separated from the group, Jason fired.

Robin turned her head away from the floury blast of the chemical extinguisher, but all the others could see that nothing touched her, as if she were protected by an invisible bubble of hard plastic. When the dust settled, she turned around and said, "Didn't feel a thing." There was a ring of extinguisher chemical on the floor around her, three feet away from her all the way around.

"Fabulous," Monica said. "How much endurance, I wonder?"

"I don't know but it feels like a lot. I didn't notice a shift in the power at all," Robin said, and all the other girls ran to the table and selected an amulet.

All of them gasped as the stone touched their skin and Monica screamed "No!" when Sara turned toward the south wall and prepared to unleash some power.

Sara stopped and said, "Oh, all right. But we need some kind of firing range to test these things out. We need to know about endurance. This--is--freakin'-- awesome!" she shouted louder with every word. Then she took the extinguisher from Jason and shot everybody in the place, and forgot that Jason wasn't wearing a protection amulet. The chemical clung to his face and he coughed and sputtered while all the women laughed and apologized and patted at him to clean him off.

Suddenly Monica turned to the south wall and said, "Somebody just went into the store. I have to go."

"Damn," Sara cried. "We were having so much fun."

"Don't worry," Robin added. "I'm pretty sure the fun has only just begun."

Thanks - 5

Monica returned to cover the shop while the rest cleaned the room and Jason too. He held a trash bag while Robin shoveled in extinguisher chemical with a dust pan and he asked, "What did Sara mean when she said something about setting a circle?"

They stood next to the corner of an area rug that covered the majority of the center of the room, under the long folding-leg table they had occupied during the castings. Robin used her foot to curl back the rug's corner far enough to show a segment of a nine foot diameter brass ring inlaid into the wooden floor.

"We had this circle cast by a metal worker. He poured the molten brass into a sand mold, I watched him do it. The brass came from found pennies with dates between 1962 and 1981 because those were brass. It's also a good idea to use pennies because so many people touch them over the years. Those things get charged up like an Eveready. We took about five years to collect all the pennies. The circle is a device to protect us if we want to conjure a spirit. If we're on the inside it protects us from anything on the outside, and if we're outside, it protects us from whatever is on the inside. Up to now, we haven't been able to use it because we don't have enough power in our coven to set it properly. With your help, we can set it and I bet it will hold just about anything."

"Why in the world would you want to conjure anything in the first place?"

"Think about it Jason," Francine tested, "what if you lost the love of your life in an accident or something and you wanted to make one last contact? What if we told you it could happen; would you want to do that?"

"Can you do that?"

"We can if we can set the circle properly."

"I'm not sure if I'd want to do that or not."

"Of course you would," Sara offered, "if she was the love of your life and you never said goodbye. Who wouldn't?"

"I would," Robin said.

Jason realized that this was a sensitive area and decided to move on. "Why would you need some kind of extraordinary protection for something like that?"

"Because, when you open a conduit to the other side, just about anything could pop through. Bad spirits, demons, all sorts of nasties," Francine explained. "Those bad guys we told you about earlier, the Unseelie, they could use it too, and we don't want any interesting surprises. It's a hole in the fabric of reality and if something on the other side sees it open, it could jump in."

"Ok then. I'm at a loss for what to do next. What now?" Jason asked.

"Now we ship your sister's amulet. We have UPS pickup every day and I'll take care of it for you, if you have Honore's address handy," Susan offered.

"I do, and thank you. Just let me know the cost and I'll take care of it."

"No cost, sweetie," Robin said.

"I insist," Jason responded.

"No Jason, you don't steal back a gift by paying for it. That takes the power out of it for us," Robin retorted.

"Besides, these amulets you cast for us are priceless. We couldn't take these and make you pay for shipping."

"Well, I won't break your arm for it, but I would like to take you to lunch, all of you."

"All of us in your little corvette?" Sara asked.

"Little Corvette? That's a 427 cubic inch 400 horsepower muscle car, if you don't mind."

"I meant it only has two seats, and I didn't mean to insult your man crutch. I swear, you guys with your cars, you'd think I was talking about the size of your. . ."

Jason interrupted Sara before she could complete the sentence, "We'd have to take two cars, of course."

"We could go to Padrino's, it's just four doors down," Sara offered.

"No, you take Robin," Susan said. "We always take turns for lunch, except for her. The rest of us have work to do anyway and Robin never has a break like the rest of us. She's the one who always covers."

"Ok, so we'll rotate over the next seven weeks then. I want to get to know all of you."

"Don't worry about that," Sara said. "We'll get to know you plenty before it's over, and I don't think it's gonna' take you seven weeks to get caught up. You're already way beyond us."

"Ok. You're the boss. But can I try to tap the line again? I feel like I left something undone."

"Of course," Robin answered. "Do you want the lights off?"

"Let's try with the lights on this time. I think I can do it."

"Go for it," Francine said, and he did.

He fought a little to bring up his second sight, but it opened and he saw the line almost as vividly as he had in the dark. Then he called the line with just a thought and it snapped to his will instead of just flowing through him. Less than a second later all four of the ladies still present felt the tug on the line, and they were not even connected, in fact, Monica felt it next door and knew exactly who had tied in.

"Can you see the line, Jason?" Robin asked.

"Bright as it can be. Why don't you join me for a moment," and they all did.

"Can you hear the grass and trees and moss?" Jason asked and the girls replied "No" in turn. "I can hear them, and I want to thank them for helping me. How do I do that?"

"You just did," Robin replied.

"It's not enough. I need more words."

"I don't know, we never communicated with plants before, but I don't see why there shouldn't be a way to thank them formally. We could do something based on the thanks we give to the elementals and the guardians of the watchtowers I suppose. They're not the same as the living plants and elements but they look over them."

"Ok, give me some of that."

"Let me take your hand, and just think about the words as I say them," and Robin took his hand.

Her sight was immediately enhanced and she saw the line in the lighted room as well as Jason, and Jason's perception barely rippled at her touch. "Fantastic," she said. "This is real power, blessed be. Ok, here goes,"

> Oh guardians of the Watchtower of the North, and spirits of Earth; and all living things and elements who have rendered assistance under your care, we thank you for helping Jason this day; and before you depart to your fair and lovely realms, we bid thee Hail and Farewell.
>
> Oh guardians of the Watchtower of the West, and spirits of Water; and all living things and elements who have rendered assistance under your care, we thank you

> for helping Jason this day; and before you
> depart to your fair and lovely realms, we
> bid thee Hail and Farewell.
>
> Oh guardians of the Watchtower of the
> South, and spirits of Fire; and all living
> things and elements who have rendered
> assistance under your care, we thank you
> for helping Jason this day; and before you
> depart to your fair and lovely realms, we
> bid thee Hail and Farewell.
>
> Oh guardians of the Watchtower of the
> East, and spirits of Air; and all living
> things and elements who have rendered
> assistance under your care, We thank you
> for helping Jason this day; and before you
> depart to your fair and lovely realms, we
> bid thee Hail and Farewell.

"Awesome. But there's something missing, something in the center, it seems like there should be acknowledgement of the guardian of the watchtower of the middle, the spirit of the life force maybe, the quintessence, maybe."

"The Goddess watches over the center, Jason," Robin said.

"Ok" he replied, and then he added:

> Oh Goddess of the Center, and spirits of
> the Life Force; and all living things and
> elements who have rendered assistance
> under your care, we thank you for helping
> this day; and beg your forgiveness for my
> inept handling, because I'm a beginner. If
> I've taken too much please forgive me,

> and allow me to call upon you again.
> Please guide me to what is right and
> wholesome and pleasing to you in your
> ancient and gracious wisdom. Now as we
> depart, please return in peace and love to
> your fair and beautiful realms, we bid thee
> farewell until we meet again.

"I think that does it just fine," Jason said as he felt the warmth of the misty words 'You are most welcome' flood his body, and Robin felt it too.

"I feel them. I hear them. Jason, I hear them," Robin said with a shiver in her voice. Francine, Sara, and Susan all rushed to grasp onto some part of Jason's bare skin. Francine took his left hand, Sara pushed his sweater sleeve up and grabbed his wrist, Susan put both hands on his neck and they all gasped in surprise as they also felt and heard the actual living beings in the lay line as the mystics said in unison:

> Jason Patrick O'Hara, friend of the living
> and seventh son of a seventh son, healer,
> maker, defender of the weak, fear not for
> it is your birthright and we exist to serve
> the righteous. We are but an extension of
> your power and as long as you continue
> on the path of your true destiny we are
> here for you with seven times seven the
> power you have called upon today, unto
> the giving of our very life force if the
> need be great and the cause be righteous.
> Hale and farewell, oh guardian of the
> living.

. . .and then the spirits whispered to themselves, not gone but now attendant of the line, waiting for another request, as they had before, for eons past and future because it was their purpose.

Jason felt satisfied and dropped the line, "Wow; that was interesting."

The four women dropped the line as well but they didn't drop Jason, in fact they smothered him in a group hug and didn't seem to want to let go. Water ran down the back of his neck and he realized it was tears from the crying women.

"Ok ladies, you're getting me all soggy."

"Oh, Jason, will you marry me?" Francine asked.

Through teary, shaking voices the other three said in unison, "You're already married Francy."

"Well, what about polygamy, how about that?" she sobbed.

"I don't think it works that way," Jason replied.

"Well why not?" Francine cried. "If you can have two wives, why can't I have two husbands?"

"First of all, it's illegal, and second, I don't think your husband would approve."

"Oh, I suppose your right, but I'd consider divorce if you were willing," Francine offered.

"As much as I'd love to, really, I'm flattered. . ." Jason began but Robin cut him off.

"That's it Francy. That's enough for today. Let's get out of here," and they stood up to head back to the shop.

"It's just a compliment, that's all. I didn't really mean it."

"Well what makes you think Jason considers you throwing yourself on him a compliment?" Sara demanded.

"Well, I'm not all that bad looking, after all."

"Francy, I'd be honored, but I'm just not interested in that kind of relationship. Thanks though," he said, and Robin deflated a little bit just under the skin.

Cats - 6

Back in the shop, Jason pulled his phone out of his pocket along with the amulet for Honore and gave Susan the address in Seattle. He wrote a note with instructions to wear it next to her skin at all times during her trip while Susan typed the address into their shipping computer and printed out a label. She placed the amulet in a nice cotton lined jewelry box and sealed it in a bubble envelope, and that went into a UPS overnight delivery box with some packing peanuts. She put the whole thing into the UPS out box, finished nice and neat where their regular driver would pick it up before the end of the day.

While Susan prepared the shipment, Sara and Francine almost attached their lips to one each of Monica's ears and whispered all of what had happened after she left. The surprise on Monica's face was evident and when they were done, she spoke to Jason, "I knew something big had happened. I felt the line quiver in here like I've never felt it before. Jason, how extraordinary," she said and shook her head.

He hesitated for a second, at a loss for words, and then said, "I can't thank you all enough, and I'm going to steal Robin for an hour or so, if you can spare her Monica."

"Don't mention it, and take your time, Robin has five years of lunch breaks to catch up on. And don't forget, straight across the bridge, no dilly dallying. And don't forget to say goodbye to the cats."

"I could hardly miss them; they've been trippin' me up ever since I walked back in the door."

The cats had been turning figure eights between and around his feet at every step.

"Ok. Come on kitties, up, up. Come on kitty kitty," Monica called from behind the counter. All three cats jumped up in front of her, and faced Jason. Pye stuck out her paw and he shook it again, but when he let go she stood on her back legs and put her front paws on his chest, stretched out to full length to rub noses. Jason complied and accepted a cat kiss to beat all cat kisses. Pye rubbed noses ten or eleven times, alternating from side to side, and then sat back on the counter. When Jason thought about it later, he figured it was fourteen times. He reached for the other two and scratched them behind the ears to the sound of massive purring.

"What are the other's names?" Jason asked.

"The calico is Callie, of course," Susan answered. "And the gray is. . ."

"Wait, let me guess. Fluffy?"

"Wow, is that the vet talking or the seventh son?" Susan asked.

"Seemed pretty obvious."

"Yeah, I guess, now get out of here, and we'll see you on Wednesday night at eight," Monica reminded. "Robin, you keep your eyes open on your way across the river, and Jason, this time I get a hug," she said and came out from behind the counter.

All the girls squeezed the stuffins out of him in turn, except for Robin, because she left with him. When they reached the car he suggested they put the top down, and after she looked around with her second sight, Robin figured they had time because there was nothing on the radar.

Jason zipped down main, around the corner at the end and across the bridge in less than a minute.

"Great, I didn't see or feel a thing," Robin said, and dropped her second sight while she let her hair down, since she'd taken her hat off to don the new amulet. As soon as she'd done it she realized it was a mistake. Her hair blew straight forward, and she asked, "What the hell, shouldn't my hair be blowing the other way?"

"Oh, yeah, that happens. You have to put your seat back and push the sun visor all the way up past the line of the windshield. I'll turn on the fan, with a little heat, to get some flow going and keep you warm."

She did as instructed and her hair settled down in a stream straight back. "That's better, but I'm gonna' get some wicked split ends."

"I gotta' think there's some kind of spell for that."

"There is, but it's not worth the cost, unless you're going to prom or something." She didn't want to say getting married, but that's what she was thinking.

"Where are we going?" Jason asked.

"Straight on down 50 toward the city. I could use a beer, but 50 West Brewery doesn't open until four. Pizzelii serves beer."

"You feel like pizza?"

"Why not?"

"Pizza it is, but we could have gone to Padrino's."

"Padrino's is great, but, it's four doors down from the shop and we go there almost every night after work, so I think a little ride and a little variety is in order."

A hundred feet above them a crow flew in the opposite direction, a spy, a demon in the guise of a crow that had been tasked by his sorcerer master to watch the eastern approaches to the city. In particular, to watch the witches who gathered at Enchanted Notions in Milford. He felt a nudge to his senses as Robin passed below, and she felt a similar nudge, but both dismissed the indication of an enemy since the feeling was so slight and so brief. In a few minutes, the spy would turn around because of a ripple in the line that he could not ignore.

How Do They Burn - 7

They listened to the husky music of the muscle car's exhaust all the way through Terrace Park and they only had a couple more miles down US 50, or Wooster Pike as it was called on the road to Cincinnati.

Jason opened the conversation, "You know, when I left the house this morning I figured I'd run into something interesting at your shop, but sister, I never expected anything like that."

"Sure turned fascinating in a hurry. And now your life will never be the same. Now you're in the craft and I doubt you even believed it existed."

"Hey, I saw the movie."

Robin giggled, "Yeah, it's just like that, huh?"

"Surprisingly similar, I must say."

"Oh really? We're just like a bunch of poser high school kids who wrecked the ocean, killed people for gain or revenge, and nearly killed each other because they were selfish and ignorant?"

"Well, I wasn't going for that exactly, and there was a Robin in there."

"Yeah, Robin Tunney . . . I guess there are worse comparisons."

"I just meant that it really works, that's all.

"You're a believer now, huh?"

"I'm totally and irrevocably in."

"That's fabulous, it really is, and I couldn't be happier. But I worry we'll smother you. Francy already proposed for heaven's sake, and then there's the whole bad guy thing. There's more to it than fairies. There are honest to God real bad guys who use the craft for personal gain. Once they find out you're around, they'll go to any lengths to get control of your gifts. But I'm pretty sure they'll underestimate you. I know we all did. You can talk to grass, for cryin' out loud. Who can do that? And this amulet, holy cow," she said and pulled the leather thong away from her skin to look at her donut shaped stone, and revealed a donut shaped burn mark right between her breasts.

Jason saw it but wasn't sure he should mention it since that would be an admission that he had peeked. But she had a burn and he should tell her, "Hey, did you notice you have a burn mark under there?"

"What? What the hell?" She leaned forward and pulled the visor down so she could use the mirror to see her chest. Of course, the second the visor came down her hair changed directions and she fought with that and the mirror at the same time, but finally saw the red donut on her skin. "Well, I shouldn't be surprised I guess. All that raw power, real fire, and lightning bolts, and silver needles. It's a wonder I didn't turn into a smoldering cinder. Should have thought about that before I went all power ranger."

"Does it hurt?"

"Naw, I hadn't even noticed. Kinda' like sunburn, I guess, when I touch it, but it looks damn funny. I'll have to go to a higher neckline for a few days. Guess I shouldn't have pulled the line through, plus I already had a little energy spooled up. I felt like I could have used the amulet all by itself, once I saw the kind of power it held. I wonder if it will drain real fast when used alone, without the backup of the line or a spool."

Robin hesitated a second, and then continued, "Whenever I cast an amulet, there's nothing like that in it. I wouldn't even think of lightning or fire, and forget needles. I need everything I can muster to just cast a calming. It doesn't seem fair."

"Don't ask me, this whole thing is brand new and I only thought it was possible because the grass and trees, fish and birds, bugs, everything alive for sure, and I think metals too, iron, copper, silver, and gold I think, they all told me it was not only possible, but essential."

"Jason, we're all amazed at how the line talked to you, and I'm sure we would never have heard it ourselves unless we were in contact through you. And I don't think metal talked to you, that was probably elementals, guardians of all that stuff. I've never even considered that before. How is it possible?"

"I can't even imagine how, but it seems like I was schooled there for a minute, the first time, when we cast the amulets. They kind of told me how to do it, and I didn't hear them the way we did at the end. I just received information straight into my head, or even deeper if that's possible. It's like they imprinted directly to my mind, or even my spirit. The impression hit me that it's my birthright, just like they said at the end. And somehow I'm not as worried about the dark stuff as you guys, not like I was before."

"You should be. There really is pure evil," Robin interjected.

"A different impression came to me, sort of how I knew about the center. . ."

"Yeah, that blew us all away, we know about it of course, but we never even mention the spirit when we call the corners, nobody does; we just follow the old books and concentrate on the corners. We knew that came from someplace else, had to," Robin added.

"You're right, but I had no idea what to do, what words to use, and your suggestion was a giant help. Thank you by the way."

"De nada," Robin answered.

"But I'm talking about more than that; I have the distinct impression that what we call the evil side is really just the other half of the good, the yin to the yang, the dark to the light, masculine to the feminine. There isn't an evil side to masculine and feminine, most of the time anyway; each is simply half of a whole. I received the impression that opposition is necessary for balance. Kind of like if there was only sunlight on the planet, we'd all burn up, there needs to be night or we'd all be living in a giant Sahara. I guess we wouldn't be alive at all."

"I see what you mean, and it makes sense, but what about the Hitler types?"

"I think there are exceptions where there is all evil, kind of like when somebody gets addicted and all twisted up, and then it's all evil, I guess that's logical. What they impressed on me though was that there are very few truly evil things in the world. Most things are a mix, like there isn't this sharp divide between the profit guys and the compassion guys. There can be profit and compassion mixed together at the same time. Ben Franklin said it was perfectly acceptable to do well by doing good. We need to keep in mind that there is good and bad in everything, and balance is what we're shooting for. I kind of think that that's my job now, not to just vanquish evil, although I think there's going to be plenty of that, but to bring balance where it's needed."

"Yeah, these weapons make me wonder what that's all about. Why give the maker such a destructive weapon? I see you as a healer and a builder for the good side, and figured we'd just need to protect you from the bad side. What you're saying is that you'll try to redeem the bad side and bring them back into balance, and the weapons are there in case they don't want to come."

Jason thought about it for a second, "Yeah, I guess that's about right," he said, and pulled into the pizza parlor parking lot.

They ordered pepperoni and mushroom, Pizzelii only makes one size so Jason ordered two, one for in and one to go, both with garlic crust. When Robin raised her eyebrows to the double pizza order, he explained that they could take one back to the other ladies. After inquiring about beer on tap, he ordered two glasses of craft that was brewed especially for Pizzelii by 50 West so Robin got her pizza and 50 West beer all rolled into one.

Ahead of the lunch rush they had the dining area to themselves. While they waited for the handmade pizza they chatted about more personal things, caught up with their lives over the years past, and Robin learned that Jason had been divorced for a year. Her spirits rose a bit and she had already noticed that he no longer wore a wedding band.

After they had discussed the whereabouts of classmates, the conversation came to a pause, and then Jason continued, "I've got about a million questions."

"I bet you do," said Robin. "I'll try my best to answer anything you ask, but you're something new to all of us. You're just rumor and folklore suddenly here in the flesh. We'll all have to figure this out as we go along. We can start by teaching you what we do know, and I guess you're bursting to get started, but rushing in can be dangerous. The kind of power you can wield is truly astonishing."

"Ok, fools rush in, I get it. And yeah, that fire that jumped out of your fingers was pretty startling, but I just kind of knew it was in there. It looked exactly like what I envisioned when I thought about what should be in the amulet."

"And the casting was directed by the line?"

"Yeah, mostly; I put my own twist to it I guess, but when I thought about Spiderman and webs, that didn't seem to take. Maybe the spiders didn't want to give up their secrets or something. I put a protection in it too, like a force field, as you saw when I shot the fire extinguisher at you. I knew it would work. And, as you already felt, there's wind in there too."

"Fabulous," was the only reply that came to Robin.

"You know, I forgot to pick up one of those amulets for myself before we left."

"Not to worry," Robin said while she wiggled a bit in her chair and produced an amulet out of her enigmatic pocket. She held up the stone pendant and Jason took it over the remaining slices of pizza.

"It's a fire breathing dragon, made of hand carved jade. It's not old or anything, or expensive, but it seemed the appropriate one to me. I should have let you pick it yourself. Does it seem right?"

"Does it ever! It's perfect and it's almost buzzing in my hand. I can feel it."

"I wouldn't put it on yet," Robin said as Jason spread the jute lanyard to slide it over his head. "We don't want you to think about fire and accidently blow a hole in this guy's pizza parlor do we?"

"No I guess not." Jason thought for a moment and added, "We need to practice a little, and I think I know just the place."

"Oh yeah, where?"

"The gravel pit over in Miamiville. It's pretty much abandoned now but there used to be a shooting range down there and it's secluded enough to keep a secret I think."

"Especially if we ward it before we go down," Robin added. "But you don't want to drive your Corvette into a gravel pit, do you?"

"No, we'll meet there later, after work, and I have a pickup truck that will go down there. One of you must have a vehicle that will make it down?"

"Francy has a four-wheel-drive Explorer and we can ride in that if the road is still passable. We can pick you up, it seats six if you don't mind cozy."

"No, cozy is good," Jason said and thought again before he continued, "I need to ask something that's been bugging me since I first heard about your shop."

"Go ahead. We don't have many secrets, and you're on the inside now. There's no reason to hold back."

"Well, I'm curious about the whole 'suffer a witch not to live' thing. Are there religious types to be worried about? Seems like the bad guys and good guys both would be after us. You know, the gremlins or whatever they are, and then the people who think they're doing God's will. That represents both sides of the equation that you have to deal with."

"There are a few, but they leave us alone because there isn't much they can do these days. No hanging, drowning or burning allowed. We had one 'person of faith' steal our Bible if you can believe that. Thou shalt not steal, except to save a Bible from the heathens, I guess. They can try to defame and marginalize us but the whole thing has sort of devolved to leaving each other alone. It gets to the root of the argument, that if they believe in witches then how can they burn them in the first place? How could a witch with real power allow something like that to happen? So they prefer to leave us alone and believe that we have no real power.

"Plus, the ceremonies in formal religion aren't all that far from what a coven might do. You know, call on spiritual beings to affect temporal life. That's what a prayer is really, just a plea to God to bless someone, with good health, or deliverance from evil, or whatever," Robin explained.

"If witches are real, then how can they burn?" Jason repeated the question. "Interesting, I never thought about it like that. It's a good point."

"No real witch has ever burned at the hand of a simple clergyman. There's no way they could do it."

"What about a warlock in the guise of a clergyman?"

"I guess back in the day a warlock might want to pose as a clergyman, to stay under the radar maybe. He could use his skills and say it was miracles from God or something. But a warlock wouldn't really want or need to burn a witch. All the hangings and burnings were done by regular men against innocent women, or at least women of limited skills. There are some people who have a knack for growing things, a green thumb you'd call it. Others have healing hands, or they can see a bit. That's the kind of witch they hung in Salem."

"What about the witch hunts in Europe back in the fifteen hundreds, or whenever?"

"Same thing, regular people were accused for all kinds of reasons and the church rounded people up, tried them, and burned them at the stake for heresy. It was mostly about power and control; land grabs in a lot of cases."

"How come the real witches didn't get involved and protect the innocents?" Jason asked.

"It's a good question, but think about what someone like me could do back then, without one of these nifty amulets you made today. I could Jedi Mind trick the inquisitors, or hex them with warts or something. I could get myself out, but without true weapons how could I protect the forty thousand people who died during the witch hunts that covered a couple hundred years back then? I don't think it would be possible."

"Forty thousand, you're kidding?"

"That's the low estimate, because there were no records kept in rural areas, only in the population centers where there were big churches. Some estimates reach two million. There are stories of entire towns being burned in Germany, including the local priest in one case."

"All in the name of God, for heresy," said Jason.

"Yeah, on the surface at least, but most of it was political, to maintain the power and authority of the church, and in a lot of cases, for gains in lands, and treasure too."

"Jeeze, pretty amazing."

Robin took advantage of the pause to nibble at a slice of pizza and sip a little beer. Jason did something similar, only nibble and sip didn't really describe what he did with the pizza and beer. After a few seconds Robin made a suggestion, "You know, I'm thinking we should practice a little while we're sitting here. The faster you can tap a line the safer you'll be. Why don't you take a peek right now?"

Jason swallowed the wad of pizza already in his mouth and washed it down before he calmed his mind and unfocused his eyes. He saw a similar version of the line that he had worked with in the shop.

"Can you see it?" Robin asked.

"Yes, it's just like in your shop."

"The river is only a couple hundred feet away, right behind Pizzelii's," Robin said and pointed to the south, right past the pizza oven and the employees busy with noon preparations. "Why don't you try tapping the line?"

"Ok," Jason said and reached out his hand. The energy snapped into him and filled him with a feeling of power, of invincibility. "It really is quite exhilarating, isn't it?"

Robin tapped the line and giggled, "Like a drug almost."

The line flowed through them, shared its power between them, cemented their closeness, forged a kinship that felt intimate beyond something as simple as sibling affection, but not quite like lovers. Then they both heard a voice, a woman called through the fog from a distance, "Beware, beware," it warned, and Jason dropped the line.

"Wait," Robin said and held out her hand to stop Jason's question. She held her eyes closed for a few pregnant seconds then dropped the line and looked up at Jason. "We have company."

Company - 8

"Company? There's nobody in here but us and the employees," Jason whispered as he leaned toward Robin across the small table.

"Outside, not to worry, I didn't get anything more after you dropped the line, but before I dropped I felt the presence of a spy, just one, and it can't seem to zero-in on us in here, but it's close. We've got time, nothing to worry about. We must have attracted the attention of something passing by—feels like a crow. We've been practicing outside of a warded space. Anything watching from not too far away would sense that."

"A crow?"

"Yeah, they're pretty smart birds and dark witches can use them to gather information. Down in the city there's a dark wizard, a sorcerer that watches us out this way from time to time. We're in the open and when we tapped the line here, it was like we'd splashed our feet in a quiet pond, sends waves out. A proper ward is designed to stop that. Stay here for a minute."

To help her locate the spy, Robin tapped the line again as she crossed the threshold, and before the door swung shut behind her she felt a separate tug on the line. Jason had tapped in too.

She heard soft murmurs but focused to seek out the spy, indeed a crow perched on a branch of a tree across the street. The crow corked at her so she cast her usual blocks; confusion, blurry vision, and a sense of danger, but this crow didn't leave.

"Oh, so that's how you want to play it," she whispered. "I've got more for you this time little birdy," and she dropped the line to keep from burning herself like she had done when she cast through the amulet earlier.

The door behind her opened and swung shut, she felt the presence of Jason as he stepped up to her left. She raised her right hand and pointed her index finger at the spy that corked again. Robin rotated the tip of her finger in small circles to call wind from her amulet and dialed up her willpower just a smidgen. A column of air darted from her finger and consolidated into a ball shape as it sped toward the crow. She held back most of the power, sent only enough to ruffle the crow's feathers. The puff of wind caused him to flap to keep his balance on the perch, but he didn't fly away.

Robin rotated her index finger in small circles pointed at the spy. She sent a little more power and the next gust evolved into a small horizontal tornado that expanded from the size of her finger to about a foot in diameter as it reached the crow. The tube of air rotated and undulated just like a real tornado, so Robin adjusted her aim to bring the wind to bear, and knocked the bird from his perch.

Head over claws the crow tumbled back and only regained control when Robin ceased the flow. He flapped hard enough to shed a few feathers, righted himself and turned toward the west, toward downtown Cincinnati.

"There we go," Robin said as the spy gained open air over Wooster Pike and climbed toward the city.

Jason raised his right hand in a fist, pointed at the bird and thrust his fingers out to launch a volley of needles that shredded the crow into a puff of feathers. The naked carcass plummeted toward the road. Feathers fluttered down from the point of impact and the needles flashed brilliant white light as they burned to vapor after they passed through the crow.

"What the hell!" Robin shouted. "What did you do that for?"

As it fell, the plucked carcass burst into flames and disintegrated to nothing but a trail of smoke that drifted in the gentle breeze left over from the tornado.

"Jason! You didn't have to kill it! A crow isn't evil; it's just under somebody's spell."

"But Robin, that one was evil. I was told to do it. That wasn't a crow at all. The line told me it was a demon in disguise and that destroying its physical form would simply release the demon and return it to the underworld, or wherever it came from. That part wasn't clear."

"Oh-my-gosh, you're kidding?"

"No, I swear it."

"Did you put your amulet on?"

"No, it's here in my pocket. I forgot all about it," Jason said and pulled the jade dragon out to show her.

"Jason, that's incredible. I don't even understand how you could fire needles without a focus object. Do you taste or smell anything?"

"Just pepperoni, I ate the last piece while the voices in the line told me about the crow."

"Amazing; you're so casual about this and so familiar already. The line talks to you while you eat pizza. I can't imagine anybody else getting away with something like that."

Robin gazed at him for a moment and noticed that he held the take-away pizza box on his left hand like a waiter carrying a tray through a crowded restaurant. "Just like that huh? So matter of fact, like you been doin' this for years. It's not fair you know."

Jason shrugged his shoulders and headed to the car. He hesitated to start the Corvette and turned to Robin, "Do you know who controlled that demon?"

"I've got a pretty good idea. The warlock downtown that I mentioned runs most of the shady, night-type business there."

"Such as?"

"Hookers, gambling, drugs, and black market stuff, cigarettes, Cuban cigars, whatever you can think of, he's into it. He calls himself Penthraig, means head dragon. I know, corny huh?"

"Pretty bad," Jason agreed.

"Nobody knows his real name because real names have power. Combine a real name with hair, or skin cells, saliva, blood, any of that can be used against you. Or for you, depending on who's doing what."

"You mean like voodoo dolls?"

"Exactly like that. Give me some spit and I can make you dance, or turn you into my love slave, or make you do things you would never consider doing on your own. I can call you into a circle with your name and a few hairs and hold you there as long as I want."

"Sounds like I have a lot to learn."

"Yep, and I guess this is lesson one, or ten, or whatever since you're so far along already. Lesson a million is probably more like it. This morning you had hardly any conscious understanding of this, and now, less than two hours in, you vanquished a demon with silver needles out of your fingertips; without a focus. That's amazing."

"Tell me about it. But it seems really comfortable, natural. Like this dormant thing is awake now. I'm a little scared but really excited, and I seem to have this urgent, almost uncontrollable desire to get in the game."

Robin studied him for a few seconds and continued, "Yeah, ok, but now we need to coach you so you can do whatever this calling is for without getting reamed yourself. You need protection from bad guys and the first thing to do is to add a name that nobody knows. We need to seal it with the line so nobody can summon you or hex you. And you need to be careful about hair and body fluids and skin cells. Let's go back into Pizzelii's for a minute and I'll show you. Your fire tools will be really handy for that."

They returned to the table, which had not been bussed yet. "Forget something?" one of the employees asked.

Robin had pulled out her sunglasses in advance, again from the enigmatic pocket in her clingy dress, and feigned their retrieval from the table. As she held them up, she waved at the employee and cast a calming, and added a deflection spell that turned the inquisitive pizza maker back to his duties. Then she picked up both beer glasses and held them in one hand by their bottoms, turned away from the counter and asked, "All clear?"

Jason checked and stepped to her side for additional protection and answered as he turned his back to the counter, "A-OK."

Robin pointed her index finger into the mouth of Jason's glass and released a puff of flame that sizzled the dregs of beer mixed with saliva that evaporated in a short second. She followed with her own glass and wiped the outsides of both with a napkin that she also used to pick up a couple crusts from the pizza tray. She blazed the surface of the metal and added a puff of wind to diffuse the wisps of smoke that trailed up. The whole cleansing took just a few seconds. The employees never even looked their direction and Jason held the door for Robin to return to the car.

Before Jason opened the passenger door for her, Robin placed the napkin with its crusts on the pavement and flashed them to cinders. After the two practitioners buckled-in, Jason hesitated on the starter, "How would we do this with a full restaurant?"

"We'd cast a nifty little spell over the whole place and do the same thing right in front of them. I have to tell ya' that this is really simple with the fire, way better than usual. We just need to keep from burning the whole place down."

Jason chuckled, "Is that really a concern?"

"I'm just worried about Sara or one of the girls trying it without a little practice first. I do most of the casting and I can feel the power in the amulet. I'm experienced enough to gauge how much to use, and your tools feel natural to me already. I used a minuscule amount of power, didn't even tap the line, and the glasses still heated up enough that I could barely hold them, even with those thick bottoms."

"So, I guess I need to collect all the hair off my comb, and keep my toothbrush in some kind of solution, and wash my underwear every day, that kind of thing?"

"Yeah, but we can ward your house and other places to help out a lot. It gets to be a routine, and we usually don't bother at home unless we're being watched, which we will be for sure pretty soon. Plus, they can't do anything really bad to ya' without your summoning name. They could give you an itch or something like that, but couldn't call you to a circle, so the risk is minimal."

"If we ward my house, does that mean my witch with a 'B' of an ex-wife won't be able to get in anymore?" Jason asked as he started the Corvette and allowed it to rumble in idle for a few seconds.

"Well, if she has evil plans for you, yeah, she'll be blocked."

"Great, things are looking up!"

Jason backed out of the space and while he turned he asked, "Did that thing report back to his boss?"

"Hard to say; he was probably out on a routine patrol, an opportunist, but Penthraig could have been watching all along. If he was, we'll be in it up to our necks a lot sooner than we want to be."

"How do we tell?"

"No real way, but that crow didn't act like he was under direct control. If he was, with the power of a demon under the influence of a sorcerer, as soon as I hit him with the wind he would have jumped the line back to his lair. Plus, it's daytime and Penthraig is a nightlife kind of guy. I doubt he knows, yet, and he won't know, at least not more than one of his minions is missing. I didn't feel a tug on the line from that direction, so I think we're ok for a while. He may never suspect what really happened. And then there's Monica. If you'd been under threat, she would have felt it and called by now, but there's really no way to know for sure."

"You have a cell phone tucked in that pocket, or whatever it really is?"

"Yeah, there's a cell phone in there, and yes it's really a pocket, but a very special pocket."

"You'll have to teach me how to make one, looks pretty handy."

"Of course," Robin answered as Jason turned onto 50, headed back toward Milford while he wondered about Robin's pocket in that clingy dress.

Jason asked another question, "Ok. So what do you mean 'jumped the line?'"

"Hey, before I answer that, let's take a quick detour. Just to be careful. I can't remember ever seeing only one crow. Those things travel in pairs most of the time. Turn right on Newtown road, so we can cross the river. We'll go down Roundbottom and over the East Fork back into Milford from the south. That'll take us across the river twice."

"Good idea," Jason agreed and headed across the Newtown Bridge.

Robin pulled up her second sight and looked around for signs of any other watchers. By the time they had crossed the bridge she was satisfied, "All clear," she said, and proceeded to answer Jason's question. "Demons can jump from place to place using the energy of the line, but it costs a lot. They usually have some kind of charm or focus object crafted from something living, like the worm we talked about before, or something bigger, like a rat or rabbit. They spool up the life force in their amulet and use the whole reservoir to jump. It's a dark magic thing and dangerous for anybody from our side. You could get trapped in somebody's circle if they're watching and they have something of yours to divert you, like some hair or even an article of clothing. If a person doesn't take the time to invoke a circle with their soul name, they can be diverted. We don't skip that part as a general rule, it's a dangerous shortcut, but I'm thinking you'd be able to just ask and get passage, seeing as how the line favors you like a freakin' rock star."

"Ok, good to know, but don't hate me because I'm beautiful, I can't help it, I was made this way."

"Oh, don't worry, I don't hate you, I'm just jealous. I've been doing this a long time, and have some talent, and more than a few skills, but you make me look like a rank amateur on your first day. Take a left just after the Shell station, on Valley. It cuts across to Roundbottom."

"Got it, so what now? Back to the shop, report in; feed the girls, then what?"

"We seal a new name for you. You'll do that alone so none of us know what it is."

"It's like a password then?"

"Yeah, but it protects your soul, not your computer files. And like I said, if the bad guys get ahold of your name, they can make bad things happen to you, even make you their puppet if they're powerful enough, and if Penthraig consorts with demons, he has the power. It's important enough to say it again."

"So I need to be thinking of a new name. Let's see, Merlin is probably out?"

"Oh jeesh, please," Robin giggled. "Although, when I think about it, you'd be more entitled to that name than anybody else. But no, make it something nobody can guess. Some people use nonsense words like 'buglump' or 'gnixlflub,' or something in Latin, because it sounds witchy, but whatever it is; only you should know it, and it should be something that you wouldn't accidentally say."

"So is that why all those books and movies use Latin phrases to cast spells, so they won't say anything by accident? Maybe blow up a pizza joint when all they want to do is heat up their coffee?"

"Well, I doubt any of the books or movies understand the motivation, and that's a little simplistic for an example, but that's essentially it."

Jason spent the rest of the ride deep in thought about potential names. They pulled up in front of Enchanted Notions a few minutes later and Robin led the way into the shop where the others responded to the call of pizza, including the cats that jumped up on the counter in anticipation. The women were surprised to see that Jason had reentered the shop.

"We thought you'd be headed home, but we're glad you're here," Monica said. "I'd be plum tuckered out after the morning you've had, as a newbie and all. Aren't you tired?"

"I'm fresh as a daisy, couldn't be better. In fact, I feel great, full of energy and raring to go some more. Apparently, I need a new name."

"Plus, there's news," Robin added as the girls jockeyed with the cats for pizza. "Jason killed a demon right out in front of Pizzelii's."

Even the cats stopped pawing at the pizza box and they all stared at Jason, stunned by the news.

Monica broke the silence, "How did you know it was a demon?"

Robin answered for him, "The line told him."

"No!" went around the circle of women in disbelief so Robin filled them in on all the details while Monica pulled pepperoni from her slice of pizza and tossed it to the cats that she'd called back to the floor.

"Oh boy, it's on now for sure," Monica said. "Robin, we need your best wards on Jason's car, his home and business, his workshop, everywhere he spends a lot of time. Do a security sweep and start with the car."

"On it," Robin said, and headed for the door.

Monica continued, "We can't wait until next Wednesday to begin training. Sara, honey, call in some backup to cover the shop, we need to practice with these amulets. Time and a half is approved for whoever you can get to come in."

"Good as done," Sara said and stepped behind the counter to make the calls.

"Susan and Francine, prep the studio for a name sealing, and we'll try the big circle since Jason is Hercules and Sampson all rolled into one," and they nodded while they turned for the door.

"Jason, if you're available and willing--and you should be, for your own good--your training starts right now."

"Ready, willing, and able," Jason replied and came to attention, clicked his heals and saluted.

Soul Name - 9

"Ok, Jason, let's give 'em a couple minutes to prepare the circle and in the meantime we'll talk about your new name, or what we call a soul name, or summoning name."

"Great, I could use some guidance."

"Perfect, never be shy about asking for advice from any of us, or in your case from the guardians too. I'm sure Robin already told you that names have power, both for good and bad. The bad side is why we keep them secret from everybody but the true guardians. It's never been an issue for us because we don't have much that anybody would want and we keep to ourselves. We don't make enemies who would use our names against us. Another thing is that we've never been able to travel in the realms, but it seems like you'll be able to go there for vacation if you want, if what I've seen so far holds up."

Jason thought about the term 'realms' for a second and decided to defer for later, "It's all so overwhelming, but in the same breath, I feel comfortable, and very excited about going forward."

"Well, that's good because this is no place for doubt or fear. You have something big to do, and I suspect that when you enter that circle in a couple minutes you're gonna' find out what it is."

"I hope so. I'm anxious to get on with it."

"Great. Now with respect to names, you can pick whatever you want. Rumplestiltskin if that suits you, but that doesn't seem to fit as far as I'm concerned."

Jason chuckled and Monica continued, "Your divine name, or soul name, should be something that gets to the roots of you. After you dust off all the cobwebs it should be an affirmation of who you really are, and if you can't get to that, it should affirm who you want to be.

"Some people take months to pick a name and in the process, some of them figure out who they are. But we don't have that kind of time for you. That's why you'll be wise to ask the guardians for help when you're inside the invoked circle."

Jason considered Monica's words for a moment and said, "I get this picture of somebody shouting out 'Jason' in a crowd, like at a parade or something, and not a single Betty will turn around, but I'll turn around every time. I hear it and obey, just like a trained monkey. My name has power over me."

"Exactly, and the same thing happens if a bad guy gets your true name and calls you into a circle, nobody else will hear it and your butt is in there for as long as the bad guy wants you there. You'll have to buy your way out and it can be real expensive if you have a lot of what the summoner wants, like all that power you've already shown today."

"Blackmail huh?"

"Yes."

"So I take it this power is transferrable or something?"

"Some creatures, some of the Unseelie for instance, can suck the power from you, energy vampires is what we call them, but for most practitioners, not really. None of us would be able to do that, but it doesn't mean the bad guy can't force you to do some big favors. There are ways, like drugs, or spells if they sneak up on you, to subjugate you. In that case they'd be able to draw a line through you and stick you with the cost.   You'd be the worm, but it wouldn't kill you. Somebody like you who can call on the line to pay would be almost inexhaustible to somebody willing to abuse you for their own gain. Plus, your power is capable of doing what the old alchemists tried to do for millennia."

Jason thought a minute and said, "You're talking about turning lead into gold, that kind of thing."

"That's it. And by way of example, they'd have you trapped in a circle, maybe they'd hold a knife to your girlfriend's throat, or hold one of us captive, and compel you to make a bunch of gold for them. Or they'd grab your sister and force you to make all sorts of amulets that they could use to wield your power, the way we'll be able to do with the charms you made for us. The nasty buggers from Unseelie and dark sorcerers would do things like that," Monica suggested.

"Geesh, it's like something out of an old horror movie."

"Not to worry, we just keep you out of a place like that and there's no problem. If they tried to hold one of us hostage to manipulate you without having you trapped in a circle, you'd be able to take them out with a backhand wave and a 'howdy do.' Nobody in their right mind would dare challenge the power of the line wielded by a seventh son."

"Yeah, maybe; of course, that's probably just the type who would try that kind of thing, somebody out of their mind," Jason implied.

"Too true, but it would still be a big mistake, on their part. We'll go over in a minute, the girls probably have everything just about ready, but before we do I want to explain a couple things about a circle."

"I'm all ears."

"Great, it's important to think of the brass circle as a planar cross-section at the very bottom of a perfect sphere, like a soap bubble sitting on one of those little bubble-blowing wands, or a crystal ball sitting on a brass ring stand. Most people think of the circle as a line bisecting the sphere, but if you do that then you wind up with a nine foot diameter ball with four and a half feet of space above the floor and four and a half feet below the floor. We want most of the sphere to be above the floor, and if you think of it like that, the sphere can be a really big space to work in. We want it like that so we can get a whole coven inside."

Jason thought about it for a moment and asked, "What if somebody forgot about that and set the circle so it was bisected, would it chop 'em in half?"

Monica answered, "No, if you touch the wall of the bubble it will burst. If it was my circle and you were standing in it with me crouched down, it would just pass right through you, and half of you would be outside the circle, unprotected. It goes through the floor, after all, and doesn't cut the wood. If you set it outside on the ground, it goes right down through the dirt. We invoke it first, that way the energy of the line shows the sphere, kind of paints over it, and if you're close to touching it you move it up, make it bigger, so it's not a problem. You set it when it's ready and not before. But if you were in a hurry to get away from something for instance, and if you set the circle at the same time as you invoked it, then it just wouldn't set at all if it touched any part of your flesh. Once you set it, if you touch it from the inside, as I mentioned, it will fall, but until then nothing on the outside can get in.

"Robin can set a circle in a couple seconds, just by crouching down and scribing a personal size circle with an athame, or a piece of chalk, or just her finger in the dirt. It's a good thing to be able to do if there's an attack. Once she's in it though, she's stuck until the bad guy goes away, or something happens to him. In fact, she was attacked last Halloween."

"Really, what happened?" Jason asked.

"We had a bunch of customers on a ghost walk, something we do every year, and we were outside the wards. There was a spy watching, a boogie or boggart or one of those nasty little Unseelie, I can't keep 'em straight. Anyway, Robin tapped the line to see if there were any ghosts around and the spy darted out of the bushes and went straight for her."

"Why, for cryin' out loud?"

"It's always for power with those things. They want to grab anybody with some skills and imprison them and draw on their power, to make themselves more powerful. Like I said, some of them are energy vampires and they need a fix, or they want to be the boss of their enclave. The end game is control, mostly."

"So how did she get away from it?"

"She didn't have time to cast anything so she dropped into a crouch and scribed a circle in the gravel, set it instantly. The boggin ran right into it and knocked itself out. Then she dropped the circle, pushed the boggin in with her foot and re-set it from the outside. When the boggin woke up it was trapped. Robin came back after the tour and forced it to buy a trip in the line back to the Unseelie court. That thing was pissed off, let me tell ya'. Anyway, we have to be a little careful, and now with you around, we need to be a lot careful."

"What did the customers think about all that?"

"Well, they didn't know what was going on because none of them had second sight, and by the time they realized Robin had crouched down they just thought she had tripped. She nudged the boggin into her circle with her toe, re-set the circle in a second and nobody was the wiser."

"Holy cow!"

"Yeah, pretty wild."

"You said she forced the boggin to buy a trip through the line. Why couldn't Robin get out of her circle with a trip through the line."

"Well, two reasons really. One, she would have been at risk for some confederate of the boggin who was watching. They might have been able to draw her to their own circle when she jumped, if they'd found out what her summoning name is. It's always better to be safe than sorry. And the other reason is the cost is high. A trip through the line is equivalent to a year off your life. It's better to just wait it out because the Unseelie are impatient and they get bored easy. It would have run off after an hour or so, if it couldn't find some leverage to force her out. Anyway, let's get you over there so you can figure out your new name."

They retraced their earlier steps to the studio where they found the long folding leg table leaned against the south wall with the legs snapped in. The carpet was rolled up and out of the way behind the table. The chairs were folded and leaned against the north wall, which Jason noticed for the first time was light purple. *They sure like purple*, passed through his mind.

In the center of the room the nine-foot-diameter inlaid brass ring stood empty, apart from unlit candles in silver candlesticks placed at each of the cardinal directions. Each candle was a different color, green to the North to represent earth, yellow in the East to represent air, red for fire in the South, and blue to the West for water. In the center of the circle the women had placed a long-nosed lighter and a dagger. Robin, Francine, Sara, and Susan stood on the outside of the circle, one at each candle, facing in.

"Everything's ready to call the corners," Robin said.

"Ok, Jason you stand in the center of the circle," Monica instructed, and Jason did. "Each candle should be lit as we call that particular corner. Once the circle is set, you'll be able to close it just by saying 'silence' and then we can't hear a thing."

"What's the dagger for?"

"We call that an ath-mey, spelled a-t-h-a-m-e, and it's there in case you need to draw blood, or whatever comes up. You can defend yourself with it too; if you need to. The blade is silver plated and will work on anything you might run into, but we don't think that will be an issue. Nobody knows about you yet, I don't think. And that's why we're here, to seal a new name for you, so nobody can abuse you when they do find out you're around. Your name right now is a matter of public record and anybody that knows it can jump right in there with you, or pull you through the lines to their own circle. For now, all you need is the lighter."

Jason picked up the lighter and waited for instructions. Robin tapped the line and instructed, "Bring up your second sight, tap the line, and repeat after each of us while you take a knee and light the candles in turn."

"Ok," Jason said as if it were a question. He tapped the line and gasped at the vision of the river of energy flowing through the room. "I still can't believe it," he added.

Robin continued, "Let it be known that a circle is to be cast," and Jason repeated word for word. Robin continued, "This circle is to be private and secure from all but he who enters and sets the casting for the purpose of sealing a new and secret name to be known by the caster and the guardians of the watchtowers and the guardians of the elements only."

Jason repeated everything Robin said and moved toward the candle in front of her, but she pointed to her left, toward the East.

Francine pointed at the yellow candle, Jason kneeled to light it and as he did she picked up the narrative, "Guardian of the Watchtower of the East, I respectfully request your attendance for this right of naming and ask you to please grant the powers of knowledge and wisdom that are guided by air. We ask in love and trust in the name of the Goddess."

Jason repeated and when he looked up at her she pointed toward the south. He noticed that a bit of the blue green line wafted up in front of Francine like smoke rising from a partially extinguished campfire, but slowly, and it followed the curve of the sphere. He stood and moved to face Sara who pointed at the red candle in front of her. Jason kneeled to light it and as he did Sara said, "Guardian of the Watchtower of the South, I respectfully request your attendance for this right of naming and ask you to grant the powers of energy and will that are guided by fire. We ask in love and trust in the name of the Goddess."

Jason repeated and watched line energy spiral up in front of Sara where it curved to meet its twin between East and South. Now Jason had the idea and instead of waiting to be pointed he rose and moved in front of Susan at the blue, West candle where he kneeled to light it and as he did Susan said, "Guardian of the Watchtower of the West, I respectfully request your attendance for this right of naming and ask you to please grant the powers of passion and emotion that are guided by water. We ask in love and trust in the name of the Goddess."

Jason repeated her and watched the smoky energy rise to connect with the other two and the entire Southern half of the circle swirled with blue green light. Jason realized that the dome being described was only four and a half feet tall. It intersected with him at the belt buckle since he was close to the edge, and even though he wasn't sure how to make a change, he thought about the sphere as if it was sectioned at the bottom and the bubble responded. The sphere expanded so that the top of it passed through the ceiling and the sides bowed out past the copper circle.

"Good, very good," he heard Monica say from her position between Robin and Francine. All the girls backed up to stay clear of the broadened wall of the orb before them.

Jason moved to face Robin at the North position. He kneeled to light the green candle and as he did Robin said, "Guardian of the Watchtower of the North, I respectfully request your attendance for this right of naming and ask that you please grant the powers of endurance and strength that are guided by earth. We ask in love and trust in the name of the Goddess."

After Jason repeated the phrase Robin waved him back to the center and continued, "You don't have to repeat anything else, the corners are called, and the circle is ready to be set. What you do now is think about the words you said to invoke the circle and think about why you want to be in there in the first place. Later, you can pick a word that represents all of that and say it to invoke and set the circle all at once. For now, when you're ready, just say 'set'. Don't forget to use silence to block the sound or we'll all know your name when you ask to seal it."

Jason turned and said, "Thank you all. It seems a momentous occasion, like a baptism or something, so thanks for your help." They all nodded in reply and Jason took the queue with the simple word, "Set."

Jason felt a pressure change that popped his ears and wind blew. The sphere around him crackled with tiny lightning bolts and a deepened energy level made apparent by the thickened, quickened, and brightened blue green swirl that defined the dimensions of the bubble. He turned to look at the women with their jaws dropped and hands clasped over their hearts and at the base of their throats. Jason felt secure, confident even, but he didn't like the look on the women's faces. Clearly, something new had happened.

"Jason, can you hear me?" Monica shouted.

"Yes, clear as a bell," he replied in his normal voice.

In her normal voice, Monica continued, "Wow, I figured I'd need to shout over the wind and all that crackling in there. Are you alright?"

"Happy as a clam so far."

"Ok, it looks pretty wild in there, but if you feel good about it, it's time to call for silence."

Jason nodded and spoke the word. The noise of the wind and electricity was blocked from the girls, and Jason stood alone. All the women felt helpless and inadequate with their new friend on the inside of a maelstrom that they'd never seen before. Robin reached out and knocked on the sphere, "Hard as concrete," she said.

Jason didn't respond from the inside, didn't even hear Robin's knock, but he did hear the voices from the line, more clearly than he'd heard them before. The voices pierced him as if they were on the inside of his head instead of the outside, and they sounded like an entire choir of men and women and children all in unison.

"Hail Jason, seventh son of a seventh son, maker and protector of the living. Welcome to your naming," the voices said in unison.

"Thank you all. I'm here to serve but ignorant of protocol and pretty much everything else. Please teach me what I need to know and guide me to the service you require."

"Well said," the choir of voices replied. "To the naming, then, and after, introductions to your true guides who will instruct you further, for it is their duty, and your destiny."

"I apologize for being unprepared. I haven't had sufficient time to think of a proper name, could you help me please?"

"Your name has long since been chosen, it is your essence as well as your entrance to the realms of the guardians. You are seventh son of seventh son, maker, and guardian of living, defender of right, protector of weak, and speaker of truth. You are warrior of righteousness, destroyer of wickedness, and you are sanctified by birthright in honesty and faithfulness to your calling. We speak it and it is so. Henceforth you shall be known to us as Jason Patrick O'Hara Sahen. Sahen being the ancient word for seven, being the shape of the sword, and further representative of the wheat sheaf, thus symbolic of the strength of many held as one. We hold and protect your sacred name unto the felling of the world. We beseech you to go forth and seek the path that will be shown to you as you tread in honor. Fear not, courage Sahen, fulfill your destiny."

"Thank you, I'm humbled," Jason answered. Before he could ask one of the thousand questions stirred up in his mind, the chorus of the line interrupted him.

"Now, Sahen, meet the Guardian of the Eastern temporal and terrestrial angle, the keeper and ruler of the very air you breathe, caller of whirlwind, tamer of tempest, most high prince of celestial intelligences and sacred angels for good, His Honor, Michael. Speak his name with reverence for he is a God to all under his purvey."

Jason turned to the east, where the yellow candle wavered in the stiffening breeze, but it did not go out. The entire sphere glazed suddenly and the air near the candle shimmered into human shape. The form developed until there stood before Jason a white haired, smiling man with a close-trimmed beard, in white robes like a senator of ancient Greece. Taller than Jason, maybe six and a half feet, Michael's hair was curly and trimmed, adorned with a wreathlike golden crown of laurel.

"Hail Jason Patrick O'Hara Sahen, well met," Michael said and offered his hand.

"Hello sir, it's my pleasure," Jason replied and went for the handshake, but Michael's hand slipped past his own and grasped him on the forearm all the way to his elbow. Michael's grip was firm and he shook Jason heartily and slapped him on the shoulder.

"Well then, it's finally time. We have been watching for you and now you are called to fulfill your destiny. Are you ready and willing to accept your duty?"

"More than willing, sir, but I don't feel particularly ready."

"Have courage, Sahen, and call me Michael. We are on familiar terms now. You shall receive the necessary instruction in the time that it is needed, for circumstances vary greatly. Do not fear, my friend, have faith that you shall be provided for. As long as you honor the calling and resist temptation to excess, you will receive all that you require. If you fall to poor decisions, your birthright will be stripped from you, and in that day you shall be as all others and subject to the reckoning of justice. Keep your birthright, keep to your work, and you shall have dominion over the elements and wield the power of life and death with the blessings of the terrestrial and elemental guardians."

"Thank you Michael, I'm humbled to receive your blessing and I will do as you command."

"Yes, fine my friend--well said. We have great confidence in you. Now, meet the prince of air, the one who will be your guide in my stead, my right hand, Cherubiel. It is he you will call upon for guidance from the Eastern quadrant," Michael said as the air to his right shimmered and developed as before into another white haired, ancient Greek senator look-alike, also with a broad smile."

"Hail Jason Patrick O'Hara Sahen, well met. I am at your service," Cherubiel said with a nod and offered his hand.

The Roman handshake repeated and Jason said, "Thank you sir, I'm pleased to meet you and humbled to be in your presence."

"Ah, so polite, and proper. Very well, Sahen, we will be great friends and close associates in the work ahead, I'm sure. And call me Cherubiel, if you please."

"Thank you Cherubiel. I'm anxious to learn my duty and will strive to be a good student."

"Wonderful, Sahen," Cherubiel replied and continued; "Now it's time to meet the Guardian of the South."

The chorus of the line spoke, "Now, Sahen, meet the Guardian of the Southern temporal and terrestrial angle, the keeper and ruler of fire, caller of flame, tamer of lightening, most high prince of celestial intelligences and sacred angels for good, His Honor, Nariel. Speak his name with reverence for he is a God to all under his purvey."

Again the air shimmered and this time an ethereal flame swirled through the sphere, and warmed Jason to the core. Outside the sphere, the women had gathered next to Robin and looked on in wonder. They could no longer see clearly, since the sphere had frosted over before the appearance of Michael, but they could see enough to know that there were now four human shapes standing inside Jason's circle.

Robin had gasped at the first appearance and said, "Holy cow, the Guardian of the East is in there with him."

"That would be Michael," Francine agreed.

When the second person formed next to Michael the women were at a loss. "Who is that?" Sara shouted.

"I don't know," Monica answered, "but I have a feeling it's gonna' get pretty crowded in there before it's over."

"What a privilege to be a witness to this," Susan offered.

"Yeah, but who are *we*? Chopped liver?" Robin added rhetorically. She didn't need or want an answer and the women all looked on in silence.

Inside the sphere Jason enjoyed the same introduction to Nariel and his assistant, Nathaniel, as he had with Michael and Cherubiel.

The Southern Guardian and his prince looked and talked much the same as the Eastern ones. Nathaniel shook Jason heartily and said, "Hail fellow, and well met, Sahen. We will work together with Cherubiel, and Tharsis, the prince of the West, and Ariel, the prince of the North, to restore balance and to retire the minion demons that have been called to the Earthly sphere by evil designing wizards.   For   now   we   will   continue   with   the introductions."

The chorus of the line spoke again, "Now, Sahen, meet the Guardian of the Western temporal and terrestrial angle, the keeper and ruler of Water, caller of cloud and rain, tamer of oceans, most high prince of celestial intelligences and sacred angels for good, His Honor, Raphael. Speak his name with reverence for he is a God to all under his purvey."

Raphael appeared as another white-haired and bearded Greek senator along with a swirl of crystal blue water that slightly chilled the warmth of the southern fire, and mixed with it to ride the winds of the East in a blue and reddish-orange rainbow of shifting color. The unlikely meld of fire and water mesmerized Jason and also the women on the outside who gasped and gaped as witnesses of the beautiful twisted air, fire, and water that swirled around the sphere. Like a cold drink on a summer day, Jason felt refreshed and fulfilled.

After   a   similar   meeting   that   included   the   now obligatory Roman handshake, Raphael introduced his prince, Tharsis. After the greeting, Tharsis spoke, "The gifts of the power of Air, Fire, and Earth have been granted to you already and are stored in the amulets of your warriors, let us now grant the power of Water as well. Hereafter you may call on water in any form, as you may call on Fire and Air and Earth. All these things are given to you in your righteous pursuit of balance and justice. May you use these gifts wisely and not to excess."

"Thank you Tharsis, and thank you all for these incredible, and generous gifts.   They will be used with reverence and temperance," Jason replied.

"Well said, and now meet the Guardian of the North," and the choir of the line introduced Gabriel. As the line called him, the green representation of the Earth ascended to join the eddied current of Air, Fire, and Water.

Gabriel brought forward his prince, Ariel, and after the standard meet and greet, Ariel spoke, "The gifts of the power of Air, Fire, Water and Earth have been granted, however, you should understand that the power of Earth includes more than silver needles. You may call upon earthquake, upheaval, magma, landslide, crevasse, any needful thing that you require. All of this is in your hands, use it wisely and avoid excess. In a moment we will allow an audience with your warriors so that the gift of the power of water may be added to their amulets, and so that we might seal their commitment to the work, in support of your duty. However, before we do that, we shall accomplish that for which we have been called, to seal your new name. Please stand in the center."

Jason moved to the center of the circle while the Guardians and their princes took their places at the quarters. Michael began the name sealing ceremony, "Jason Patrick O'Hara Sahen, by the power and authority of the Guardians of the Watchtowers of the four quarters and on behalf of Hecate, Goddess of magic and the crossroads between temporal and spiritual realms as mediator and advocate of the righteous, holder of the keys of the gateway, and protector of the worthy, we seal your name in harmony with the essence of all living things and grant you access to the realms of the guardians and passage along the lines of living energy throughout the temporal world and as necessary throughout the realms of spirit. You are seventh son of seventh son, maker, and guardian of living, defender of right, protector of weak, and speaker of truth. You are warrior of righteousness, destroyer of wickedness, and you are sanctified by birthright in honesty and faithfulness to your calling. We hold and protect your sacred name from any and all who seek to do you harm and command all the Privy Council to honor your righteous requests. We beseech you to go forth and seek the path that will be shown to you as you tread in honor. Go forth and fulfill your destiny."

Jason felt something beside him, or rather with him, perhaps within him, a presence of warmth, love, understanding, and even sanctification, as if he'd been filled with a special entity or companion, a motherly presence. From the outside, the women saw a shining womanly shape in flowing robes and golden hair adorned with a spiked crown. She held a torch in each hand and the women watched her meld with Jason in the center of the circle for a moment and then dissipate into wisps of light that joined with the other colors that twisted and roiled around the inside surface of the orb.

"Could that have been the Goddess?" Robin asked to nobody in particular.

"I'm not sure who else it could be," Monica replied. "Which one, I couldn't guess."

On the inside, Michael continued, "The naming is accepted by the Goddess and sealed with the life force of the line and all living things. Now, if you will make a passageway for your combat team to enter the circle, we will secure their commitment to support you in your work and grant them full power and authority to act on your behalf."

"I've never felt anything like that. I'm overwhelmed. Thank you so much. I beg your forgiveness, but I'm not sure how to make a passageway," Jason said.

Cherubiel offered instruction, "Take up the athame at your feet and simply cut a door."

"Just like that, then? Nothing to it?"

"It is your circle. You may alter it at your need. Touch it only with the blade, for if you brush it with your hand, it will dissipate, and us with it, but we still have work to do."

Jason picked up the athame and knelt to push it into the translucent swirling colors that still moved around the entire inside surface of the globe where the bubble met the floor. Half way between North and East, right in front of the women, he dragged the blade left to right along the floor, up the right side of an imagined door, and along the top rail, and down the left. When he pulled out the athame, a door shaped section of the bubble dissipated. He noticed that the wall of the bubble was about three inches thick.

The stupefied girls stared at Jason through the open door, "Well, would you like to come in?" he asked.

Teamwork - 10

Robin stared at Jason through the open door in the bubble, hesitated a moment and then said, "You're supposed to ask us how we enter the circle."

"Ok, Robin, how do you enter the circle?"

She took Jason's offered hand, stepped across the threshold and said, "I enter with peace and love, and pray for the trust of the Goddess."

"Monica, how do you enter the circle?"

She stepped across and said, "I enter in peace with perfect love and pray for the light and love of the Goddess."

All the women entered with similar phrases and each followed Robin around the circle with the dip of a knee and a bowed head to greet the Guardians and their princes in turn. As they progressed around the circle, they were more and more overcome, and all of them snuffled with tears from pure emotion. The Guardians greeted them in warm tones, "Hail and well met sister Robin. I am Michael, Guardian of the East and this is my prince Cherubiel. Welcome one and all." Similar greetings happened all the way around until all the women were in.

Jason wasn't sure how to close the door, but the impression came to him that he simply needed to place the athame into the color at the header and draw it down. He did so and the door filled in like a window shade with no seam or any indication at all that a passage had ever been there.

Everybody shuffled to make room and Michael asked the Western Guardian, Raphael, to grant the power of water to the women. He did so with great reverence and similar instruction to that which he had given Jason. As he blessed each woman he touched their amulets with the tip of his index finger.

Michael continued, "Do you all commit your time, your talent, even your very lives to the work which will be laid out before you in support of your leader, Jason Patrick O'Hara, in order to return balance to the earth and to bring justice to practitioners of evil and to retire demons that have been called to the Earthly sphere to do harm and mischief?"

The women each with their head bowed and sobbing voices said "I do."

"Very well," Michael continued, "You have all received powers similar to that of the seventh son; you have been set apart and sealed to the work. Go forward with confidence and courage, for your task will be difficult at times, but we will be there at your need, to guide you and guard you. However, the task is yours and you are expected to fulfill it, call us sparingly because we do not seek to alter the balance too far, there must be opposition for free will, and anything else is contrary to the point of existence. You must have choice and only balance offers choice to all.

"We shall leave you now, and be advised that the local inhabitants are eager to stand in support of your mission. Great shall be your rewards in this life and the next if you mind your task in proper form with humility and avoidance of excess. Hail and farewell," Michael said as he wavered into nothingness.

All the Guardians and their Princes left in a similar manner. After they were all gone the women wept and huddled to the center in a group embrace. Jason noticed that the globe had returned to its original look, with the blue green energy of the line wafting over and around it. The glaze was gone and it was easy to see through its walls.

Jason cleared his throat to break into the attention of the group, and said, "I think I need to thank them and the Goddess before we leave the circle. Anybody have anything to say?"

The women opened their group and Robin reached out to pull Jason in where they smothered him with hugs and tears. After a long few seconds, Monica said, "Yes, a thank you would be nice, Jason. Please go ahead, for all of us."

Jason bowed his head and raised his hands with palms up and offered, "Oh Goddess of magic, life, love, and liberty, and Guardians of the Watchtowers with your princes, and spirits of the Life Force, we thank you for our wonderful blessings and for the power and authority to act in your name for the good of all. Please forgive me for my inexperience, and pardon all of us if we must call upon you again. Please guide us to what is right and wholesome and pleasing to you in your ancient and gracious wisdom. Farewell and return in peace and love to your beautiful realms, until we meet again."

A moment later all of them heard a response:

Friend Jason Patrick O'Hara, seventh son of a seventh son, we exist to serve. Hale and farewell, oh guardian of the living…

. . .and the spirits whispered to themselves, now attendant of the line, as they had done before.

Sara bawled out, "I heard them plain as day. How wonderful! Jason, seventh son, thank you so much," she said as she grabbed him around the waist and pulled his chest into her face as she wept into his shirt.

Jason hugged back as the others surrounded him again, showered him in tears again. "Hey guys, were you aware that we have company?"

The women pulled away and rubbed the tears from their eyes as they scanned around the room to find families of raccoons, squirrels, and rabbits, a dozen mice, and twenty or more large flying insects that glowed and talked in high pitched voices, in English.

"Holy Shit," Robin said, along with the rest of them in varying degrees of exclamation as they realized that the bugs were little women, fairies no doubt.

"What the hell?" and, "Oh-my-God!" they said over each other.

The bug sized women spread out around the globe and sang as one:

> Oh lovely hall of magic ones,
> We come in peace and trust,
> To help and serve the seventh son,
> With honor as we must.
>
> In perfect love we serve the right,
> And battle evil in the night...

Jason touched the wall of the orb and it vanished with a rush of air and a pressure change that blew their hair with a soft pop. All the animals and poetic insects scattered toward the back door. They were all gone in an instant and Monica asked, "How in blue blazes did they get in?"

The women ran to follow and found the door ajar when Francine offered an opinion "Must have been one of the guardians. Michael said the locals would be eager to support us, how about that for cool?"

"Way cool," Susan replied.

Jason joined them at the back door and said, "Well, what next?"

Monica took charge as their natural leader, "Robin, you take Jason home and to his business and get those wards up. The rest of us will get the shop in order and meet you at the gravel pit for some target practice. I, for one, can't wait to try out these new weapons. After that we'll discuss how to move forward."

"Sounds good," Jason said. "No time like the present. See you all at the gravel pit."

Robin and Jason returned to the Corvette and Jason felt something when he reached for the passenger door handle. He hesitated to touch it and turned to Robin, who said, "You feel it don't you?"

"Yes, it's like static electricity or something. What is it?"

"I put a couple layers of wards on there. I'm pretty sure the amulet helped me make it much stronger than usual. I'm really happy with it, because you normally wouldn't feel anything unless you had mischief on your mind. And I'm happy not only that it's more powerful, but that you can feel it. Your senses are developing. That's pretty amazing for the first day. The Guardians want you on the job right away, it seems."

"Well, let's get to it then," Jason said and opened the door for Robin. They headed back out of town over the bridge as they had on their way to Pizelii's only this time they turned right, toward Miamiville.

They drove to his home in Loveland while Robin replayed the events of the day with enthusiasm.

"We saw the Goddess meld with you. How did that feel?"

"The whole thing is a whirlwind pretty much, but I'd have to say that part was the most engaging on a personal level. It felt like a warm bath with an oil massage at the same time. Pretty amazing really, I wasn't sure what was happening but I knew it was good. I felt loved and protected, and accepted. More than accepted, I guess justified is another word, not a better word, but another one added in, sanctified too I guess. It's hard to explain, but it was a great feeling.   Like nothing I've ever experienced."

Warding - 11

Jason pulled into his driveway and Robin responded, "Well aren't you the yuppie poster boy? This place could be on the cover of Urban Professional magazine, if there was such a thing."

"Yeah, Karen kind of insisted on it. She especially fell in love with the breezeway between the garage and the house, if you can believe that. We had most of our meals in there, when we sat down for one that is, which wasn't all that often. I'm in debt up to my eyeballs for it, but I guess it works ok."

"Lovely," Robin said as she stood next to the Corvette to study the manicured grounds. Tasteful beds bloomed with spring flowers and the lawn was trimmed like a fairway.

Jason joined her and continued the conversation, "Karen's moved up to the country club set. The place she lives in now makes this place look like the servants' quarters."

"Too bad, this house would suit me right down to the ground. This is a place for raising a family with three kids and a dog. Idyllic upper middle class, the American dream. All you need is the picket fence."

"Yeah, I like it, but it seems a little much for a bachelor pad."

"You won't be a bachelor forever, will ya?"

"I don't know. I guess I'll have to see how this warrior for truth and justice thing works out. Maybe I won't even survive it."

"Don't worry honey, you will, and I'm gonna' help make sure of it by plasterin' this place with enough protection to keep Genghis Khan and the Mongol hordes outta' here. Let's get started on the inside."

Jason opened and held the front entry door while Robin stepped in. She hesitated at the threshold and noticed a six pointed star in a roundel on the mat. *H'mmm, hex sign*, she thought, *probably not the wife.*

She pulled something that looked like a small faceted rock out of her magic pocket, "What's that?" Jason asked.

"This is a smoky quartz crystal and we need one at every entrance, front, back, side, whatever you have. We're setting up a grid that nothing evil can penetrate."

"You have enough rocks in your pocket to do all that?"

"Doubting so soon Thomas? I thought you were all in?"

"I am, it's just that pocket of yours defies logic."

Robin giggled and said, "Just minutes ago, you stood in a magic sphere with eight mystical Guardians and melded with a Goddess, and you're worried about my little pocket?"

"Well, when you put it that way I get all embarrassed and feel stupid."

"Not stupid, sweetie, you're just a noob. Don't worry about it. How many entrances do you have?"

"There are three; this one, the back, and the breezeway from the garage."

Robin pulled five more crystals from her pocket and continued, "Ok, we'll add one to the door from the garage to the breezeway too. I presume there are doors on both sides of the breezeway in addition to the garage and house so we'll cover those too."

"Yep, six in all."

"Let me concentrate for a sec and I'll speak out loud so you can get a feel for what's going on here."

Robin tapped into the line, pulled it in from all directions because the land was flat and a mile from the nearest river or valley. Jason tapped in too. "Good, you felt that."

"Yep, and I'm getting better at joining you."

"Great, now be still for a minute and concentrate on the crystals in my hand. We'll call on one of Hecate's court, Enodia, the watcher over entrances."

Robin closed her eyes, dropped her head in reverence and prayed, "Mother Enodia, guardian at the gate, with perfect love and peace we call upon you to bless us with your protection on the house of Jason O'Hara, a seventh son, called and sealed to the work. Please grant us this favor in the name of the Goddess Hecate and seal this house in protection against accident and evil and ill purpose of all kinds. Thank you and blessed be."

Robin bent at the knees and waist to place one of the crystals on the floor next to the door but before she completed the task, a voice pierced her mind and Jason's too.

"Sister Robin Rae Stapp, daughter of Mother Earth, esteemed practitioner of the craft, lioness of battle, defender of right, and protector of weak, hail and well met. Brother Jason Patrick O'Hara, seventh son of seventh son, maker, and guardian of living, defender of right, protector of weak, and speaker of truth, warrior for righteousness, destroyer of wickedness, called of the Guardians and sanctified of Goddess Hecate. Hail and well met."

Robin was almost there already so she kneeled in submission and respect with her head bowed and eyes closed. She clutched the crystals over her heart and shivered as the beautiful Enodia shimmered into existence in front of them in brilliant white silk and jet black hair. Her hair and robes seemed to gently float in a breeze that neither human could feel.

Jason seemed unaffected and when Robin failed to say anything he offered, "Mother Enodia, fair Goddess of gateways, protector of the righteous, hail and welcome to my home, and thank you for blessing us with your presence. We are humbled and thrilled."

"Rise sister Robin," Enodia said, and waited for Robin to comply. "Great shall be your need and great shall be your support. My angels will attend the doors of this home and all other places you see fit to protect. I shall personally attend with a flaming sword to cleave asunder any who would threaten the gates, doors, and passages of entrance and escape in support of the mission of the seventh son. Fear not, for I am tasked to perform on your behalf. I do so with pleasure. This special dispensation I bestow upon you, sister Robin, look upon me and receive the blessing of the Goddess."

Robin looked up to drank in the radiant visage of the raven haired beauty before her. Enodia dressed in the flowing robes that Robin had always imagined as the garb of a Goddess, topped with a silver tiara for a crown, she gazed with crystal green eyes into Robin's egg blue eyes. The Goddess pointed her index finger at Robin's chest, and touched her between the collar bones. A flash of light burst from the point of contact, then Robin filled with a warm glow that rushed to permeate her body.

Enodia turned her head to Jason, "Farewell," she said with a smile, and vanished.

Robin slumped but Jason grabbed her around the waist before she hit the floor. He struggled with the door because of his awkward position behind the limp woman in his arms. He lowered her while he worked his arms around to pick her up, with one arm at the knees and the other at her back. He carried her to the living room sofa where he gently laid her down. He checked her rapid pulse at the carotid artery and watched her chest rise and fall with shallow, almost panting breaths. Not knowing what else to do, he ran to the kitchen to wet a hand towel.

When he returned she moaned and stirred as he folded the towel and placed it on her forehead. A few seconds later she opened her eyes to find Jason kneeling on the floor next to her. He held her hand in both of his.

"Are you ok?" he said.

"Oh God, did I pass out?"

"Yeah, you went limp, like a wet noodle."

Robin stirred in an attempt to sit up but Jason pressed on her shoulder, "Just stay there for a minute, until your pressure comes back up. We don't want you going out again."

"Ok, I'm content for the moment. Tell me what happened."

"She touched you and light flashed. I saw a glow spread through your whole body; like you were one of those cylinders you put a candle in, or a better description is when you put your hand over a flashlight. The glow was inside; it shined through your skin all over your body. She turned to me and said 'farewell' and vanished. Then you just went limp. I caught you on the way down and carried you in here."

Robin used her free hand to pull the washcloth from her forehead and ran it over her face. Jason stood and pulled her to a sitting position with the other hand and sat beside her. She ran the towel behind her neck and across her collar bones as Jason released her, "How do you feel now?" he asked.

"Much better, almost normal. Give me a couple more seconds."

"Take all the time you need."

"Geesh, I'm such a girl. No wonder you boys get all the cool stuff."

"What? You were just infused with the power of a Goddess and you're still whining with the penis envy? Maybe a man wouldn't even have survived whatever she did to you. Maybe that's why she touched you and not me. What about that? I was just an observer this time."

"Yeah, I guess you're right. Sorry, it seems a little ungrateful doesn't it? I'm just geared to trigger on the feminine, have been for a long time. I guess I need to adjust that a little."

"You have great strength of character, Robin, don't change a thing. I like you just fine the way you are. There's nothing wrong with fighting for what's right."

"Thanks, I get it; just pick the battles a little better, huh?"

"So what's next? Do you feel like continuing?"

"Of course; that's what we're here for. Just let me get a drink of water first."

"Stay right here, I'll get it for you," Jason said and headed off to the kitchen.

Robin stood to test her state of being and everything felt good. She looked around the room, *definitely the touch of a woman with good taste, expensive taste,* she thought. Artwork on the light blue walls, plush cream colored carpet, claw foot furniture, everything matched all around. Antiques spread here and there, classic dental work and fluted column mantelpiece. Crown molding and wainscot painted white and live plants all around. "Very nice," she whispered. And on the wall to the right and left of the fireplace she noticed two more roundels, both with a curious bird in the center, one facing the other across the chimney. "Distelfink," she whispered to herself.

Gotta be his mom, she thought just as Jason returned with a heavy lead crystal tumbler that brimmed with ice water. She drank half of it in one go. After a moment she pointed at the pictures and asked, "Probably from your mom?"

"Yep, she's a Shultz, just steeped in Pennsylvania Dutch."

"Do you know anything about those pieces?"

"Yeah, I guess I do, Mom painted them herself."

"Oh my gosh! They're so good. I had no idea your mom was so talented."

"Runs in the family on that side I guess."

"Did she tell you what it means?"

"Yeah, she said it was representative of a goldfinch, the good luck bird. She painted those for all us kids when we moved into our own homes. Some of them have "Wilkum" lettered under the bird, for 'welcome' obviously, and that one usually has two birds on one roundel. I never asked why mine didn't have the lettering, and she never offered. That's about it; she was a little cagey about all the barn signs. She used to say she did them just because they were pretty, but when the curiosity bug bit me I spent some time on line and learned all about hex signs and all that."

"Well, your mother was a very wise woman, and I suspect she knew more about what you were than she let on. She would never leave an open invitation, in your case. At least I wouldn't and I guess she wouldn't either. I bet that's why there's no welcome lettering. Not everything is welcome here." After a few seconds of thought, Robin continued, "She must be very proud of you."

"Yeah, if she could see me now, huh?"

"Oh, she sees you now; I'll betcha' my last nickel."

Robin drained the rest of her water and the clinking ice cubes reminded her of quartz so she asked, "What happened to the crystals?"

"I'm not sure. I guess they're on the floor by the front door."

Robin finished the water and handed the tumbler back to Jason, "Thanks, let's go see."

Jason set the tumbler on a coaster already in place on the end table and led Robin back to the front door. The six small stones were scattered in the entryway but they were easy to find because they glowed with soft amber light.

"Wow, look at that will ya'," Robin said.

"Pretty amazing, but that kind of thing gets less unusual all the time," Jason replied.

"Well, I guess the crystals are done. We just need to put them by all the doors," and they did. They returned to the house from the breezeway and Robin led Jason to the northwestern most corner of the first floor. She pulled another crystal out of her pocket and was surprised to see that it glowed just like the smoky quartz now in place by all the doors, except the glow was purple. "Huh, Enodia thought of everything. This one is amethyst and we'll put one of these in each corner of the house, on both floors," and they did.

The master bedroom was upstairs on the southwest corner, perfect placement for Robin to slip a small heart shaped rose quartz charm next to the amethyst. She didn't mention it to Jason because the rose quartz was there to promote calm, gentle, compassionate love, as well as heated passion at the right moments. In the back of her mind a subtle desire bubbled that she sensed but tried to ignore. "What the hell. You never know," she whispered as she tucked the small heart in the corner.

Jason waited at the door, "Did you say something?"

"Just a little invocation, that's all. Now we need to go to the property corners. Can we grab a spade or a hand trowel? We need to bury a stone in each corner."

"Sure, there's a potting shed attached to the back of the garage. Should be whatever you need out there."

They exited through the north door of the breezeway where Robin noticed another building that she hadn't seen before. "That's my workshop," Jason said as he guided her along a stone path that split off from the one that lead to the workshop. They curved behind the garage where they came upon a nifty little deck with a roof that extended off the back wall. Under the roof was a massive wooden potting table with a cobalt blue tiled surface and two heavy shelves above. Hand tools of every variety; pruners, loppers, and trowels were hung from wooden pegs on the side of the table. Shovels, spades, hoes, rakes, forks; all the long handled tools hung from a rafter to the side of the table. Pots and water cans were organized on the shelves with bags of fertilizer and potting soil stored on a shelf beneath the table top.

Robin stepped up onto the deck and selected a trowel, "You built this didn't you?"

"Yeah, a surprise for Karen, but she wasn't much for doing her own gardening. She hired everything out. My yard guy loves this thing and brings his wife with him to do special pots for the house. There are live plants all over the place, and it's a pain in the neck for me to water all that, but I guess it's worth it. Reminds me of my mom's place; homey, you know, a woman's touch."

"Live plants in the house are a good thing Jason, and believe me, I noticed. Too bad Karen didn't get it."

"Best thing that ever happened to me, but I don't want to talk about it, if you don't mind."

"No problem, and as long as we're back here, we should do your workshop. I can't think of a better place to cause an accident than a shop full of power tools."

"You're kidding. Somebody would try to hurt me in my own shop?"

"You betcha,' once they get a load of what you can do, they just might be inclined to trip you into a table saw to chop off your casting hand, or something even worse. They'd burn the thing down with you locked inside; if they thought they couldn't control you and decided to just do away with the problem. And believe me, you're gonna' be a problem for them. You already dispatched a demon and barely batted an eyelash over it."

"Should I have remorse for that, d'you think?"

"No, not at all, I'm just sayin' who'd be able to do that on the first day of practice in the craft? That's all."

Jason opened the door to the shop and Robin was impressed with the layout and all the machines. Everything looked brand new, with the exception of the corner that held the blacksmith tools. All of those looked like antiques, including the anvil. Everywhere else one could eat off the floor.

"Wow, you sure keep this place clean. Every other shop I've been in is covered with sawdust and wood scraps."

"Yeah, I have to keep it pretty clean because of the forge. It's well vented but sawdust can be explosive. I have a big dust collection system in its own shed outside and that takes care of most of it. Whenever I turn on a tool, the dust collector runs, and each tool has a collection hood. The valves operate automatically to connect the running tool with the collection ductwork. It's a novel system that I designed and built myself."

"Of course you did. I continue to be amazed." Robin placed smoky quartz at the entry door and the big rollup door. She added amethyst in the corners and they left the way they came in. "Now to the property corners," she directed.

Robin used the hand trowel to open the earth where she placed black tourmaline, smoky quarts, amethyst, and clear quartz; all of them glowed with Enodia's blessing.

Robin tamped down the grass and at the last corner said, "I put the same kind of stones in a small purple felt bag that I placed in your glove compartment. That's part of the protection that I invoked for your car. The bag also includes feverfew, an herb that helps transmute energies in moving vehicles. The clear quartz magnifies everything else."

"What do you mean transmutes energies?" Jason asked as they headed back to the potting table.

"When a bad guy fires a spell at you, the energy needs to be converted to something less potent, or changed to something positive. A protection grid on the move kind of lags behind the car, the line energy drifts away in the slipstream. All the protection trails out behind the car, where you don't need it. Feverfew saturates with the protection energy from the crystals and helps carry it along, and it absorbs or converts whatever energy is cast at you from the outside. I'm not as worried as I used to be, because now I have your amazing amulet with its own built-in protection bubble that's better than anything I've ever seen."

"Ok, what's next?"

"Well, this house is only a few years old so we probably won't have to sage it. I should have had you open your second sight in there so we could see if anybody's hangin' around. This was Shawnee land and some Iroquois made it down into here too, even some Seneca maybe. Anyway, there were Indians, pardon me, Native Americans, all over this place long before we got here. You never know when there might be a pissed off native ghostie around lookin' to get some payback. That's not really why we're here but it wouldn't hurt to check. I guess we could do that another time and head over to your business now to lay some wards down there too."

"My partners should be locking up at about 6:30 so we better wait until they're gone, don't you think?"

"OK, that's probably a good idea. Let's go back in and see if anybody's around, but let me set the protection grid first."

Robin drew line energy to her and waved her hand from the northeast corner all the way around the yard to finish back where she started. She closed her eyes and whispered, "Praesidium posuit eget."

Jason tapped into the line energy immediately after Robin and when she murmured her phrase he saw the blue green mist thicken and snap in an instant into walls that surrounded the entire property. The color lightened where it curved over the house to join all four walls together high above. "Wow, looks like a fortress now. How high do the walls go?" Jason asked.

"Only a couple hundred feet, we don't want to interfere with airplanes, but demon crows that try to fly over will get a nasty surprise."

"What was the phrase you used?"

"It's just Latin for 'set protection grid.' I'm not even sure if it's really how to say it, but it doesn't matter if it's correct as long as I have the right intent. That's what it says to me and that's what matters."

"Awesome. I guess you said it in Latin to keep from using it accidentally, like you mentioned earlier?"

"Well, yeah, but not so much for that, since you wouldn't normally use a phrase like that unless you intended to set a grid. I could have said it in English, but when I dreamed it up, I associated deeper meaning with the Latin phrase. I meditated about protection grids a while back, and used the Latin phrase to hold all the intent that I could build into it, sort of a code phrase, like we talked about. It would be like using a single phrase to make one of your amulets. All the stuff you crammed into those things took a while to build. If you wanted to do it with a phrase or even a single word, you would meditate, build all the things you want into the image in your mind and then associate a code word or phrase with the whole thing. That way when you use the special word, all that intent would dive right in without the need to go through the whole process again. I use that little shortcut all the time. As long as you build it right to begin with, you can use the word over and over for an indefinite period."

"Awesome," Jason replied and they returned to the back door of the house. Jason held his second sight open the whole time. He saw the protection energy as it boiled around the door and all the windows in the back. The breezeway was also heavily protected. He suspected that the tingle that wafted across his skin as he entered was from the energy of the spell.

As soon as they stepped across the threshold Robin instructed her student, "Ok, keep your sight up, and just walk around. Look into every corner, every closet, all through the house and concentrate on spirits like the one you helped cross over earlier today."

"Oh man, that was today. Seems like a year ago, and it's hard to believe I had a part in it at all," Jason said as he strolled around the first floor. They spent a slow twenty minutes to check every crevice, including the basement and the crawlspace in the attic. "All clear," Jason announced when they were done.

"Great, but I expect it won't stay that way. Your seventh son thing, now that it's awake, will draw spirits to you. You'll be a lighthouse on a moonless night to them. You won't have to worry about evil or mean ones, because they won't be able to get past the wards, but tame ones, lost or confused, will see this place like a beacon. When they show up, don't waste a lot of time on them, just send them on to the light. Some might have a message that will be a comfort to their loved ones, or maybe they'll help solve a crime. Whatever it is, you can pass it along at your convenience, or not at all if you don't want to. It's not your responsibility, and I'll help with that to keep them from bugging you too much."

"The surprises just keep on comin'. I know now that anything is possible so how could I still be surprised?"

"Like I said, you're a noob."

Enter the Dragon - 12

Twenty miles to the west, in the heart of downtown Cincinnati, Penthrag, the head dragon, entrepreneur and sorcerer-in-chief stirred from a druggy sleep. He was crime boss of what is called locally the 'tri-state' area, where Ohio, Indiana, and Kentucky meet. He'd partied at his club, Caleo, last night and mixed his poison with far too much enthusiasm. The loose translation of Caleo is "hot and bothered" in Latin.

The buxom blond woman who was passed out facing him snored away on her side, but didn't look familiar to him at all in the low light that filtered in from the bathroom. He slid the silk sheet from her shoulder down past her hip to see if the large breasts, slender waist, and shapely hips conjured any memories, but he remembered nothing.

He gawked and thought, *I wonder who she is? The problem with having so much fun is that you don't remember having so much fun. I'll have to start all over with this one though; keep her around a while. She's amazing. I wonder if the boobs are real,* he pondered, and cupped one to see. *Fake, but who cares, they look fantastic.*

The woman stirred, opened her eyes and said, "Hej sotnos." She realized that he had no clue what she meant and continued, "It means, 'hi sweetie.'" After a short pause she said, "You want to go again? So early?" and stretched like a cat, with an arched back that displayed her assets to their fullest.

"I hate to say it, but it's not early, baby. It's past four in the afternoon, and I have business to take care of. You stay right where you are and feel free to make yourself at home. There's food in the fridge or you can order out if you want, just tell them to put it on my tab. All the joints around here cater to me special, like I was the King of Siam. We'll get reacquainted later tonight."

"Thanks honey," she said and rolled back into the silk to snooze a bit more.

Penthraig showered in the spacious granite-appointed bathroom that was the size of an entire bedroom in most houses. He'd converted an old three story business building on Vine Street, not far from the University of Cincinnati. The brick building had been a clothing store at one time, then a hardware, then electronics, and now it was the hottest club in all of Cincinnati. The store fronts all along Vine had come to life after years of abandoned neglect. Now the Over-the-Rhine district, or as it's called by the initiated, the OTR, is the place to be any night of the week.

Named by German immigrants, the OTR grew up as Cincinnati's brewery center. Beer brewing served as the city's socioeconomic center for decades. Then, like many cities, decades of decline followed.

When Penthraig learned his craft and made deals in the dark, the area came back to life. The old breweries were restarted or repurposed. The old Schoenling building was now a Samuel Adams brewery. Kaufman had become Christian Moerlein. Findley market, the oldest farmer's market in the state, had been completely refurbished and once again drew customers for fresh produce from all over the greater Cincinnati area.

Vine Street was lined with two and three-story brick buildings, had been for a century, and a large percentage of them incorporated storefronts on the street level with apartments or offices above. Most of the buildings had been boarded up, infested with rats and clandestine drug factories, before Penthraig came along.

When Pen, as he was called by his friends, used his influence, or better stated as his dark magic, unresponsive investors became enthusiastic supporters and financial backers. OTR grew, and prospered, which on its face seemed like a good thing, but under the surface, young women and young men were turned to drug abuse and prostitution. Illicit drug manufacture continued but now it was organized and sanitized under the direction of businessmen and city leaders who gleaned the fields for protection and participation.

During the day, legal trade drew upward-progressed professional types with families. During the night, illegal trade hidden under the guise of legal nightlife plied the fast lane and drew coeds with rich boyfriends as well as seasoned denizens with money who were on the prowl for excitement.

Caleo packed 'em in on the weekends and weeknights buzzed but at least there was shoulder room. The real action happened underground, in the old brewery tunnels. Most of the buildings in OTR were built before 1900, before refrigeration, so Lager was brewed and kegged underground to keep it cool. Bottling changed the game in a big way, and necessitated means for the transportation of fresh beer to the bottle works across the street. The easiest and most temperature controlled way to do that was on the same underground level, so the brewers honeycombed OTR with tunnels.

Pen had uncovered passages that city planners would never find on any plat map. Prohibition had driven frenzied activity below ground and tunnels lengthened at an exponential rate during that time. Of course, illegal activity was best left undocumented, so nobody really knew the extent of the tunnels until Penthraig ferreted them out, added a few of his own, and improved them for his purposes.

Caleo operated at street level as a legit night club, but underground there was anything and everything that the dreams of a hedonist could conjure. On the second floor of Pen's building there were four large offices to keep track of his holdings, and the top, third floor was his living space. There were four decent sized apartments up there originally, but he'd had it gutted, walls removed and massive pillars set in their place with steel beam cross members to hold up the twelve foot ceiling. He liked to call the design "postmodern industrial" and it was full of stainless steel, glass, granite, and marble. Full length electro-chromic windows darkened to opaque at the flip of a switch, and even the walls to the bedroom were made of glass.

One of Pen's favorite ploys was to invite a new girlfriend to make herself more comfortable in the bedroom and then with impeccable timing enhanced by his abilities, he'd grab his remote and turn off the glass wall so he could see her in whatever state of undress she'd happened to reach. He loved those little surprises. The girls almost always acted embarrassed and grabbed for something to cover up, but he couldn't understand why because they'd gone in there in the first place to prepare for his entrance, pun intended. Every now and then he'd find one that would simply saunter over to the window and press her breasts to the glass. In fact, he just recalled that 'whatshername' did that very thing last night, or was it early this morning? He was foggy on the whole evening, but bits were coming back as he rode his discreet elevator down to the lowest level, to his private, secret office.

A rough looking mobster goon type with a pocked face and big nose rose from a desk as Pen entered, "Hey boss, we have the daily brief ready and there's a couple things on there that you're gonna' wanna' see," said his adjutant, Alastor. Al for short was Pen's right hand man and privy counsel for the entire Pentraig Empire. If Al didn't know about it, it hadn't happened yet.

Pen insisted on a daily brief just like the President of the United States, a comprehensive secret document that presented all of Pen's holdings and the state of every business. Each section began with a snapshot for quick information. If Pen wanted more details, they were there. The document also listed specifics of the protection detail including the spy network he used to keep an eye on prospective competition, potential threats, and opportunities.

"Ok Al, give it up," Pen said as Al handed him a three inch ring binder packed with individual sheets. First were the immediate action items, and on the top of that list was a tip from a source in the District Attorney's office about an upcoming investigation in the disappearance of one Adalie Suzanne Becker.

"Where is Ms. Becker at the moment?"

"She's our best producer so she's down in number nine. That's the best room we have. She's only been on the line for a month and she's already the top girl. She seems pretty happy too, what do you want to do?"

"Regardless of how happy she is, I'm not sure we'll be able to avoid prosecution for kidnapping and prostitution charges leveled by loving and irate parents."

"We could do something with the parents."

"No, the family line, in general, is inexhaustible and sooner or later we'd run into real trouble going that way. No, I think we'll send Ada out to California, or New York, where she can phone home with the usual boyfriend story. I suppose they tripped to the girlfriends, their last sighting, something like that?"

"Yeah, that's the way the report reads."

"We'll have to speak with the boys on the floor, again. They're supposed to be more discrete. I guess we can't make 'em all perfect, but it won't hurt to point it out one more time. Have Stoli take care of the girl."

"Ok, as soon as he checks in I'll let him know."

"He's not back yet?"

"Overdue by two hours now."

"He ever come back late before?"

"Not to my knowledge, he's one of our best imps. Loves his job and he's always on time."

"Except for now,"

"Right."

Pen closed his eyes and tapped the line that flowed along the mighty Ohio, a mile away but so big that it felt like he stood right next to it.

"Where's he patrolling today?"

"Out East."

Pen turned his attention to the East, upriver, in the direction of the flow of the line, and called to Stoli with his soul voice. There was no answer.

"That's funny," Al said. He had tapped the line at the same time as Pen. "Can't believe you can't reach him; I tried a few minutes ago and just thought it was me, since I don't have your moxie."

"We should be able to reach him, but I can't feel him at all. Who's his relief out East today?"

"Cali, but he's on fours and probably isn't even out there yet. The next winger is South, and that's Edgi. He's due back at sunset."

Pen directed his thoughts to the south, which was problematic because the terrain on that side of the river went straight up from the banks a couple hundred feet. The virtual cliff dammed up the line and made communication spotty to the South. "I'm not getting him either, but that's probably the Kentucky shoreline. Any wings come home lately?"

"Yeah, there's Beti, she was spelled by Edgi. She's probably down in the cafeteria, hangin' out with the rest of the mornin' shift."

"Get her in the air to the East. Find out where Stoli is, or what happened to him. I'm not optimistic. Tell her to cruise by the folks at Enchanted Notions. If Stoli got in trouble out East, those ladies are the only ones out that way who could do any damage. Tell her to stay high. The witches don't have much reach, I don't think, but I'd rather they not know she's there if we can help it."

"Ok boss. What about Ada?"

"I'll see to that myself. Is there anything else in this report that I need to see right this minute?"

"Nothin' that won't keep for a bit; a day or two probably."

"Great, see you back here in twenty."

They checked with the line energy to make sure the tunnel was vacant and entered the tunnels through a hidden entrance that looked like the rest of the bricks that lined the wall. Al turned in the opposite direction from Pen. After a five minute walk that uninformed guests could never duplicate without breadcrumbs, Pen stopped in front of a door marked with a gold script nine. He tapped with his knuckles.

"Come in," sounded extra sultry through the door.

Pen entered and found Ada sitting up on a short divan, "Hello Ms. Becker," he greeted.

"Ada, please, Mr. Pendragon," came the silky siren call.

Now I see how she's risen so fast, Pen thought. *She's a true charmer. Wonder if it's natural or enhanced. Probably enhanced, our madam is the best in the world.*

"Ok Ada, I need to talk to you for a second."

"Are you sure you only want to talk?" she asked and rose to show her five-eleven model figure to her boss.

"I'm quite interested Ada, but I need to just talk for a moment."

"Oh pooh, that's no fun. I'm not in trouble am I?"

"No, you certainly aren't in trouble. I'm going to send you on a little vacation to New York or California. Which do you prefer?"

"California is wonderful, they say," she said and glided closer, and stared into Pen's eyes.

Lovely, he thought. *Eyes as blue as a glacier and a natural blond, she could be a cover girl at any agency in the world.*

When their eyes connected, Pen drew on the line and pulled Ada's thoughts to him. She had been under a spell the whole time she'd been a working girl in Pen's establishment. He recognized the traces in her mind, he'd seared them into her brain himself. Now the spell was a part of her psyche, and he began to alter the traces without her permission or knowledge; one of the dark sorcerer's powers. A dog or a goat would have to die later to replace the spooled energy that Pen drained to grasp control of the lost girl in front of him. She was his slave in reality, but she didn't know it, and she would not remember it.

He didn't need to use words, but he found the sound more comforting for the receiver, "Adalie Suzanne Becker, I command you to forget all you have known in this place. Hereafter you will wait in this room until someone comes to take you with him to, where shall you go? I see in your thoughts a warm sun and sandy beach, so you will travel with your companion to San Diego, where you will spend a lovely weekend on the beach to swim and surf and see the sights. On Monday morning you will call your home and talk to your Mother. You will tell her how much you were in love with a traveler who met you at Caleo, the best club in the world. You will tell your mother that you were enchanted with his charms and you will apologize for not calling sooner. You will beg forgiveness and refuse to name the boy because you were at fault and foolish. You will tell your mother that he never made any promise other than to show you a good time in California, where you always wanted to go. You will tell your mother that you want to come home and beg her for a ticket on the first available flight. After that you will do as your mother commands and you will not remember anything from this place where you served many, except in pleasant dreams. Now sleep and dream until you leave for San Diego. You will awake when you are safely on the road, and you will believe that you are in love and traveling to a wonderful future, until Monday morning when you will feel remorse for leaving without saying goodbye, and you will call your mother to do as you have been commanded. Sleep," he said and touched her forehead. She lay down on the bed and closed her eyes.

"Sleeping beauty, it's so easy," Pen said and left the room.

A ten minute walk away in the other direction, Al had just filled in Beti with her new mission. She stared up at him with knitted brow and a frown from her five foot two altitude. Her brown hair was tied in a bun, and she pierced Al with falcon-like eyes, jet black pupils and yellow irises, like sunflowers.

"Of course I'll go out. Stoli's in trouble,"

"Report back as soon as you know anything," Al said, and Beti sprinted down the tunnel to a half circle shaft of light. In mid stride she shifted to her winged form, a Kestrel Falcon, and darted up through the air vent at sidewalk level in the side of the building as her clothes dropped empty on the tunnel floor.

"I'll never get used to that," Al said and turned for the return walk to Pen's office.

Outside, Beti the falcon imp soared skyward. She climbed to the South over Vine Street until she was high enough to clear the buildings and then continued her climb eastward. Navigation would not be a problem; every demon in the employ of Penthraig knew where the witches to the east of Cincinnati practiced their craft. She'd follow Columbia Parkway all the way to Milford, with special care around Lunken airport. Birds and airplanes just don't mix well, but on this beautiful day, she could see a small private airplane from fifty miles away. Perhaps she'd swoop down to follow the Ohio and then up the Little Miami. No, the river would take longer and Stoli was missing.

$\mathcal{P}$*ractice - 13*

Back at the shop, Monica, Susan, Sara and Francine prepared to pile into the Explorer for the trip to Miamiville.

"Sorry Amanda, thanks for coming in early, we appreciate it."

"Hey, no problem Monica, I'm glad to get the extra hour."

"Ok then, we have our cell phones if you need anything, but we may be out of contact for a while. Go ahead and feed the cats if you will, please. It's been a hectic day, good hectic but hectic nonetheless."

Amanda had been around long enough to know she was better off not asking what had made the day such a trial that the cats were neglected. She watched the four practitioners exit the rear of the shop and waited for them to pull out of the back lot. She shook her head and returned to the counter where she opened the cat food and shook some dry kibble into each of the three bowls. There was plenty of water for them so she sat in the tall chair against the red brick wall and opened her staff book to work on a new song. Her talent lay in the music field and she had little desire to learn the ways of a sensitive, but she loved the little shop and had brought her organizational skills to bear. The jumbled up shop had gained a natural flow that enhanced the shopping experience and increased sales. Her real ambition lay in Nashville, and she had the voice, looks, and connections to make it a reality. She wanted to succeed on her own and refused the offers from the witches to light the way before her. It wasn't that she didn't believe or appreciate the sentiments, she just wanted to do it under her own power and the girls respected her for that.

The cats stood sentry on the back window sill, not hungry, just concerned.

Francine turned right after they crossed the bridge. While Sara had her second sight up before they reached the bridge, she let go after they crossed. She was eager to discuss how they intended to practice with their new amulets and had dropped her guard in the belief that they were safe from any spies once they reached the other side of the river.

Perhaps if she'd kept her sight up, and had looked high in the direction of Cincinnati, she might have seen the speck of a Kestrel Falcon on an intercept heading, but probably not.

Beti had just arrived at the outer reach of her station when she saw the four witches exit the rear of their shop. She didn't need to search for auras, she could see their faces, recognized every one, and required no other confirmation. She decided that a stakeout on the shop would be fruitless with four of the witches gone, so she followed them. The thermals had diminished in the evening air but she only needed an occasional flap to coast along with the Explorer, 'ghosting' the technique was called, and she was perfectly suited for the mission.

In Loveland, Robin and Jason were back in the Corvette, headed to the rendezvous with the girls. They'd spent the last half hour discussing the events of the day and were just headed out to the office when Monica texted Robin to meet at the gravel pit at 7:00. They figured the timing was good and they'd beat them there by a few minutes.

They'd meet and instruct the girls on their new weapons and practice a little. Perhaps they'd find the limits to the power they were called to wield on behalf of good versus evil.

Jason and Robin did arrive first and leaned against the passenger door of the Corvette as the girls pulled up. Francine stopped to take on their new passengers but Robin rotated her hand in the universal roll down your window signal.

"The entrance is blocked by a big 'ol log. I guess the owner doesn't want anybody down there. Maybe the road is washed out or something," Robin said.

Francine pulled ahead of the Corvette where the log was evident, "Oh brother, that's a big one. I guess were going to have to walk down or find another place to practice," she said and turned off the motor. The girls exited the Explorer and gathered at Jason's car.

"What now?" Monica asked.

"I've been thinking about it for a minute and maybe we're not out of luck after all. I have a hunch, so let's see what we can do," Jason offered and led the women like ducklings to the obstacle.

"What are you thinking? Like we're Navy Seals in training and we're supposed to pick up that log, put it on our shoulders and carry it down to the bottom?" Sara chided.

"Hey, you wanna' be a lumberjack you gotta' handle your end of the log, right?" Jason teased. "No, I'm thinking something else entirely. It's not chained or pinned that I can see," he said and held out his right hand with the palm up, fingers curled in, but not in a fist. He extended his arm a little and opened his hand toward the log. A whirl of air flowed from his fingertips and tested the log just ten feet in front of the group.

Jason crouched down and bounced his hand up and down at the wrist still palm up and pivoted his arm from the elbow, like he was tossing a ball up and down. The wind strengthened and rotated into a little tornado that curled under the right end of the log. He raised and lowered his arm and hand in an undulating motion and the log rocked.

"Lookit' that would ya?" Sara said among gasps from the rest of the women. "Wonders never cease. Regular ol' Jason my ass!"

The log lifted on the right end about a foot and pivoted away. When it reached the berm of the gravel road Jason slowed his hand motions, the log settled gently and laid there as if it had never been moved at all.

"Well folks, let's get to the bottom of this, literally, and fire up these amulets. I'm itchin' to get witchin.' Shotgun!" Sara shouted and jumped into Monica's traditional spot in the Explorer.

"Not so fast Sara honey. We need protection. We're gonna' send tidal waves down the line unless we ward the snot outta' this place," Robin said. "It's big so everybody help out please."

Sara hopped back out of the Explorer and Monica asked, "What are we using?"

"You're not gonna' believe it, but Enodia visited us at Jason's house, and we have a promise," Robin informed the ladies.

"Oh, you're kidding," Susan nearly shouted to be heard over the gasps of the other women.

"Cross my heart," Robin replied.

"What was the promise?" Monica asked.

"She promised personal protection, help from her angels at every door, gate, and passage, including Enodia in the flesh with a flaming sword if we need her."

"Oh—my—God!" Sara blurted out.

"That's not all," Jason added. "Enodia touched Robin right between the collar bones and she went out like a light. Or I probably should say she went on like a light and went limp as a wet dishcloth."

"What do you mean, 'went on like a light?'" Francine asked.

"When Enodia touched her, her skin lit up. Just like your hand looks when you put it over a flashlight in the dark. She glowed for a full twenty seconds. She fainted, but I caught her on the way down and carried her to the sofa, and she glowed like a firefly the whole way in there. By the time I set her down, she looked normal again; flushed, but normal."

"Fainted huh; you big sissy," Sara said.

"I know, jeesh, it was embarrassing," Robin replied.

"And that's not all. The crystals glowed from then on. They were still glowing when we left," Jason offered.

Robin pulled a black tourmaline from her pocket and all the women gasped again because it glowed like a hot coal at the end of a campfire.

"Robin, I'm not sure you'll need us for this one," Susan said.

"Well, haven't we all had the interesting day?" Monica said and 'tsked a couple times while she shook her head.

"I wonder," Robin said as she rattled the stone around in her caged hands.

"Wonder what?" Monica asked.

"I wonder if I can set a grid with one stone?" Robin answered and rolled the glowing tourmaline like a die to the edge of the road.   Before it stopped she said, "Praesidium posuit eget."

They all saw it even without opening their second sight. Not a square, as they expected, the ward flowed out from the stone like a live river of fog and followed the irregular edge of the gravel pit all the way around. It looked like the hole in the ground had been filled to the top with a thick fluffy cloud.

"Oh man, that's the coolest thing I've ever seen," Sara offered.

"You mean cooler than the Guardians and the Goddess earlier today?" Francine challenged.

"Well, you know what I mean."

"Yeah, I do, and Jason, honey, are you sure you won't marry me?" Francine offered again.

"What? I had nothing to do with that, it was all Robin. She's the one with the blessing from Enodia, not me."

"Well, none of it would have happened if you hadn't shown up at the shop this morning, so the offer stands."

"You better be careful, I might just accept one of these days, and then what will you do?"

"I'll get divorced and marry you, that's what," Francine finished.

"That's enough, Francy, for God's sake, give it a rest," Susan said.

"Ok, are we sufficiently warded?" Sara asked.

"Yeah, I'm pretty sure," Robin answered. "One thing about not being able to see in is that we won't be able to see out either. We won't know if something's coming."

"Well, I'm for taking the chance, plus, you have a promise, so let's get our asses in gear."

They loaded up the Explorer and rolled down the access road with great care, in case there was something wrong with the gravel, and because she couldn't see very far in the fog. After a few feet of descent, they cleared the fog roof and could see all the way across the pit with no difficulty at all. Still, Francine proceeded slow and careful.

But Sara wasn't interested in careful, "Come on Granny, get off the damn brakes. I wanna' shoot fire from my fingertips."

Francine rounded a bend where she could see the rest of the road and rolled a little faster, but still with care.

"Over there, right next to the pond in front of that pea gravel mountain," Sara directed as she pointed to the west wall of the pit. The gravel there extended up from the pond all the way to the crest, 150 vertical feet of backdrop.

"That's where the shooting range used to be," Robin said.

Before they had rolled to a complete stop, Sara jumped out and sprinted toward a self-designated firing position. She skidded to a stop, tapped the line, flicked out her right hand and fire blazed from her fingertips. A horizontal cylinder of pure flame blasted the pea gravel.

The blow torch of fire was so loud that Robin figured Sara didn't hear her shout, "Sara! No! Don't tap the line!"

If she heard at all, she ignored the advice because she didn't hesitate for a second; she was caught up in the moment. She fired again, this time with both hands, double barrel cylinders of napalm splashed into the pea gravel. Steam burst from the mound and sulfurous smells wafted toward the group who watched with rapt attention. They all wondered if Sara would spontaneously combust with all the fire she sent downrange.

Now she fired alternately, left hand then right hand over and over while she shouted, "Yeee hawww!"

Suddenly, she stopped and clutched at her chest, then pulled at the lanyard around her neck. Something was caught in her sweater, "The amulet," Robin guessed aloud.

"Holy shit!" Sara shouted as she ripped her sweater off, and then slapped at her chest. She yanked her bra off over her head and continued to slap at her chest, boobs swinging all over the place.

The group was dumbfounded and at a loss for what to do, but Robin ended the logjam and ran toward Sara who broke for the pond at the base of the target area. She was short and fast so Robin didn't catch her before she long jumped into the pond. She sputtered back to the surface and fought for the bank that she'd just vaulted from, "Holy M-mother of God, this water is ice f-freaking c-cold."

When she regained the bank her teeth literally chattered and she crossed her arms in front of her breasts more for warmth than modesty. The women pulled her into their circle and Jason faced the other way.

"Sara, you've been branded," Susan said with alarm as she pulled the amulet away from the scarlet skin and rotated it on the lanyard to Sara's back.

The women each studied the scald mark between Sara's generous breasts. Not only had the circle of the amulet been scorched into her flesh, it seemed the sweater had melted and stuck to her skin over a five or six inch diameter around the charm.

"You're blistered, honey, we need to get something on that right away. I've got a first aid kit in the car," Francine said and headed away from the group.

"Wait a second," Jason said.

"Jason, she's burned to a crisp. She needs the aloe vera from my car, and probably a shot of penicillin to cover whatever microbe is spawning in that mucky pond."

"Hold on, please," Jason asked and held out his hand in a stop sign to Francine. "Sara, do you mind if I take a look?"

"W-well, I d-d-don't imagine it'll b-be new to you at this p-point," she chattered out. "B-b-be m-my g-guest, d-doc."

The women rubbed Sara's bare arms and back to get some warmth back into her shivering body. Jason inspected the mark on her chest, scarlet red with white blisters that folded into her cleavage.

"Ooh, that's a good one, much better than Robin's."

The women all looked at Robin and she raised a corner of her mouth in a half smile as she pulled at the lanyard of the amulet that covered her own burn mark. "Sorry hon, I tried to warn you."

"Robin, don't you think that information would have been useful before we got to the bottom of this pit?" Monica asked.

"Sorry, I forgot, it's been a busy day."

"O-k-k. We can p-piss and m-moan later. J-Jason, c-can you d-do something?"

"I think so, I'm pretty sure. Feels like I can. Let me try."

"H-have at it," Sara said and let her arms fall to her shivering sides.

"I'm sorry, but do you mind?" Jason asked and motioned back and forth with a finger at the large breasts that hung in front of all creation.

Sara exhaled and turned her head to the side as she pulled her breasts apart, one in each hand. Jason and the women couldn't help noticing that her nipples were erect, hard as rocks.

Sara knew what they were thinking and stuttered, "I-it's the c-cold."

"Ok," Jason said and closed his eyes at the same time as he placed his right hand over the burn that had already cracked in places and seeped a yellowish fluid.

Sara felt the hot spot on her chest turn cool; the rest of her cold flesh turned warm. The pain left her the moment Jason's hand touched her.

The women knew something had happened because they had continued to rub Sara's bare skin and they also felt the cold flesh turn warm at the instant of Jason's touch.

"Seventh son of a seventh son, healer, maker, and protector of the living," Sara said without a single tremor in her voice.

Jason pulled his hand away but kept his eyes closed. Sara and the women inspected the place where the burn had been, but now there was clear skin, just as it had been before the burn. The melted sweater had fallen away with no sign that it had ever been there.

Sara wrapped Jason in a hug, bare breasts and all. Jason hugged her back and spoke over her head, because the top of her head only came to his collar, "Could someone get her bra and sweater? I'll just hang on for a minute until then."

Sara hugged him the whole time it took for Susan to retrieve the clothing, "This sweater is toast Sara. It's all melted in the front."

"Damn polyester crap," Sara said but didn't let go of Jason. "Francy, you can forget it, because he's mine now."

Francine ignored the challenge and said, "Hey, I have a whole sack of my daughter's dirty laundry in the back of the car. I'm sure there's a sweatshirt in there; might be a little tight but should do."

She ran back to the car to fetch the clothing. When she returned, Sara let go and turned her back to Jason, who also turned his back, to recoup at least a little sense of decorum.

"Ok, so how come you didn't do that for me earlier?" Robin asked as she stepped around in front of Jason.

"It never occurred to me at the time, but I'm available right now."

"Go for it," Robin said as she jammed her fingers in her cleavage and pulled her breasts apart without taking anything off.

Jason tossed the amulet over Robin's shoulder to get it out of the way and repeated his earlier healing, closed eyes and all.

When it was done, all the women inspected Robin and found perfectly clear skin where her burn mark had been.

"Ok, anybody else want Jason to feel 'em up?" Monica asked. "No Francy, not you," she said as Francine stepped toward Jason. "That was a rhetorical question, and I was being facetious, or whichever one makes grammatical sense. Let's get back to the reason we came here in the first place. I'm gonna' guess that we all learned something important. Don't tap the line before you use these weapons."

Sara's pants dripped with scummy pond water, and Monica seemed to be the only one who noticed, "Francy, you got any dry pants in the car for Sara's bottom? She's gonna get cold again, or maybe she'll take her pants off so Jason can grab her bare ass and warm that part up for her too. What the hell, let's all get sky clad and pass Jason around like a doobie."

"We're in luck," Francine said, with the hope of moving past Monica's rant. Sara, if you don't mind a co-ed's dirty sweat pants, I can fix you up. They'll be extra-long on you, but we can roll up the cuffs."

"Guess that's cleaner than what I'm wearing now, after a dip in that cesspool. Glad she's got some baggy stuff in there, I'd never be able to shimmy into those skinny jeans she wears. Probly' get crabs though."

High above the gravel pit, Beti communicated with Al through the line without fear; because she knew the witches were perfectly isolated under their ward.

"The witch Robin brought a friend," she said. "He used a spell to move a log that blocked the entryway. Before they descended, the witch Robin cast a glowing stone and a ward cascaded around the gravel pit in the passing of seconds. A ward the likes of which I have never seen. The hole in the ground filled with fog, and when I used my second sight, it became a mirror of the sky. I could no longer see the bottom or any portion of the pit at all. When they descended even their auras were obscured. Only a minute passed before strange lights flashed beneath the mirror and steam rose from its surface. The smell was of brimstone. Surely they were conjuring with great power, much more power than I have sensed from the witches ever before. I sensed nothing new while they were above, but what I saw when they were beneath revealed great power.

"Thermal flight is no longer possible so I will not be able to remain on station for much longer. If I land within sight of the entrance, they will surely sense me when they exit."

"Very well," Al replied. "Stay as long as you can, then return to base. You've had a long day and the boss will want to hear all about this before you retire. Good work Beti."

Back in the gravel pit, Robin instructed the group, "Like I said, you don't need to tap the line.   In fact, it seems pretty dangerous if you do."

"Yeah, that amulet was still warm when I pulled it off my melted sweater," Sara offered. "It was stuck on there and I can't believe the stone didn't crack."

"That's why we buy nothing but quality stones," Monica said.

"Yeah, like we knew they'd have to hold up to something like that," Susan stabbed.

"Alright smarty pants," you're up first, Monica directed.

"Ok with me. I'm gonna' try water, since nobody has yet," Susan said and braced herself for the attempt. She pulled up the sleeves on her own sweater and extended her right arm while she imagined a fire hose, and that's what she got when she flicked her fingers out. Just like the fire weapon, a horizontal column of water six inches wide rushed from her fingers and impacted the pea gravel very near the spot where Sara's fire had hit. Steam burst from the nearly molten gravel. Susan shut down the hose and pulled her amulet out by the lanyard. "It's cool," she said. "No problem."

"Remember, we can call on water in any form," Jason said and gestured toward the pond that Sara had used to quench her burning chest. A wave leapt up in the middle of the pond and Jason controlled it from one end to the other. He gestured again and a basketball sized orb of water rose from the pond and traveled over the pea gravel where it burst like a soap bubble and rained down in a short torrent.

"Awesome," Sara said, but she hesitated to call on any of her powers, because her first experience had ended in so much agony.

"I'd go with the fire," Robin suggested. "Get back on the horse sweetie."

Sara nodded and flicked out her hand. Fire blasted out of her fingers and scorched the pea gravel where the water had just splashed down. Steam rose and gravel popped as it exploded from the rapid change in temperature.

Now the women were in a line, firing each of their weapons in turn. They experimented with the pond water and found that they could craft shapes, geometric at first, then organic including animals and humans. Francine fashioned a dolphin that stood on its tale and sprayed a stream of water out of its blow hole.

Susan experimented with wind and when she fired both barrels at the same time she learned that she could point her hands down to the ground at her feet and rise on the twin columns of air. With a few tepid tests the entire group decided that sustained flight was possible, but nobody wanted to risk it until they knew the limits of their power. Plus, once off the ground, their hands were occupied and useless for any other purpose.

"I don't feel any change at all in the power level," Monica offered. The women affirmed her observation in turn. They'd been at it for almost an hour and so far there didn't seem to be a limit.

Jason practiced as well, and remembered that Ariel, the prince of Gabriel, had said that the power of Earth included more than silver needles. In fact, they could call upon earthquake, upheaval, magma, landslide, crevasse, and any needful thing.

Hmm, that's really kind of vague, Jason thought. "I wonder," he said aloud and called upon the earth to bring forth iron in its raw state.

He held out his hand and drew it back in, as if he were collecting air to himself, and the women noticed.

"What's up?" Sara whispered to Robin who stood with her attention not on the target area but on Jason.

"Jason's up to something cool, I think," Robin replied.

A moment later the ground trembled, "Earth quake?" Susan stated more than asked.

All the women migrated to Jason's side as he concentrated. "I don't really know what I'm doing," he said. "Let's just see what happens."

The women weren't sure what to expect, but they had said they would never truly be surprised again at anything Jason did. They thought back to the words of the Guardians and worried a bit about crevasses and upheavals, since they weren't sure what Jason was after, but soon they were rewarded by their patience.

The women witnessed the first ever migration of iron ore as rust colored pebbles rolled along the ground toward Jason with his outstretched hand. He gathered in with his intent and the earth responded. Close on the heels of pebbles were rocks, and then boulders began to break the surface of the earth in front of them. Soon there was a dump truck sized pile of rock a dozen yards in front of him.

Jason changed his intent, and suddenly rusty colored flakes broke off the rocks. Soon the group was surrounded by an orb of rust bits that aligned themselves like iron filings on a sheet of paper during science class magnetism experiments. The women felt like they were back in the circle at the shop with the colors of the Guardians swirling about them, only this orb was monochrome in a reddish-orange hue.

Jason gestured with a wave and the rust flecks formed into a solid, stationary, twelve inch cube a couple yards away. He withdrew his hand and walked over to the cube. He tapped it with his toe and it didn't even budge. All the women did the same thing with exclamations of the surprise that they had claimed to no longer experience.

Moments later they realized that the sun had set and each expressed their disappointment out loud, "Damn, and I was just getting the hang of those tornados," Susan complained.

"Time flies when you're having fun," Francine added.

"Time and tide waits for no man, or woman," Jason said.

"Ok, I guess we better get home," Monica chimed in, "before any more clichés pop out.

Darkness dropped like a curtain in the pit, so Jason sent a tiny fountain of fire up over the group as they walked back to the car. At the top of the hill Jason replaced the log while Robin retrieved her stone. The ward fell with a sizzle.

"Wow, that was interesting," Monica said. "I never heard one do that before."

"A day of firsts," Jason said, "for all of us."

Everybody hugged and shared farewells.

"You goin' back with us Robin," Francine asked.

"I guess," She answered and looked to Jason, hoping he'd suggest something like a drink.

Jason hesitated a moment, sure that Robin had sent a signal, but he jibed away with raised shoulders, "I have to work tomorrow." He wanted her company, he did not want the day to end, but he had only met her true self just this morning, and he wasn't sure that romantic involvement would be a good thing in the first place. After all, he was supposed to battle evil in the near future, and she was one of his warriors. The Guardians had said so.

"What about your office?" Robin wanted to go with him so bad she could taste it, but she couldn't--wouldn't--throw herself at him. She wanted more than what would come from a one night stand. *It's too cheap, too meaningless,* she thought. She wanted to know him on a cellular level. She wanted a lifelong companion, she wanted him to fall in love with her, because she was in love with him, had been for a long time really, but fear held most of the cards at the moment. There would be time. She knew it in her bones.

"I totally forgot about that. You want to go now?"

Robin sensed the hesitation and decided to pass off the stone so Jason could do it himself, "We could go now, or, I tell you what, take this," Robin said and produced the glowing black tourmaline from her pocket. "Stick it in the corner of the building and say the words. Do you remember them?"

"Prasdium postute eget?"

"Close, but no. 'Praesidium posuit eget.' If you want it to mean the same thing you have to say it the same way."

"Praesidium posuit eget--Praesidium posuit eget--Praesidium posuit eget," Jason repeated.

"By George, I think you've got it," she said and walked him to his car.

"Thanks for everything Robin. This has been the most extraordinary day, and I want a thousand more just like it."

Robin's heart skipped. *That's the kind of thing a girl wants to hear*, she thought, but said, "I don't know if I could take another one just like that, but a thousand more a little less intense would be nice."

She tilted her head and looked out of the corner of her eyes and smiled. Jason hugged her and kissed her on the cheek, and the day seemed over, for them.

Beti Reports - 14

Beti landed on the roof of Caleo as the sun dropped below the horizon. Pen had crafted a special area, like a helicopter landing pad, for the flying demons, with access to spare clothing and their own elevator that stopped only on the roof and at the first tunnel level. She had transformed from bird to human, feathers morphed to the fine hair of a human body, and she had pushed the call button when she heard a door open a dozen yards behind her.

"Mr. Penthraig, how nice to see you on the roof."

"Hello Beti, I hope you had a nice flight and that you're not too tired to give me a personal report." He pulled open the closet door next to the elevator and selected a robe for Beti. He held it for her while she threaded her arms in and cinched it closed over her perfect body.

"Not at all sir, would you like to accompany me down to the offices where we can include Alastor?"

"Al is waiting for us right now in my personal area. I have refreshments set up and we won't keep you any longer than you need to make your report. Then you can get some rest."

"As you wish," Beti said and followed Pen to the stairway that served as a fire escape for his top floor living spaces.

The first exit in the stair well down from the roof led to a spacious balcony that occupied the entire length of the back side of the building. The sun was below the horizon for Pen and Beti at the third floor, but the taller buildings downtown still reflected the orange light as the horizon line ascended the glass covered Great American Tower, and the stately stone Carew Tower.

Pen paused a moment to enjoy the upward creep of night. "Beti, did you know that the Carew Tower was the model for the Empire State Building?"

"No sir, such things are beyond my purview, but it is noteworthy. Thank you for sharing. The light is beautiful this evening."

"The thing that I like about a crisp sunset is how the dark rises, not the light.

"I beg your pardon, I misunderstood."

"Don't bother, it's natural for a Falcon to enjoy the light, with your eyes and flight capabilities, but I would have suspected that the demon in you would be a bit more attuned to the dark. There is power in the darkrise, if you know how to use it."

"Forgive me Lord Penthraig, I meant no offense. The long years of service in the daylight in my bird form has taken a toll it seems."

"Never mind, Beti, stay just the way you are. You're a good being to have around and I wouldn't dream of altering your evolution as a living entity, just as long as you serve according to your agreement."

"Of course my Lord; I have no desire to return to the realms. My life here is fulfilling, and wonderful. To be able to feel, to taste, to be alive is the greatest reward of all. I am content to serve and wish to stay on this plane as long as you will have me. In the realms, I had no physical being and existed as little more than a slave to greater demons."

The darkness enveloped what was called 'Princess Diana's tiara' at the pinnacle of the Great American Tower and Pen turned toward Beti, "Not to worry. I'm perfectly satisfied. Now let's join Al for your briefing."

The glass wall that partitioned the balcony from the living spaces was black, opaque and nearly seamless. Pen walked toward the wall as if he intended to crash right into it, but at the last second a panel whispered open like a very quiet grocery store automatic door.

Beti followed Pen in and found Al reclined at a sunken lounge area framed by sumptuous built-in soft leather sofas in black. Black marble adorned the floors and walls with highlights of figured granite in earthy shades of brown and rust. The table in the center of the lounge was a heavy granite cube with a smoky glass top that extended out from its sides. The table had been set with a myriad of finger food that included two kinds of chilled caviar (red lumpfish and black whitefish) in a yin yang divided serving bowl that was cradled on a bed of ice.

Al scooped an unsalted cracker through the lumpfish caviar and held it out to Beti, "I think you'll like this, just pop the whole thing in your mouth and chew slowly," he said, and she did.

Beti's sunflower eyes opened wide and the Falcon inside her back-flipped, "Oh my! May I try the black?" she asked.

"Help yourself," Pen encouraged with a hand gesture. "Champagne? It's traditional with caviar, or if you're a purist, a shot of vodka is preferred. I like it with Champagne myself."

"I couldn't imagine how soiling the flavor with a beverage of any kind would improve it in the slightest," Beti said before she realized it might be impolite, or at least impolitic; to chide her master as he offered her the finest delicacy that worldwide cuisine had to offer.

"I think we've created a caviar snob, Al. Whatever shall we do," Pen said with a laugh.

"I beg your pardon again my Lord. I'm mostly unaware of social conventions."

"Don't worry about it Beti. And in my personal spaces please just call me Pen."

"Thank you my Lord, I mean Pen, I'm honored and humbled."

Pen plied her with additional exotic foods and he wasn't surprised that the fish dishes commanded most of her attention. *I guess you can take the demon out of the underworld but you can't take the falcon out of the demon,* he thought. When he noticed her slowing down, he returned to the subject, "Ok Beti, if you're refreshed and feel up to it, how about that report?"

She related all that she had told Al while she was still on station.

"Interesting, the witches have a boyfriend, Al, and he seems to have some power. We need details on this guy."

"On it boss. He sounds like he might be a candidate for the succubus."

"Maybe, we'll see. Beti, what about Stoli? Get any leads on what happened to him?" Pen asked.

"I called to him and searched the area for his aura, but found nothing. He seems to have vanished," Beti replied, and at that moment, Ms. Plastic Boobs crashed in from the public elevator lobby.

The curious woman flustered with a half dozen shopping bags draped from her elbows. She wore a skin tight very short black dress, sleeveless, backless, with the neckline cut to the bottom of her breastbone.   Boobs were on display both in the middle and on the sides. Stiletto heels troubled her on the slick marble. "Hi guys, I'm gonna' need rubber soled shoes to walk around here without breaking my neck. The floor's so damn slick!"

"Hi honey, welcome home," Pen greeted.

"Hi Pendi, hi Al, I'll just take these things into the bedroom and leave you three to your meeting. Sorry to interrupt."

"Don't mention it sweetie. I'll collect you when we're through."

Tits and ass wiggled the length of the open space and entered the blacked out bedroom at the far end. The door slid shut behind her, completely silent from the forty foot distance.

"Sorry about that. Anything else Beti," Pen asked.

"I need to report the noises. I heard something like jet engines on afterburner, lights flashed, as I mentioned, and there was cheering, and then there were the sounds of distress, as if someone were injured. I heard water splash and women shouted. There was a silent period and then there was more splashing water and wind and lights. I was forced to retire while all continued in the pit. It was very strange, like nothing I've ever seen. That is all I have to report."

"Ok, you can take a plate with you if you want, and use the main elevator that. . .whatshername. . ."

"Marta," Al inserted at the hesitation and gesture for help from Pen.

". . .That Marta just arrived in. We'll talk tomorrow once Al and I have a plan for you and the others. This is priority one until we find out who the new guy is and what happened to Stoli."

"Thank you Pen, I've had a wonderful feast, and I'll await your instructions," Beti said and bowed as she left.

After the elevator door closed, Pen scratched his head and said, "Marta? Help me out Al."

"Wow, you really don't remember?"

"I remember waking up next to a goddess this afternoon, that's it, pretty much. You know, she's a true blond, I figured that out right after I realized there was somebody in bed with me. I do remember that when I played my little game of peekaboo with the glass wall, she didn't even hesitate. She was in nothing but high heels and a thong. Walked over to the wall and pressed flesh, amazing."

"So I gave her a credit card I guess, by the look of the packages, but who knows? I'm pretty sure it was worth it. Wish I could remember."

"Boss, you need to back off a little. These blackouts are getting longer and they happen more often."

"You're right, Al, I don't want to croak myself, at least not before my empire is complete anyway. Maybe I'll stay in and get re-acquainted with Marta. . ." Pen hesitated and rolled his wrist.

"Marta Johannsen, originally from Sweden, by way of South Beach. She doesn't need your credit card, by the way. Her ex is a big developer over in Europe and dabbles in Miami. That's where he dipped his wick in a coochie dancer and Marta dropped him like a hot rock, took half of his entire holdings, I hear. No pre-nup, and that means she's loaded. She stays in her South Beach penthouse most of the time now. Bought some boobs and runs with the jet set down there."

"This just gets better all the time. How did we meet?"

"Part of her settlement was a chain of motels and she came here a couple days ago to see to tri-state business. She heard about the joint and stopped in with friends last night. The friends went home to Miami without her and she spent the night up here with you. You comped' her whole party, ten grand, she was impressed, and a little high, and I think you used some mojo too. She seems to enjoy the freedom of single life. Anyway, that's the skinny on her. Time for me to go, I have surveillance to set up. Enjoy your evening," Al said and left via the secure elevator to the tunnel office.

Marta Johannsen, let's see what you're up to, and maybe I can catch you with your pants down, so to speak, Pen thought as he stalked like a panther toward the bedroom. He found the remote for the chroma-window and punched the button for clear. Marta had her back turned as she stepped into a new white dress that nearly matched the black one she'd taken off a minute ago. She wiggled it up past her thong, but the change in light alerted her to Pen's ploy. She had experienced the same trick last night and knew that Pen was playing his game again. She decided to put on a show and spun around with the dress held at her waist, breasts fully exposed because she never bothered with a bra, that's what the implants were for after all. She feigned surprise and snatched the top of the dress up as she squeaked and raised her eyebrows, and formed her mouth into a perfect 'O'.

She saw the delight on Pen's face so she wagged a finger at him, "Naughty boy," she said. Then she stepped with a seductive bump and grind to the glass wall right in front of her new boyfriend. She turned sideways and arched her back, still covered at the top, but then she slid the dress back down with one hand while covering as much of her breasts as she could with the other hand and arm. She stepped out of the dress and turned her back to the wall, spread her legs and gyrated, and then she pressed her ass to the glass. She'd done the boobs last night, so the other end seemed appropriate. She wiggled her legs and peeked over her shoulder where she saw that Pen had unbuttoned his shirt and his excitement was evident at the zipper level. She continued to grind against the glass and crooked a finger at him. Invitation received, and answered for the next hour.

The first time was against the glass where she stood, the second time was on the bed in the middle of the new dresses she had laid out earlier. The third time was in the shower.

"What a way to start an evening," she said as she tugged back into the white dress. She didn't even bother with the thong, since she figured Pen would come on to her again during the evening and she decided to leave the gates of paradise unguarded. "Let's go downstairs and dance like we did last night, ok honey?"

Pen nodded his assent, "Whatever you want baby, to half my kingdom."

"You're so sweet," she replied. "Zip me?" and he did.

Sex with this guy is amazing. He must eat Viagra like M&M's, she thought as she watched Pen button up a fresh silk shirt.

Perhaps she wouldn't care if she knew that Pen's size and stamina was not drug induced, but black magic.

Jump the Line - 15

Jason pulled into his driveway and just out of curiosity opened his second sight. He wanted to see what the line energy and protection on his property looked like at night.

He gazed at the blue green light that flowed around his house, and thought it looked more like a pond of energy rather than the stream he'd seen at the shop and the pizza place. _Flat land far from the river_, he surmised and at that moment voices plowed into his mind.

"Hail Jason Patrick O'Hara Sahen, seventh son of a seventh son, maker, healer, and protector of the living."

After a moment of hesitation Jason responded to the greeting, "Hail voices of the line. How can I be of service?"

"It is we who serve you, Sahen. We must inform you of happenings earlier this evening. During your time of practice with weapons you were observed by your enemy. A demon in the guise of a falcon followed the witches to your rendezvous. Through our energy conduit which you call the line, the demon imp sparrow hawk Beti reported flashing lights and sounds to a half demon, Alastor, a possessed human minion of Penthraig. The imp mentioned that she was unable to locate the demon imp crow, Stoli. She was unable to see more due to the ward of the guardian Astrath, angel of the Goddess Enodia, who serves witch Robin in her efforts to protect the seventh son; however, we of the line suspect there will be more surveillance on the morrow. We were unable to communicate with you during that time because only one member of your group had connected to the line. The witch Sara did not hear our warnings for the brief time she was connected."

"Very well, and thank you. What course of action do you suggest?"

"It is for you to decide, Sahen, we only observe and report. You may ask help with decisions from any of the princes of the elemental Guardians."

"Pardon my insolence, no insult is intended, and your information is greatly appreciated, but you informed me earlier of the crow, and advised me to destroy it, 'to send it back to the realms from whence it came,' if I remember the words correctly."

"Your challenge is well received, and we were instructed by the prince of the air, Cherubiel, to inform you in that instance. We are instructed to inform you to retire all demons as they are encountered, presuming we are able to contact you. Beyond that we have no instructions, and it is not ours to make decisions for the Gods. To we of the line, humans are as Gods. We serve."

"Ok, I thank you and I ask for information about traveling through the lines. I've been informed it's possible. Is such a thing possible, in fact, and is it safe for me to do so, and if so, how is it accomplished?"

"You have but to ask, Sahen. It is our command and pleasure to serve the righteous. It is safe for you to travel the lines and to visit the realms at need. Where would you like to go?"

"I can go anywhere?"

"Within the limits of the energy of the line, yes."

"Can you tell me where Robin is right now?"

"The witch Robin reposes at this moment in the circle where you received your name earlier today."

"Can you bring her here?"

"We can, if you say her summoning name."

"Can you send me to the Enchanted Notions store."

"Of course, as you know, they have an excellent circle that will protect you from being abducted by one with evil designs upon you."

"So that's something to worry about, but I suspect the bad guys don't really know about me, and they don't have my name. Is that true?"

"They do know about you in general terms, and yes, it is true that they do not have your name. They will not receive your name except from your own lips, but beware, they are masters of blackmail. They have no moral boundary to abduction and torture, or murder, or any other method used by evil ones to obtain leverage against the wholesome."

"Thank you for your wise advice. What about something inside the circle, will I materialize inside a chair or table, because the witches usually have those things set up in there?"

"Such a circle will eject obstacles, and you would not be at risk of such a thing even without a strong circle. We of the line will protect you from solid objects."

"Do I need a circle to travel the lines?"

"For you, it is not necessary, for others, it is advisable. The circle focuses energy and allows we of the line to generate the necessary power to accomplish such things. You, seventh son, healer, maker, are infused with a birthright of great power, quickened from the Goddess Hecate, and you may travel the lines at will."

"What about demons, they travel and communicate using the lines, don't they."

"Demons on this plane wield their own forces and usurp our abilities. We of the line do not like the Demons, but we must obey or suffer. Demons kill for power, and we of the line are subjugated against our will. Many living things would die if we were not obedient to the demons who force themselves upon us. Demons have been known to destroy entire forests to force we of the line to do their bidding. We are happy that there is one who will bring balance again."

"Thank you for the clarification. Can they use such influence to force you to reveal my soul name?"

"We of the line have been tasked to protect the seventh son to the end of the earth, and so it shall be. Also, the demons know that if they were to force we of the line to reveal any secret, that we have the power to reciprocate. They will protect their own secrets above their need to learn yours."

"Thank you. I really do appreciate the instruction because I'm a novice and only began to realize anything at all just this morning."

"We of the line are happy to serve."

"Ok, what do I have to do to go to Enchanted Notions right now?"

"You have only to ask, Sahen."

"Ok then, please take me through the lines to the circle at Enchanted Notions in Milford."

"Very well, Sahen." The voices of the line responded as one and suddenly Jason felt as if he'd grabbed a static generator in a high school science class. His skin tingled and his hair stood on end. The world turned green and blurred. Suddenly he stood in the middle of the circle at Enchanted Notions with chairs and women scattered on the floor around him.

The witches had driven back to the shop after weapons practice, as they'd agreed to do before they left. They decided to have coffee and discuss the events of the day in the studio. The cats were with them, and the cats listened with great interest from the laps of Monica, Robin, and Sara.

Their chairs were in a loose circle and just as they settled into an inventory of the day, the cats suddenly abandoned them and scooted to the front door.

"Uh oh, what's happening?" Monica asked an instant before the women were scattered with the force of a two handed shove well past the diameter of the bronze ring set into the floor.

"Jeeze Louise," Sara shouted.

"What the hell," and similar were the comments from the rest.

"Jason!" Robin shouted as soon as she could gather herself after her roll across the floor along with her chair and coffee cup.

"Oh, sorry, I guess I should have asked if the circle was clear before I came across," Jason said and vanished the orb with a touch. He progressed around the room, and pulled the dazed women to their feet.

"Jason, you jumped," Monica said with wide eyes.

"Yep, the voices said I could go anywhere I wanted, within the limits of the line energy. I guess that means anywhere but mountain tops or something."

"Well, we're glad to see you but flabbergasted," Monica responded. "I didn't know the circle would chuck us out like that. Then again, nobody's been able to use this one until today, so how could we guess? How did you know what to do?"

"Apparently all I need to do is ask," Jason replied, "but that presupposes I know the question."

"Jason, you scared the livin' daylights out of all of us." Sara chided. "Next time tell the line to beep a horn or flash a light or somethin' so we can get out of the way."

"My point exactly; if I'd known to ask for something like that, I would have."

"None of us would have thought of it," Francine added.

"That's right, especially since none of us has ever actually jumped through the line," Susan said.

"The cats knew," Monica offered, "but we didn't understand the message."

"Is everybody ok?" Jason asked as he pulled Robin up last, and received positive comments all around except for Sara.

"I'm gonna have a bruise on my ass as big as Dallas," she said.

"That's not so bad when your ass is the size of Texas," Monica responded. "You just want those healing hands again, I bet."

"Well, it hurts, and he can fix it," Sara answered as she rubbed her bottom.

Jason raised his hands and cocked his head.

"Forget it Sara. Let's move on shall we?" Susan asked to nods all around.

"Well, to what do we owe this auspicious visit, Jason? Were you just curious or is there some reason for this?" Francine asked.

Jason had gathered the tumbled chairs during the rejoinder, and grabbed another for himself. He gestured to the women and when they were all seated he told them about the spy.

"Oh jeesh, I dropped the line right after we crossed the bridge," Sara offered. "I might have seen it if I'd watched better. We might have known long before we got there."

"We didn't tap in at the pit because of the weapons; except for Sara," Susan added.

"The voices of the line said they tried to contact Sara but she didn't respond," Jason offered.

"Maybe we wouldn't have heard them anyway, because of all the noise the fire makes," Francine suggested.

"Robin would have heard," Monica submitted.

"Well, that gives us a couple of problems that we need to address, beyond the fact that a spy was at the pit, and that they probably know about Jason now," Robin said.

"Yeah, we can't tap in when we use weapons, and we're not necessarily in contact with advice even when we're connected to the line," Monica summarized.

"Well, that might be true for some of you and maybe not. We can practice to find out. And that's a reason I came over. I felt like I should inform you, and I wanted to try travel through the line, and I think we need to do some testing back at the gravel pit tomorrow. We should make sure our protection is adequate, and maybe we can say hello to that spy. I also wanted to ask for some guidance regarding our next steps. Once we have control of the weapons, and when we feel confident that our protection will stop whatever they throw at us, we need to know what to do with it," Jason said.

"When you say 'ask for guidance' I'm guessing that you don't mean from us?" Monica asked.

"Well, if you have an answer, that's good enough for me, but I asked the line and the voices told me to get help from the guardians. I suppose that means one of the princes," Jason replied.

"You mean right this second?" Robin asked.

"No time like the present and the circle is right here."

"Ok, let's go for it," Susan encouraged.

The women retrieved the same candles from the earlier invocation and placed them at each of the cardinal directions; green to the North for earth, yellow in the East for air, red for fire in the South, and blue to the West for water. The long-nosed lighter and athame were placed in the center as before. Robin, Francine, Sara, and Susan took their places at the candles and Monica stood next to Robin, but on the inside this time. Jason moved to the center and picked up the lighter, he'd done it once before and needed no prompting.

"Everything's ready to call the corners," Robin said, or we could use my shortcut phrase.

"Ok," Jason said. "What do I have to do?"

"Just light all the candles first and leave the rest to me." Robin continued as Jason did as she requested, "Let it be known that a circle is to be cast. This circle is to be private and secure from all but we who enter and set the casting for the purpose of seeking guidance from prince Cherubiel of the guardians of the watchtowers only." After invoking the prince of the watchtower of the East she said, "Placiat."

The pressure changed and popped their ears and wind blew. Just as before, the sphere around them crackled with tiny lightning bolts and showed a deepened energy level made apparent by the thickened, quickened, and brightened blue green swirl that defined the dimensions of the bubble.

When the sphere had calmed, Jason asked, "Is that all you had to say to cover the whole thing that we went through earlier to call the corners?"

Robin nodded and whispered, "Quiet."

The voices of the line pierced them as if they were on the inside of their heads.

"Sister Robin Rae Stapler, daughter of Mother Earth, esteemed practitioner of the craft, lioness of battle, defender of right, and protector of weak, hail and well met. Welcome to all the members of the team of the seventh son. Make your request and we shall serve to the best of our ability."

Robin continued, "Thank you voices of the line and we come to serve as we have been directed. We seek guidance from the Prince of the East, Cherubiel, in order to successfully fulfill our quest."

"Cherubiel, the prince of air, the right hand of Michael, Guardian of the East has been summoned at your request. He comes," the voices of the line said as the air shimmered and developed into the white haired, Greek senator that the team had met earlier in the day.

"Hail Robin and all of Hecate's chosen. Make your request and allow me the opportunity to serve," Cherubiel said with a gentle bow.

"We beg your pardon for bothering you twice in the same day prince Cherubiel," Robin apologized.

"I am glad to serve and understand your need. It has been reported to me that you have been exposed to the sorcerer Penthraig, whom you have been tasked to rehabilitate or destroy. He is surrounded by spies and minions that you must approach with caution. What advice would you have of me that you have not already received?"

Robin turned to Jason for guidance, and he said, "Thank you Cherubiel, we are honored by your presence. I'm contemplating an idea that would give us information but I was unsure, due to my inexperience, whether it would work or not. I'd like to capture Beti the demon spy and turn her to our side, sort of a counter spy, so that we can learn of the enemy. Now that we are exposed, it seems our timetable must move up, before Penthraig moves on us."

"Your idea is wise and reasonable. What you need to know is that when you capture a spy such as the one who witnessed your practice earlier tonight, that demon is in your power to return to the realms or to control at your pleasure. Beware that making slaves of your own will cause you to enter the opposite side of the balance. You will become as Penthraig."

"Ok, I get it, we need to turn the spy and offer freedom, not lever her into indentured servitude, or any kind of unwilling service. The spy must agree to work with us, not to serve out of fear of banishment or other leverage at all," Jason explained to himself more than asking a question.

"Well said," Cherubiel replied. "Now go forward with confidence but caution, as your guides will not intervene, but will give to you in time of need. You have already received most of what you need, and further instruction will come to mind as appropriate."

"Thank you Cherubiel. We are humbled and vow to serve as the Goddess has tasked us all," Robin said with a bow.

"I leave you all with my blessing of health and good judgment. May you fulfill your destinies with honor." Cherubiel bowed his head and faded to mist. The group stood still and stared at the space where the prince had vanished.

Jason broke the silence, "Ok, let's talk about the plan that's been brewing in my head ever since I heard about our spy."

"Ok, Jason, we're all ears," Monica said.

"I presume we all have work in the morning, and that we can meet again in the evening to practice at the gravel pit?"

"Sounds good to me," Monica replied.

"Why don't we set a little trap and see if we can glean some inside information from one of our little friends?"

Jason hashed out the plan, simply to arrive early and trap the imp Beti. He touched the side of the circle to drop it instantly, "Pretty freakin' cool," he said.

The women hugged him individually and then all together and Jason held his second sight open while he asked the line to take him home. The ladies stepped out of the circle and Jason shimmered for a second before he vanished.

"What a difference a day makes," Susan said.

It's a Trap - 16

Friday—Day 2

The next day passed like molasses for the entire team. Jason cared for three dogs with fleas, two cats with ear mites and a little guinea pig named Buster that had a tummy ache from too many treats. Jason discovered that he had been using part of his seventh son ability all along. He had always attributed his success with animals to a sixth sense, or intuition when it came to diagnosis and treatment, but now he realized that he simply knew what was wrong as soon as he touched an animal. His healing gift allowed him to perform to a level that the assistants noticed was way more effective than the contract vets in the building. Jason owned the shop and the others paid for space and shared expenses for technicians. All of the others knew Jason was special.

Now all he had to do was lay his hands on and concentrate. He thought, *this is going to save a lot on meds and supplies*, but his concentration was lacking, he was troubled with worry about how he would fight demons and keep up his shifts and other responsibilities at the business. Finally the decision reached him that he'd cross those bridges when he came to them, and realized that everyone had left for the day at 6:30 in the evening; he was alone in the office.

He decided to place the stone and invoke the wards when he realized that the northwest corner of the building was inside a storage closet. He worked his way through boxes of cleaning supplies and placed the black tourmaline from his pocket in the corner. It still glowed as it had when it was blessed by Enodia so he spoke Robin's phrase, 'praesidium posuit eget,' and felt the ward slam into place over the office. He positioned the boxes so that the least ordered product was stacked in front of the charm and made a mental note to ensure they never ran out of the stack.

He drove his pickup to the gravel pit, moved the log, and hid his truck at the bottom with judicious application of wind on loose brush.

He called Robin on his cell phone to let the girls know the game was on. He walked back out of the pit and secluded himself in the graveyard behind a curious marker in the shape of a sofa or maybe better described as a bench with a back and arms. The name inscribed on the gravestone was 'Bonnell' and generations of visitors to the graveyard just to the west of the gravel pit had wondered at such an inviting structure. *How odd*, Jason thought, but it was a perfect place to lie in wait for aerial spies.

Meanwhile the witches piled in the van behind the shop while the cats sat on the window sill to watch, with Amanda behind them. Beti fell into high trail as the witches crossed the river. Sara kept her sight up this time and verified that they had a spy.

"Oh yeah, there's a big 'ol sore thumb up there alright, sticks out big as Dallas," Sara reported. "I wonder how Jason's gonna catch a little bird up so high?"

"He thinks it'll come down low once we set the ward over the gravel pit. After that I guess he'll use our new weapons. This will be interesting," Robin replied.

A few minutes later Jason saw the women stop in front of the road down into the pit and Robin cast a ward with her last black tourmaline. The Explorer rolled into the foggy pit and Jason watched the sparrow hawk circle lower.

Beti thought she'd be safe above the ward, the witches couldn't see out if she couldn't see in, and she wanted a better vantage point to listen. She landed at the edge of the access road and changed to human form. Buck naked she tiptoed into the brush and up the dike of earth that served as the berm of the pit.

Jason watched from concealment while Beti crouched down to listen to the beginning of the witches' weapons practice. He emerged with stealth from the imp's blind side.

When the noise of witches blasting fireballs reached a crescendo, Jason broke into a dead run, vaulted the three-rail fence at the border of the cemetery, and felt Beti's senses become alert to his presence, he knew she had tapped the line. She turned to rise into a combat stance, extended her right hand and fired an energy ball of some kind at Jason. Instinct dropped him, rolled him out of line, and from his prone position he hit Beti with a blast of air that knocked her off her feet. He rose to rush her and she fired again from a sitting position. This time he was too close to react and the energy ball hit him in the stomach, but it dissipated around him as if it were a gentle puff of air. He didn't even feel it and Beti was so surprised that she failed to fire another shot but she scrambled to her feet. Jason bowled into her and they both tumbled over the rim of the pit right through the shimmering surface of the ward. Beti screamed and her flesh singed as they fell through. They rolled down the face of the same hill of pea gravel that served as the target range below.

The witches stopped to watch a sizzling ball of flame with a trail of smoke tumble down their target hill. It stopped just before the scummy pond.

"What the hell," Sara shouted.

They saw Jason stand up with the blackened body of a naked woman cradled in his arms. He jumped into the fetid pond with her and the girls heard a sizzle like hot iron quenched in a blacksmith's slack tub.

Jason waded to the witches' side and called to them for blankets. Francine fetched three from her car and ran to the edge of the pond where she spread them on the rocky ground. Jason laid the burned imp on her back.

Her breath was rapid and shallow, she was unconscious, but Jason placed his right hand on her breastbone. He closed his eyes and called in his mind for all his healing power. After interminable moments, the imp's skin began to clear from Jason's hand outward.

"Wow, look at that wouldja?" Monica said.

"She looks like an athlete, like an Olympic gymnast, check out that body," Susan offered.

The white skin of the imp's head showed that all her hair had burned away. She opened her eyes and darted looks at the semi-circle of women around her. Jason had not yet opened his eyes when realization burst into her countenance. She struggled to move but Jason held her pinned to the ground with the full force of his being.

He opened his eyes and said, "Demon Imp Beti, you have been vanquished and are in my power. I will not hesitate to destroy your human form and return you to the realms if you resist in any way. Will you comply with my wishes? Choose now."

Beti stopped wriggling, "There is no choice sir, I am compelled to comply. I wish to remain in this form on this plane and will serve you as my new master. But how am I not destroyed already? We fell into the strongest ward in my experience. I surely burned, but now I feel perfectly well. What wizardry can this be?"

"You were all but dead," Sara said, "you sizzled like bacon, but you came under the healing grace of the seventh son of a seventh son. Blessed be."

"Blessed be," all the witches repeated.

Jason took her hand as he stood and helped her up.

"Clothes please? Francine, do you still have your daughter's clothes in the back of the van?" Jason asked.

"Oh, yeah, right. I do, and they're clean, I was going to take them back to the dorm at UC after our practice session," she answered and ran to the back of the Explorer just ten yards away.

While she was gone, Jason explained, "Beti, I'm not your new master. You may choose to join our team. If you do, you will be free to come and go as you please. You'll be as one of us with your own life. You'll exist in this plane at your own pleasure. The only thing we ask is that you decide right now that you will not harm any living thing by any direct or indirect action, except in your defense or in the defense of another. If you do harm for self-interest, I'll know and I'll dispatch you to the realms, but it's up to you to choose. You can join us and work with us on our behalf, or you can make your own way in the world on your own terms. If you want to, you can return to Penthraig where you'll remain our enemy and the next time we meet, we will do our best to kill you—at least your earthly body. Or, you can join us to help fulfill our sworn duty to return balance to the innocent. As I mentioned, the other option is to leave and live on your own, never to reveal what you know about us and never to cause harm to any living thing. Choose now."

Francine returned with the same sweat suit that Sara had used the day before, but this time it was way too big. As she dressed, Beti noticed that her hair was gone and Jason noted her reaction.

"Your hair will grow back, I'm sure," Jason offered.

"My hair is the representation of feathers when I change to bird form. I'll look like a plucked squab and flight will be impossible."

Jason placed his hands on her head and concentrated. Within seconds she sported a mottled brown pixie cut and Jason asked if that would do. Beti felt her new hair with both hands, stared into his eyes for several seconds and bowed her head to respond.

"Thank you. There has never been such a generous offer in the history of my clan. I have made promises to Penthraig, but you have vanquished me in combat and that erases my former commitment. By rule of covenant I am your slave."

"I release you from that rule and ask you to be my friend. Join us and serve good at your own free will rather than evil as a slave."

"My choice in the past has been forced servitude here or abject slavery in the realms of my makers. Penthraig treated me well but always with the threat of rendition. I live with many restrictions, but I have a body and love my existence on Earth. I accept your terms and will join your team for I know nothing of living on my own, and Penthraig will find me. He will not be happy."

"Don't worry about Penthraig," Monica said. "We're gonna' scout him out tomorrow night, and by Sunday afternoon, he won't be a threat to you anymore. Now, tell us what you know about his operation, and we'll figure out what we're going to do with you. I'll give you a job at the shop, and the cats are gonna' love ya'. In the meantime, we have work to do."

"Yes," Jason agreed. "I have something in the truck that I want to use as a test, for when we actually get into combat, so you guys show Beti some of your skills and I'll be right back."

Jason walked to his concealed truck and uncovered it with a blast of wind while the girls practiced with their weapons. When he returned, he carried a pistol.

"Woa, what's that for?" Susan asked.

"Well, I kind of think it's only academic at this point, since Beti hit me square in the middle with an energy ball that I didn't even feel, but I wanted to make sure our protection could stand up to all kinds of weapons, not just fire extinguisher chemicals."

Robin turned to the imp, squared up and pointed her finger, "You shot Jason?"

"Yes, I was under attack. I was taken by surprise and I was so shocked that the plasma ball had no affect that I hesitated and he overpowered me."

"Can you shoot one right now, at the gravel?" Monica asked.

Beti tapped the line, turned and fired a ball of light at the gravel. The effect was similar to the column of fire the witches wielded a few seconds before, but vastly reduced in power.

"Your weapons are far superior," Beti admitted. "I am a child in comparison."

"Don't worry Beti, knowledge is a far more effective weapon," Jason offered. "Your first strike in the battle for balance is more important than any plasma ball. Tell us about Penthraig's operation, his numbers and methods, his strength in magical powers, and his location."

And she did.

"Well, he's surrounded by a lot of people, human and demon alike, but we have the edge in weapons," Jason summarized. "Now, let's get back to some practice."

Jason brandished the pistol, a Colt .45, just like the cowboys use in the western movies, and asked, "Can anybody shoot?"

"You intend us to shoot at each other?" Monica queried with her head askew and eyes squinted.

"My dad taught me," Robin said, "but he also taught me to never point a gun at anybody, ever."

"Well, how about this, I'll shoot, because I only want to see what happens if I shoot near you, not right at you. I'll shoot a few feet off to the side and then get closer until I hit the shield. We saw from the fire extinguisher that the shield goes out to about three feet all around. I'm guessing it's a six foot sphere, or however tall you are, Robin, plus a couple inches, and we need to find out if it can stop a bullet."

The women shuffled their feet and looked back and forth at each other and Jason. After a few seconds, Robin stood up straight and said, "I believe in you Jason, let's do it."

He positioned her on the edge of the pond with the water extended out behind to the pea gravel backdrop. "I'll stay close, don't' worry."

"I'm not worried," Robin offered with a crooked grin. "I guess I am a little bit."

The others stood behind Jason and huddled together, with Beti nearly in his hip pocket. Jason pulled out sponge style earplugs and as he rolled them between his fingers into long thin versions of themselves, he turned to the witches and Beti and said, "You might want to cover your ears, this thing is a 'mighty big number,' as they say, and it's real loud."

Once Jason's plugs were inserted, they expanded to their original size to block the report of the pistol. Robin put her hands over her ears and nodded. Jason pointed the .45 off to the right a full five feet and cocked the hammer. The blast startled all the women, including Beti, even though they had their ears covered. They all jumped and some squealed as a geyser of water sprang up 15 feet high from the surface of the pond. The smoking barrel moved a little closer to Robin and Jason fired again. The women jumped again but none squealed this time. The geyser rose again, and Jason pointed a little closer. This time when the gun went off they all saw a spark where the bullet hit and a shimmering blue green half ball all around Robin. The water geyser was ten feet off to the right and was half the height of the two previous shots.

"That obviously deflected it," Jason shouted as he pointed the gun at the ground and left the hammer alone.

"What?" Robin asked and removed her hands from her ears, as did all the other women.

"I said, that obviously deflected it," Jason shouted again. With his earplugs in, he didn't realize that he was still shouting.   Robin nodded and Jason continued to shout, "Are you willing to go a little closer?"

Robin nodded again and held up her hand with her index finger a quarter inch from her thumb.

"Ok. Turn sideways and I'll shoot low in case it goes through the shield. That way it will only hit you in the ass," Jason shouted.

Robin knit her eyebrows and frowned but she turned to the side and put her hands back to her ears. She arched her back and stuck out her butt. This time she closed her eyes and Jason moved back to his firing position. The others covered their ears while Jason aimed just six inches to the right of Robin's cheeks and pulled the trigger.

Nobody jumped this time. Robin's ball of protection flashed blue green and sizzled a bit where the bullet hit, but there was no splash in the water. Robin looked around and felt her ass, all was well, and she noticed a tendril of smoke three feet away on the ground. She stepped over and said, "Lookit that!"

The group gathered at the wisp of smoke and saw the bullet lying intact on the ground, "I guess the shield absorbed the energy of the bullet. Maybe the high angle of the first shot caused a deflection and the acute angle caused the field to just suck up the energy and drop the bullet straight down. Pretty cool. Robin, I want you to try it on me, only aim for my stomach."

"What! No way you big dummy, I'm not gonna' point a gun at anyone, especially you."

"Beti?"

"As you wish."

"Might as well, you tried to kill me once tonight already."

"My plasma ball would not kill, only incapacitate for a short time. Only long enough for me to escape."

"Ok, step right up. Do you know how to shoot."

"It does not look difficult."

Jason moved Robin out of the way and taught Beti a short course on firearms. She stepped back a few paces, to the spot where Jason had stood, and fired center body mass. Jason's shield flashed blue green and sizzled where the bullet hit, exactly the same as Robin's. The telltale tendril of smoke rose from about three feet away. The bullet lay there on the ground.

"Impressive," Beti said. All the others stood with mouths agape.

"Ok then. I guess that shows us what we want to know. One more test, to make sure. Would all you ladies line up here, next to me, except Beti. Either side is fine," Jason directed, and they did.

"Beti, would you please fire plasma balls at every one of us in turn?"

Before the women could raise a protest, Beti tapped the line and rapid fired a ball at each of them, right down the row, five shots in under three seconds. All were unaffected as the plasma balls diffused against their shields. That fact didn't stop the women from screeching epithets at Beti.

"Now now, keep it civil ladies. I just wanted you to have the experience of enemy fire. Beti, I suppose Penthraig has more powerful weapons?"

"Certainly more powerful than mine, but nothing compared with yours."

"Ok then," Jason continued as he stepped away from the line of witches and turned like a duelist who fires on the count of six instead of ten. He shot from the hip, even faster than Beti had fired, and brought searing flames against his own team--with no effect at all.

When the smoke cleared the women were all on the ground, having hit the dirt the instant Jason fired. All exclaimed with renewed epithets against Jason, and they even went so far as to question his mother's respectability.

"Damn it Jason," Monica said as she stood and rubbed her knees that had been abused against the gravel. "I'm gonna have gray hair in the morning. You took ten years off my life."

"Sorry, but we had to know before we got into a fight with the bad guys. If we can survive our own fire, we can survive theirs."

"Thanks a lot for playing with our lives, without a warning and without our permission," Susan spat.

"Scared the bejesus out of me but I knew inside there was nothing to worry about," Sara offered. "Plain 'ol Jason my ass, seventh son if there ever was one."

"I wouldn't have fired on you if I weren't absolutely sure there would be no harm."

"Well that's comforting now, jackass. That was uncalled for and unnecessary," Francine snapped with a pointed finger.

"I don't think so, you needed to know for sure and now you know."

"What she means is that you could have asked," Robin tried to clarify.

"I'm not so sure any of you would have agreed to plasma attacks from either Beti or me until it was proven that your personal shields would hold up. At any rate, forgive me. I needed to know, and I thought that was the best way to find out. Penthraig certainly won't warn you before he shoots."

"I guess you have a point, but we're on your side for crying out loud," Robin added. "Give us the benefit of the doubt, wouldja'?"

"Ok, ok. I'm sorry, it won't happen again, but there's one more thing I need to do."

The women all took defensive stances, except for Beti. She attached herself to Jason's side like a well-trained dog at heel. Her behavior was more a reflex than a conscious decision, as her training demanded. He could pull a knife and stab her in the heart and she would bear it without complaint, and barely even flinch.

Jason stepped toward the witches and they parted like the Red Sea. He held out his hands and closed his eyes. Soon the pea gravel mountain that served as a target began to quiver. Suddenly several thousand silver needles backed out of the mountain and levitated across the pond to gather at Jason's feet. Many of the needles were bent and flattened; some were blobs where the practice fire had heated them to the melting point. He gestured with a flourish of his hands and the needles reconstituted themselves into four solid bars of pure silver that any jeweler would gladly buy, at slightly less than market rate, of course.

"We'll use this to begin funding our mission. And later we'll travel out to Stone Lick Creek where I read on line that we can find gold."

Beti bowed to one knee and said, "Surely the master of elements has spared me for a great task. I am your servant."

Jason pulled Beti to her feet by the shoulders and looked her in the eye, "Beti, I want you to be my friend and team mate, not my servant."

She bowed her head and said, "As you will."

"Ok, lets head back to the shop and make plans for tomorrow night--time to go to work."

As Jason walked to his truck with Beti glued to his hip, he turned to Monica and nodded. Monica nodded back and the others piled into Francine's Explorer.

"Monica, do you trust Beti?" Susan asked as they followed Jason up the exit.

"Well, I'm pretty much convinced, but we'll know for sure in about ten seconds," Monica answered.

"How's that?" Susan replied.

"Well, when we get up to the ward, if Beti has any designs at all, if she's not totally committed to our side, she'll burn. And this time, Jason won't save her."

$\mathcal{P}$*lans - 17*

Beti survived the trip through the ward without notice. Jason waved a thumbs-up out the window and the witches knew that Monica had used her connection to learn of Jason's plan to test Beti. The explorer stopped for Robin to drop the ward. She picked up her black tourmaline, and used a small tornado to lift the log gate back into position all in a few seconds.

Back in the Explorer Robin said, "You knew," and stared at Monica in the seat next to her.

"Yes, he connected with me using the bond we cemented when we crafted the amulet for his sister. I didn't even know he could do it until that moment. He was just there in my head."

Robin slumped, and Monica sensed a bit of jealousy. "It's alright honey; he has the hots for you, not me. But don't get anxious, he won't bring it up until we handle this Penthraig guy."

Robin turned back to Monica and cracked a smile, just a little one. "Well then, we'd better get busy," she said.

The drive to the shop took ten minutes and the sun was on the horizon when they crowded into the healing studio. After arranging chairs in a circle, Jason opened the discussion.

"Ok, tomorrow's Saturday and we need to flesh out our plan for casein' Penthraig's joint."

"I think we should just go there to dance and drink and see what's what," Robin offered.

Susan chimed in, "Yeah, Beti already knows how to get down to the tunnels and where everything is."

"Beti's gonna' sit this one out. We don't want Pentharaig to know she survived our encounter," Jason replied. "I'm pretty sure that if he finds out she's with us, he'll pull out all the stops to make sure she doesn't give up his game plan."

Susan continued, "She could draw maps and coach us on everything we need to know."

"Yes, I can draw excellent maps," Beti offered.

"Good point, but I still want to get the lay of the land, and I think it's best to see it in person. After we reconnoiter tomorrow night, we'll go in Sunday morning when everybody is hung over and sleepin' in."

"Dancin' and drinkin,' sounds like a good night out on the town. I'm in," Sara said with a clap of her hands.

"We're all going," Monica insisted. "We're a team and we're strongest together."

"Steve would love a night out," Francine said. "And so would I. Besides, he wants to meet the guy I'd leave him for."

"You told him about that?" Susan asked.

"Yep, keeps him honest."

Beti stood suddenly, "It's Alastor, my handler. He's calling for a report. Shall I answer?"

"No," they all said in unison. Monica continued, "How is he calling you Beti, when we can't hear it?"

"Wait," Jason urged. He held out his hand and closed his eyes and bowed his head. "I have it; it's just a slightly different frequency of energy, lower. Monica, can you hear it?"

"No, what do I need to do?"

"Tap the line and listen, but shift your focus to the lower tones in the line. The voices of the line are up high, but the demon is low. Can you hear it?"

All the witches tapped the line with Monica as she bowed her head and closed her eyes. Slowly she discerned the voice of Alastor, like a baritone in a choir. "I have it," she shouted.

"Careful," Jason whispered, "we don't want him to know we're listening in."

A few seconds later Monica dropped the line and looked up at the same time Jason opened his eyes. "He dispatched someone named Edgi to search for Beti," Monica said and Jason nodded.

"This is freakin' great! We can listen in to the enemy's transmissions, just like the army did to the Germans and Japanese in world war two," Sara added.

Jason turned to Beti, the 5'2" of her at eye level with Jason in his chair, and she explained, "Edgi is a demon imp like me, but his form is a crow. He is an excellent watcher and will search the area around the gravel pit thoroughly. He will come here after that to observe the witches lair. He will remain high, across the river, for protection."

"Can he cross the river if he wants to?" Susan asked.

"Of course, flying imps are beyond the effects of the river if we stay above a hundred feet or so. Cali, the wolf in Penthraig's stable, would have more trouble. He could swim, provided he had enough spooled energy, but that would exhaust his power. He can cross a bridge with little difficulty at any time. Edgi will stay on the other side of the river because he believes that your reach will be affected due to the diffusion of the river; also, and to maintain better communication. We've long suspected that the line should be an excellent conductor of signals, but experience shows otherwise. Perhaps the line resents its abuse and disrupts contact under the guise of water diffusion."

"So the line victimizes demon communication in retaliation, that's what demon's think?" Susan asked.

"Yes."

"Probably true," Jason added. "We already know that the voices of the line fear and resent the blackmail that demons use to manipulate power."

"Interesting," Susan continued, "a whole new class of victims. There seems to be a lot of power and control in victimhood. It creates an almost family bond. A kindred of anger and bitterness that drives a group to work together to right a perceived wrong. It doesn't seem to matter that sometimes the victims caused their own problem to begin with."

"Thanks for that, Voltaire," Sara chided. "What are we gonna' do about it?"

"Why don't we just take care of Edgi when he shows up? Francine asked. "I'm sure those wicked needles will reach him up there."

"Maybe he's Beti's friend," Robin answered. "We shouldn't just kill him; maybe he could be recruited, like Beti."

Beti turned to face Robin, "He is a friend, and he would turn if vanquished. It is required."

Jason responded, "First of all, we wouldn't be killing him, we'd just return him to his own realm. And no Robin, it's not the same thing. Plus, it's really a part of our charter. The imps don't belong here; they've been suborned into service by a dark wizard. We've enlisted Beti of her own free will, because it strengthens us to have her help. I think it would be better to not telegraph too much more. As far as Penthraig knows, the first one was hit by a truck or something. He's now informed that we have something going on and another of his minions is missing. To take out another one now would put him on very high alert, if he isn't already. I think it's best to just let Edgi see a normal evening in the life of Enchanted Notions and let him report back that he hasn't found anything.   Tomorrow, we'll go dancing, and scout Penthraig out based on the information Beti has already given us, and Sunday morning, we'll move in force against him."

"Ok, you're the boss," Monica said. "Beti, you'll be staying with me and Amanda. We'll need a nice big hat for you, so you can move around without detection. Let's get over to the shop before your friend shows up," and Monica pulled Beti by the elbow out of the healing studio.

Jason continued as Monica and Beti exited, "Anybody know what time things get rockin' over at this club, what's its name?"

Robin answered, "It's called Caleo, means hot and bothered, I think. On the weekend it starts early and ends late. You can order sandwiches and pizza for dinner and after about nine it gets crazy in there. Kids from UC, desperate old cougars and rhinos, and everybody in between is there lookin' to hook up."

Eyebrows were raised all around the table, so Robin continued, "Yes, I've been there a time or two, and no, I didn't despoil a college kid. Just sayin' it's a fun place to hang out. If you're there alone, a million guys will buy you drinks and ask you to dance. And they all wanna' go home with you. I'm not bringing anybody home and I'm not gonna' get laid on a frat house futon with a tie on the doorknob to ward off roommates."

"Blessed be," Susan said to roaring laughter from the others.

"Right, ok. Let's meet down there so it doesn't look like we're raiding the place with a conquering army. Monica can bring Amanda, Beti stays home, Susan with . . ."

"Mike," Susan answered.

"Sara with . . ."

"Dave is my husband's name," Sara replied.

"Francine with Steve, and Robin with me," Jason added.

"Awesome," Robin smiled. "What time should we get there?"

"I don't know, what would you suggest, since you have the experience."

"I'm thinkin' that we don't want to be too conspicuous, so we should get there about the same time as the crowd starts to gather, which should be about nine or ten."

"Nine o'clock then, tomorrow night. We'll stagger by ten minutes per couple I guess. Monica and Amanda can go first, then Sara and Dave, then Susan and Mike, Francine and Steve, then you and me Robin, at nine forty, how's that?"

"Couldn't be better," Robin answered.

"Ok, I'll pick you up about nine thirty then, if you'll give me your address?" And she did.

Proper Sendoff - 18

Edgi spiraled down over the western edge of the gravel pit. Sulfurous scents wafted up to him and he reported back to Alastor that there was no sign of Beti or the witches, or the new man, but he noticed and reported burnt marks in the pea gravel hill and someone had gone swimming because there was water on the ground leading from the pond, and the floating vegetation had been disturbed.

Alastor directed him to cruise over to the witches' shop and stay on station until relieved, so he did. By the time he arrived it was dark. Edgi's vantage point from 500 feet above and across the river prevented a perspective of the front door to the shop, so he didn't notice Jason as he entered his pickup and pulled away from the curb.

Edgi saw the truck as it rounded the bend before the bridge but the truck had no wards on it so he let it go. A minute later, he saw the witch Robin exit from the rear of the shop and get in her Outback that was covered in wards. Her car was the last one in the lot and Edgi reported that the shop was closed for the night and that there was no sign of Beti or the new guy. Alastor commanded, "Follow the witch," and Edgi did.

Her headlights cast out double fans of stark white and he cataloged the blue and green glow of her wards in his mind, like a signature, as she rounded the block back to Main Street where she turned left at the light. Round the bend and left on High, right on Lila, left on Forrest, left on Miami which turned into Price road. He had descended in trail to keep a close watch and when Robin turned into her driveway, he saw her exit the vehicle where she hesitated before she closed the door.

She felt his presence, brought up her second sight and looked to the sky.

The witch turned her eyes toward him and Edgi saw them as miniature headlights just like on the car but with a blue cast. The mysterious searchlight eyes locked onto him just a hundred feet above the trees. The intensity of the beams were like nothing he'd ever seen from any of the witches, something was different. He tapped the line to report, and then suddenly stood in the realms of his makers, in his ethereal demon imp body, confused and disoriented.

Robin witnessed the firework-like burning carcass of the destroyed crow as it dropped and vaporized. Feathers fluttered down covered in mystic purple light that glowed like phosphorescent paint for a few seconds before they grounded out and disappeared in the dark leaves of the trees that surrounded her driveway. She scanned the sky for more threats and found none. She pulled her cell phone from her pocket and called Jason.

"I sensed that he was about to report. Something about my second sight startled him and I felt threatened when he tapped the line, so I blasted him with needles. Let me tell ya', those things are awesome, and in the dark they blazed with their own light, sort of like tiny rocket trails I guess, and when they passed through the crow they burned to a vapor that flashed so brilliant white that they hurt my eyes. I surprised myself a little and I'm kind of shocked at my lack of remorse. Normally I'd be distraught at killing something."

Jason interrupted her, "You didn't kill anything Robin. There is nothing to feel remorse about, so I'm glad you don't, and our mission requires it."

"I know, thanks, and I know you wanted us to let Edji go, but I made a snap judgment based on my fear; he was right there, followed me home. I hope that didn't ruin our plans for tomorrow?"

"No, I think you did the right thing, Robin," Jason answered. "If he was following you, I guess that means they suspect that you had something to do with the other two as well. I'm sure they'll be on high alert, but I'm confident that we can go ahead as planned. Why don't you call the others and let them know. We'll have Monica and Amada switch places with us in the order tomorrow night. I'd like to be first in, just to make sure before everybody else shows up."

"Ok, I'll let 'em know," Robin said, and she did.

Downtown, in the top floor apartment of Penthraig, the head dragon, his right hand demon possessed human, Alastor, sensed a ripple in the line. He had been connected all along, and had been in contact with Edgi just a few moments before. He stayed connected as he waited for the report. He had received a bump, as if Edgi were about to say something, and then the line jerked. He called and called, but nothing. He decided to climb the stairs to the imp landing deck for a better connection, but that didn't help either. He dropped the line and pushed the button for the elevator. On the way down to the tunnels he mused about the situation and came up with only one explanation. They were under attack.

Just a few feet from the elevator was the hidden entrance to Penthraig's secret office, where Alastor spent most of his time, and where he could find his boss at that moment.

"Edgi is gone," he reported.

"What do you mean 'gone'," Penthraig asked with knitted brow.

"I don't know for sure, but I was in contact with him and told him to follow one of the witches. He was just about to report when the line rippled, and I mean it yanked on me pretty good, and then he was just not there. I think the witch Robin whacked him."

"Did he find anything out about Beti?"

"Nothing; he reported that there were burn marks and sulfur smells at the gravel pit where Beti was last dispatched, but no sign of her or the new guy, and nothing out of the ordinary at the witch's shop. He was there when the witch locked up for the night so I had him follow. A few minutes later he was gone."

"Shit, are we at war?"

"I don't know for sure but our imps have been dropping like flies. So I'm thinking it's possible."

"What the hell did we do to the witches?"

"Nothing at all, we've just been watching like always. There was definitely something going on in that gravel pit. Beti saw and heard things that can't be explained."

"Any more information on the new boyfriend?"

"Nothing at all . . . Edgi didn't see him or anybody but the witch Robin. They'd all gone home by the time he arrived over the shop at about 8:30."

"Ok, it seems to me like they're taking out our imps because they have something to hide. It's not war really, more like they have some new toy that they don't want us to know about. They're hiding under wards in a gravel pit that lights up like the fourth of July, wards like nothing the imps have ever seen, mind you. Let's pull all our assets and get them out east. I want to know everything there is to know about that place and the people in it by Monday morning. Find that new guy, and if he's the toy we'll bring him in and suck him dry. Better make that Monday evening, I've got plans for the weekend that won't leave me in any kind of condition for an early Monday."

"You got it boss. By all assets, you mean the humans too?"

"Everything, and everybody. Where's Marta, by the way."

"She's at the bar, sittin' pretty with a dozen guys around her. That new red dress is smokin' hot."

"She likes to tease, that's for sure, but all those guys are gonna' be disappointed when I waltz in and snatch her up right out from under them."

"And then she'll be under you, right boss?"

"Under, over, and sideways . . . you better believe it. If there was ever a Kama Sutra candidate, this one is it. She'll try anything and loves all of it. We've made it through about half of the positions already . . . can't wait for the other half."

At that same moment, Jason arrived at the mouth of his driveway and opened his second sight. He saw somebody turn onto the sidewalk and head toward his door. His wards were up, as strong as when Robin invoked them, so he knew the person meant him no harm, and in fact, as he continued down the drive and hit the garage door opener, he realized that the person was transparent. Then he watched the man walk right through the front door.

Jason stopped the truck in the drive and ran to the house. Inside he scanned with his second sight. Everything in the room was tinted with the blue-green light. It was different from the shop, like a pond rather than a river, and he noticed that a swirling path indicated where something had passed. He followed the disturbance into the kitchen where his guest stood at the sink and gazed out the back window. Standing still, the man looked like he was waist deep in a pond of blue green light that filled the house up to his navel.

Jason said, "Hello," in his softest voice, in an attempt to not startle the visitor. The six foot tall man wore blue jeans, cowboy boots, and a plaid shirt with a light jacket. The colors were obscured by the blue green light of the line energy, but Jason figured the jacket was cream colored in real life. The man's hair was short, like John Glenn in the 60's.

"What is this place?" the man asked.

"This is my home," Jason answered.

"You glow like a campfire."

"Is that a good thing?"

"I don't know," the man said. "This whole place shines like silver in the sunlight. I saw the light from far away and walked here to see what it was. I was a little disappointed it was just a house. I wanted to find my wife; I don't know where she is. We were on a train and the next thing I knew there were a bunch of us passengers just wandering around. Most of them walked to a light and disappeared, but I needed to find my wife, so I looked around for her. Pretty soon I was lost and have been walking a long time. I don't know where to go and decided I'd come here, because the light is different."

"Do you still see the light the other people walked into?"

"Yes, it follows me, it's out there right now, just past the fence," and he pointed as he turned to look out the window, "but I can't go there because how will I find my wife?"

"I think that you'll find her if you go to that light. I'm sure of it. Will you trust me?"

"You're different, you look nice. You wouldn't trick me I don't think, would you?"

"No, I won't trick you, and it's part of what I'm supposed to do. I think that's why I shine, so you'll know that you can trust me and go into the light. I'm supposed to help you do that. I'm sure your wife is in there waiting for you."

"Ok then, I'll try," the man said, and as soon as he made the commitment he pointed again. "There, I see my dad, and my mom, and they're so young, like I remember when I was a little boy and there's my brother Joey like he was all grown up. And there, there she is, there's my

Maggie. She's calling to me, she's waving. I have to go, thank you sir, thank you," the man said and reached out to Jason, to shake his hand.

Jason stepped forward and took the man's hand, because it seemed like the right thing to do. As soon as they touched, Jason felt warmth permeate his entire body, all the way down to his soul. The man's entire life history flashed into Jason's brain and he knew the man had lived a life that deserved to be reunited with his family. The handshake was not solid like a real handshake, but there was a surreal substance to it, like warm air that radiates from a heat lamp.

They separated and the man walked right through the kitchen sink and the wall beyond. The light reached out in a conduit as the man quickened his pace across the back yard to a full run. The light flooded the back yard, a blazing bright white light that stirred the blue-green mist of the line and drew it up like smoke into a chimney as it pulled the man in. He was gone and the light faded away after him.

Jason inspected the house for the telltale signs of ghosts who had recently disturbed the line energy and saw nothing similar to what he'd just experienced. He felt a sense of satisfaction, mixed in with creeped-out, and lonely.

On the opposite side of Milford, away from Jason's home in Loveland, Beti had just been settled into a spare room when Monica felt a tug on her chi. "Jason," she whispered and looked toward the north. "Oh poor sweet Jason," she muttered and pulled out her cell phone to call Robin.

"He needs you hon. He needs somebody, a friend. He just sent a spirit across on his own, and he's had a long couple of days for a noob. He already knows you're coming. Yes, I used my connection to tell him. He's waiting for you."

Fifteen minutes later, she stepped out of her Subaru and found Jason seated on the front stoop with his head in his hands, weeping like a child.

"Oh sweetie," she said as she sat on his right and pulled him close with her left arm around his shoulders. She tugged his chin out of his hands and turned his face so she could kiss the tears away from both eyes. He wrapped both arms around her and nuzzled his face into the crook of her neck. Tears ran down her chest into her cleavage so she fished a little pack of tissues from her pocket and dabbed at the stream.

After long moments he blubbered an apology and tried to pull back, but Robin held him close, "It's ok honey, you've had more emotions to deal with in the last couple days than most people do in a lifetime. You just go ahead and cry it out," and he did.

After what seemed like a very long time, Jason's tears dried up and Robin let him go, "I'm such a cry baby," he said.

"Not at all sweetie, you've been under some massive stress with all the changes. A couple days ago you were just a pretty good vet, and now you're vanquishing demons, sending sprits to their rest, and building an army of righteousness. I would think less of you if you didn't have some kind of emotional release, and forget about what you're thinking right now."

"And what would that be?" he asked between snuffles into the last tissue in the pack.

"You're worried that a crybaby can't be trusted to lead an army. Who could follow a crybaby? Something close to that, I'm guessing."

"Well, that's pretty astute as a matter of fact."

"Don't worry about it sugar, we all know who you are and we can only guess what you're capable of. We'll follow you to the gates of hell, and if you need to cry once in a while, well that's just icing on the cake to us ladies.

The strong sensitive type is like candy to us, or at least me anyway. Shouldn't speak for the entire gender, I suppose."

"Now I'm embarrassed and feel stupid, but I'm really glad you came over. Monica was right; I needed a friend, thanks."

"De nada, sweetie . . . are we good for the evening?"

"Yeah, thanks a million."

"Don't let this get into your head, and I'm not taking advantage, but I need to do this right now," Robin said and kissed him full on the lips, soft and long. When she was done, she stood up and turned to leave.

"Robin . . ." he said but she interrupted him.

"I got it, too complicated. Don't worry; just know that I'm here for you whenever you want me, if you want me."

"Oh, I want you, I've wanted you from the second I saw you in the shop the other day. Or yesterday, was that yesterday? Anyway, that's not the problem. . ."

"Nuff said, I get it," Robin interrupted again.

"No really, I just mean we should wait to see what happens."

"Ok then, after," she said and embraced him in a goodnight hug, which he returned, and then he kissed her full on the lips, soft and long, and teased with his tongue until Robin went week in the knees and nearly swooned.

"That's just to show you I'm serious; now go home and get some sleep. If we're still alive on Sunday night, we'll start from scratch."

"Oh brother . . . we're way beyond scratch," she said and patted his cheek before she turned away to her car.

Drop Like Flies - 19

Saturday—Day 3

Jason woke in the middle of the night from a bad dream. The memory motion picture still plagued him; a Russian mobster had accosted him, or not him, somebody else, a woman, but was it a dream? He was sure that he was awake but the movie still played in his head.

He felt he had to finish the dream in his awakened state to resolve it or the fight would continue as soon as he drifted off again.

But this was different from the usual bad dream that one finishes to their satisfaction after waking. This dream continued on without him, and then he realized that it was not his own dream but Monica's, through their psychic connection, or whatever it was, that allowed him to see. In fact, he found he could participate from his awakened state, so he stepped in behind the mobster and slapped him upside the head.

When Ivan turned around to confront the unseen threat, Monica, the original victim of the mobster, kicked him in the balls from the back side. The bad man wilted and Monica slipped into a quiet place, a field of flowers and a warm breeze, so Jason separated and lay in bed to think about the potential embarrassment that might result from such intrusions if they worked the other way. He glided back to sleep and dreamed disquietly about Monica looking over his shoulder while he was at a urinal in the restroom of Pizelli's.

He woke Saturday morning a little later than normal at 8:00 with a strange feeling that nagged him, a pull that tugged at his spine. He searched the sky out the bathroom window and noticed a crow up high. Jason was scheduled at the office for the morning shift to start at nine, but was mostly distracted with thoughts of his upcoming invasion of the enemy's space later that evening, and with memories of bad dreams, and of Robin's visit from last night.

Again he felt the now familiar tug on his senses, which he began to associate with a silent alarm, in the direction of the wooded area at the back of his property. He knew something was there but didn't spot anything so he opened his second sight and noticed an indefinite shape, a purple glow beyond the fence. He retrieved his binoculars from the closet.

Jason scanned the tree line, and there he found a coyote, or was it bigger than a coyote, maybe a big dog, or even a wolf? *A wolf, in Loveland?* The back of what must be a wolf was as high as the top of the three tier split rail fence.

Jason threw up the sash and fired silver needles that found their mark after he walked them up the line between the wolf and the window. The wolf named Cali ceased in the Earthly plane with a blaze of blue green flame and a wisp of white smoke.

The crow above wheeled toward Cincinnati and Jason fired a wild blast of needles that missed their mark but vaporized in pinpoints of red flame as they passed the crow. He ran down the stairs and out the front door where he fired again, this time on target. The demon imp Macki burst into flames and plummeted never to hit the ground, but a few feathers drifted down to encounter the top of the dome shaped ward where they fluttered right on through, because feathers have no intent. The wind drifted them into the trees where the wolf had tried to hide.

"How the hell did they find me?" Jason asked to the gentle breeze that blew the smoky tendrils of evidence into obscurity.

The witches were all at the shop even though they weren't all scheduled to work. The air was electric and they sensed that multiple eyes were on them. Monica noted Jason's attacks and nodded with her senses so Jason could hear that his lighthouse beckoned to all with the sight and she added, *be watchful, be careful. For now, drive the truck to work so they can't trigger on the wards in the Vette,* and he did.

A few seconds later a man came to the Enchanted Notions door; the cats hissed and ran from the window. When the man reached for the doorknob he shouted and jumped a foot in the air.

"Got one," Monica said, and the others gathered at the counter.

"Don't they ever learn?" Susan offered.

"I haven't seen him before," Sara added. "They probably sent him in as a guinea pig and he got the snot shocked out of him. I imagine he's spittin' an earful back to the hacienda right about now. Hah! That serves 'em right."

"I guess they think a human minion might be able to get in here," Susan added. "All they really need to do to beat the wards is hire some rube to come in and take a look, and report back. As long as he's not involved he wouldn't trigger the wards."

"Yeah, but they don't trust anybody like that. They think they need a convert with a mojo tiller to do their bidding," Sara continued. "Hell, if they wanna' know what's goin' on inside, all they have to do is ask any of us."

The bell at the back door tinkled and Robin entered. "Well sleeping beauty, glad you could join us," Monica chided. "We just had a little visit from one of Penthraig's human trolls."

"I'm not surprised," Robin replied, "I had a tail all the way here from home, a human. When I turned off Main to go around to the parking lot, he went straight. I pulled a u'ey and saw him edge in a few spaces down from the front door. I guess he tried to come in while I rounded the block to park my car in back. Was he a big dumb lookin' jock type in a black Range Rover?"

"Big tall dumb and lumpy is right, but we didn't see the car," Monica answered.

"Well, I guess we should expect something like this, since I vanquished that demon crow last night."

"Yeah, wicked! How was that anyway?" Francine asked.

"Surprisingly unemotional--just seemed like the right thing to do, and since he only went home and didn't actually die, I didn't even feel a little bit bad. It was satisfying in an odd way; odd in the sense that I felt no remorse at all. But now they're on us. We'll have to work some misdirection to get out of here later."

"Already done," Monica assured, "I called the other shops first thing, because I had a tail too, and Jason dispatched two more imps just before I left. His house is lit up like Macy's at Christmas. I arranged with the other shops for a passage cleared all the way to Allen's Coins. The 'Head Dragon,'" she emphasized with quote fingers to lend an accent, "isn't the only one with access to tunnels. We have another spy out in the bushes in the back," Monica giggled, "a human, the skinny black guy that followed me in. The dummy thinks we can't see him. He has no idea what's going on out in front and the knucklehead that just tested the wards is probably half way to the city by now. The poor baby needs some magic to salve the stinging in him's widdle finders."

They all laughed and Susan added, "All this scrutiny means we can't use warded vehicles to get downtown tonight if we want to be discrete."

"Right, I already told Jason to bring the truck instead of his Vette. Everybody else will have to figure out something. Amanda would never allow me to ward her car, she's a skeptic you know," Monica said with raised eyebrows. "So we'll ride in her car. I told her to park down past Allen's before she got here."

"Mike knows too," Susan added. "He thinks it's just a night on the town and his car's never been warded to begin with. I tried it without his permission. He caught me. It wasn't pretty. Now he checks his glove compartment on a regular basis."

"Steve can pull the bag from his, if he'll do it. Or he can borrow the neighbor's pickup; it's kind of a community car anyway. Everybody uses it to haul wood chips or take stuff to the dump," Francine thought out loud as she held a fingertip to the corner of her mouth. "We should all be able to get away clean."

"Well," Monica challenged Robin, "are you gonna make us drag it out of you?"

"What?" Robin answered.

"What . . . duh, like you don't know. What happened with Jason last night dummy?" Sara fired back.

Robin turned pink in the face and dropped her head a bit, "Nothing. I went over there to console him, that's all. He had a rough night. Besides, I guess Monica already told you all about it," and she had, "so there's nothing more to tell."

"You kissed him," Susan said.

"And he kissed you back," Francine added.

"All true," Robin replied, "but now I'm feelin' a little bit like I was kissing Monica too."

"No honey, it doesn't work like that. There has to be a threat, unless he calls me. I picked it up when Jason vanquished a wolf and a crow this morning." Monica thought for a second and continued, "We'll need to figure out how to compartmentalize certain things. Anyway, those two imps were friends of Beti's; I called her, and Cali was the wolf, they only had one, and Macki was the crow, probably."

"How is Beti, by the way?" Robin asked; glad to have a change in the subject.

"She's a trip," Amanda broke in as she stepped up into her tall chair by the cash register behind the witches. She was on duty and had been in the storeroom while mostly ignoring the talk of wards and vanquishes, but she was beginning to see things that couldn't be explained away. "She's not ashamed of her body, I can tell ya' that. Not . . . at . . . all. She came down for breakfast bare-assed and buck-nekked. Monica gave her a football jersey before both of us turned lesbian; I swear that girl is built. Then she gobbled down bacon and eggs like there was no tomorrow, and when I said something about it, she said, 'Of course, I'm a raptor,' whatever that means. I get that raptor means meat eater, but she made it sound like she was a tyrannosaurus in an earlier life or something; freaky."

"Amanda, are you ready to convert?" Robin asked.

"How do you mean?"

"She means that you're about to lose your virginity," Sara said.

"That ship sailed a long time ago, or haven't you noticed my daughter hangin' around here."

"That's not what she means," Susan said.

"No," Monica jumped in. "What she means is that you have to let go of your innocence, your denial. It's time you embraced what's really going on in the world around you."

"I don't really understand," Amanda said as she turned her head to take in the whole team.

"What if I told you that Beti is a sparrow hawk?" Robin asked.

"So? You guys were all eagles, isn't that what you told me?"

"Yes, we did, and we are," Robin answered. "But that's just because our high school mascot is an eagle. But Beti, she can change into a sparrow hawk with feathers and all. She can fly, and she can fight in human form with balls of energy that would knock you right on your butt."

"No way."

"Yes way," Sara said. "She flew in yesterday evening while we were practicing, and she shot Jason in the stomach. Jason tackled her and dragged her through a ward that fried her. Jason brought her back, healed her just with his hands, and now she's on the team. We're hiding her for the time being, at Monica's house. And get this, she's not really human at all, she's a demon."

"Oh for cryin' out loud, will you guys quit makin' up stuff to scare me. You know it doesn't work on me. Peddle your fantasy to somebody more gullible, will ya'?"

"Ok," Robin offered, "but don't say we didn't warn you when your little house of cards tumbles down around you and you're forced to believe."

"When that happens, I'll buy one of your hats and you can baptize me in the river, or whatever it is you guys do. No slit wrists and blood sacrifices or anything like that though. I don't care how wrapped up you are, or how 'real' magic is, I won't do that."

"We don't do that either," Monica said.

Downtown, Penthraig was roused by a buzzing phone. His new roomie snored softly through the sound. *What's her name?* he thought as he reached for the phone on the nightstand, *Marta, that's it.*

"Yes?" he said into the phone.

"Sorry to wake you, boss, but we have a full scale crisis goin' on," said his right hand man Alastor, the possessed human. "We've lost two imps, one of them Cali."

"The wolf?" Penthraig interrupted.

"Yes, the wolf, Cali."

"Oh damn, I liked that guy. What happened?"

"I don't really know for sure, he just dropped off the grid. I was in contact with both him and the crow Macki through the line when Macki shouted that they were under attack. He was yellin' something about Cali when he just stopped. The energy just wasn't there anymore. I think both of 'em got whacked."

"How? Wasn't the crow up high, like we told them to be?"

"I'm sure he was, reported that he was, but you know how those crows are when they get upset, he was cacklin' somethin' about strange weapons, but it was mostly quacks at that point then he was just gone, like Cali, both of them gone."

"Where were they, out at the witches' shop?"

"No, they were on something new. A big ward out in Loveland that they said was lit up like the Astrodome at night, only it was visible in the daytime, from miles away. They were thinkin' it was the new guy. The witches have him buttoned up like Fort Knox."

"So, the witches do have a new toy, just like we thought."

"Just guessin' but it sounds right. And just to remind you, Edji, another one of the crows, never came back from his shift last night. I had him on the witch Robin. He reported that he was following her home and that's the last I heard from him. He never came back."

"I remember that last one, vaguely. I've gotta' slow down a little if we're under attack. This missing time and memory loss is getting to be a problem."

"And that's not all. This morning I put a couple humans on the witches, one on the witch Robin and one on the witch Monica. Right after we lost Cali, the human Robert tried to enter the shop, under my direction, and he got the shit shocked out of him soon as he touched the doorknob. Says all the skin on his palm is burned, boy is he pissed. I told him to come in for treatment and the human William is on station behind the shop, where the witches all park their cars. So far, he says there's nothing unusual to report."

"Sounds like there's plenty of 'unusual' going on to me, our imps are dropping like flies. How many do we have left?"

Alastor thought for a moment, "Eight imps, five humans, and the succubus."

"How many have we lost?"

"Two for sure, the others just disappeared and I figure they're gone too. Five in all."

"Including Beti?"

"Yes."

"Damn, she was my favorite." Penthraig cracked his knuckles and added, "Bring 'em all in, we need to figure this out."

"Will do," Alastor finished and left the roof for the office in the tunnels. "I'll gather them in the cafeteria at four o'clock. That should give everybody time to make it in," he said as he entered the imp's landing area elevator.

Penthraig finished as the doors closed, "Except for the human on the shop, leave him there until the witches leave. Make that the witch Robin. We know she's the one who tapped Edji, so tail her 24/7, leave the others alone for now. "

"Got it boss," Al answered as the doors sealed.

Back at Enchanted Notions the day wore on, the witches were anxious to get to Caleo so they could begin a serious campaign, as they had been instructed to do by the Guardians. Robin had contacted Jason by phone to let him know to pick her up in front of Allen's store down the street. Steve, Dave, and Mike would do the same at ten minute intervals starting at eight thirty. Monica would ride with Amanda who would come back after her shift was over. They all looked forward to an exciting evening.

At noon, Larry and Ida Lee arrived for their shifts.

"Hey, what's up? Is there a company meeting I didn't get the memo on?" Larry asked.

"No, no, we're just hangin' out today," Monica answered.

"Oh, that's good. I was thinking the same as Larry," Ida Lee offered as she stepped up behind the crowd at the counter.

Larry practiced Ashati and Crystology. He was a Shaman as well as an ordained minister of the order of Melchezidek. He was also a Reiki Master and tuning fork practitioner. Ida Lee was a natural Medium and a certified spiritualist. A level two Reiki practitioner, she also worked with natural elementals.

They were scheduled until eight and Monica told them to go ahead and do the normal close of day but to leave the lights on, so that their watcher wouldn't trip to the fact that everybody was gone. Normally, the lights would go off between 8:30 and 9:00 during their summer hours. Monica figured their spy would be there until the lights went off.

"We have a watcher?" Larry asked.

"Yeah, but don't worry about it. He'll stay out of sight I think, and we're gonna' slip out through the tunnel to keep him here as long as the lights are on. You might pick up a tail on your way home, but don't worry about that either. Just be on guard like the last time we had one."

"Oh dear," Ida Lee offered. "I take it this one is human? I didn't see anything unusual when I came in."

"Yeah, he's human, but I think he's new and getting familiar with the place. Don't worry, just be careful."

"Will do," Larry said for both of them.

Jason had helped three cats, four dogs, and a parakeet, but this time he simply looked at them, touched them, called for healing power from the line, and sent them home healthy and happy. Over the last two years, ever since he opened his clinic, he thought he'd just had a knack for diagnosis and treatment. Now that he realized that his talents were far more significant, it kind of took the fun out of it. He enjoyed the search for the problem and the treatment was satisfying when it solved the problem. There was sort of a private eye, investigative research component to triage and diagnosis. He skipped right over that now. The day dragged for him too, just like the witches, in spite of the miraculous healings.

He was relieved of duty at four, but he sat in his office for a couple hours fiddling with paperwork. With an absent mind he ran over and over everything that had happened in the last two days when the phone rang.

"Hey big brother, are you there? Hello? Hello?" assaulted him when his sister, Honore, broke him out of his self-imposed, sedated state of mind after he had announced his business name by rote in the phone receiver.

"Oh, Honore, sorry, I guess my mind was on my work. It's so good to hear your voice. How's the preparation going for the big trip to the top of the world?"

"It's great Jason, and even better with this nifty amulet you sent. Thanks a million. It's beautiful, but what's up with the 'bare skin at all times even during sex' thing?"

Jason didn't answer directly; instead he asked his own question, "Hey, have you ever heard those old stories about seventh sons of seventh sons?"

"Everybody I know has read Orson Scott Card, or seen that Jeff Bridges movie, or both, but you've changed the subject Jason."

"No, I'm trying to explain."

"Alright, ok, I know you're a seventh son of a seventh son. Big deal, you aren't going to forge a magical golden plow or anything, are you?"

"No, I forged a good luck charm instead."

Silence from the other end, then "Ok, this is not helping. Explain please, in detail," so he did.

When he was done, she hesitated for a long few seconds, and said, "I'm not sure if I can believe all that Jason. I mean holy cow, fire, and water, and silver needles, and Goddesses. How can you blame me for not thinking you've gone completely mental?"

"What if I told you that you don't have to believe, that you can have proof, right now?"

"What? Are you going to teleport me to Loveland and shoot fireballs out of your ass?"

"No, just take the medallion into the closet or any dark room. Have you touched it yet?"

"No, it's still in the box, inside a plastic baggie."

"Take it out, hold it in your hand, and then take it into the closet."

"Come on Jason, you're scaring me now. . ." she said as she pulled the amulet out, and then she gasped, "Jason, it's warm, and I feel awesome suddenly, like a shot of adrenalin. I feel like I could fly."

"It's the amulet, Hahn," Jason replied, using a short version of Honore with the silent 'H' not silent but pronounced with gusto, his endearment for his baby sister. When they were growing up, Jason had teased her, "Hahnore, you have an 'h' on the front of your name, it should be pronounced."

He used herbal essence commercials when they popped up on the TV to justify his position, and drove his sister nuts with them. "It's erbal erb," he'd tease, and then pronounce the 'H' in Honore. Then 'Hahnore' had become 'Hahnoree' as he applied the same logic to the silent 'e'. When they matured, he used Hahn for short, and she finally accepted it as an honorific, or hahnerific, in Jason speak.

"I can feel it Jason, it's obviously the medallion. I'm taking it into the closet right now."

Jason heard rustling and the close of a door. Honore said, "Oh My God! Jason, it's glowing like a night light!"

"I know Hahn, I made it."

"And you think it will protect me like you said?"

"I'm pretty sure. Everything else that I told you is true; I cross my heart, so I can't see why the good luck charm won't do exactly what it's intended to do. And that's why you need to put it on, right now, and not take it off until you're back, or ever, in my opinion. What's there to lose anyway? Can't hurt, after all."

"I've got it on right now, and believe me, it's staying right there. Oh Jason, I still can't believe it, but it must be true. It fills me with warmth and energy. I feel so secure and safe. My big brother, who'd a guessed? Thanks doesn't seem enough."

"It's all good, baby sis. Be careful and go climb a mountain."

Penthraig Prepares - 20

When Alastor woke Penthrag earlier that morning, Marta woke as well, but they'd fallen asleep almost instantly after the phone call. Later in the afternoon, when he returned to the bedroom from the adjoining shower, Pendi, as she'd come to call him, was surprised to see her on the phone. She'd just placed the handset back in the cradle when he approached, in nothing but a towel wrapped around his waist, exactly one towel more than Marta wore at that moment.

"Mornin' babe," he said.

She'd sat on the edge of the bed while on her call and she rolled onto the sheets, pulled her knees up and arched her back in a seductive stretch. After a sigh of pleasure she crooked a finger at Pendi, but he hesitated.

"Much as I'd love another go, I have to get ready for a meeting, sweets."

"Ok, Pendi, but you've only got one more night. I just called for the jet. I'll be leaving tomorrow morning, or late tonight, whichever comes first."

"Business?"

"Yes, deals to zip up, contracts to sign; 'betala för lek' as we say in Sweden, gotta' pay for the play. You know that as well as anybody."

"Believe me, I know about pay. But you could close up shop and stay here with me."

"What are you asking, Pendi? Was that a proposal?"

"No, sorry, more of a proposition, I guess."

"Listen honey, it's been a blast, but I never expected roses and a diamond ring. Let's just move on while we're ahead. I've had my fill of the commitment thing. There's nothing but pain in it at the end. So let's just skip all that, ok?"

"A woman that gets it, finally; I think I love you, for a few nights anyway."

She giggled and rolled out of bed to the shower with a bump-and-grind the whole way.

"Damn meeting, maybe I should postpone it a couple hours," Pen called after her.

Marta poked her head around the door jamb, smiled and then slid one leg out with a pointed toe, "To hell with the meeting, they can all wait 'til I'm ready, I'm the boss for cryin' out loud," Penthraig shouted as he dropped his towel and went for another shower.

An hour and a half later, at 4:30, he showed up for the 4:00 meeting and didn't even acknowledge that he was late. The cafeteria normally accommodated 20 employees, because they came and went in shifts, but this meeting held every employee at once, including the upstairs 'executive' staff that didn't normally come in on the weekends, and the club staff that had been called in early. There were a hundred and twelve in all, crammed into the small cafeteria and most of them had coffee, some had a sandwich.

Alastor called for order as he handed a cup of coffee to the boss, and the Head Dragon began, "Thanks for coming in early and on your off day for the office staffers. It's important and I appreciate your time.

"I'm sorry to inform you all that we have a situation that needs everybody's attention. We have lost. . ." Pen hesitated and looked at Alastor who held up five fingers, "Five imps in the last two days."

Murmurs ran through the crowd, except for the demon imps in attendance, who were already aware. They stood against the rear wall with arms crossed and a scowl on each of their faces, obviously informed and interested in payback.

"We're pretty sure they've been dispatched to the realms by the Milford witches. Another of our group. . ." Pen hesitated again and looked around at Alastor, who added, "The human Robert was burned when he touched the doorknob at the witch's shop," and Robert raised his bandaged hand for all to see.

After the murmured comments calmed down, Pen continued, "So, it's pretty obvious that we're under some kind of attack. It's all been out East, and we probably don't have to worry down here for the time being, until we find out what's happening, but in the meantime I want everybody on high alert. Keep your eyes open, and that means second sight checks all night long for those of you who can do it. Business as usual, but you Caleo staff people, keep your guard up for the indefinite future. You all know what we do here, and I think you all like the work and the benefits, not to mention the pay, so we have to protect it from the do-gooders and busybodies that would rather see us out of business altogether. We'll put on extra security tonight and if you see something say something to one of the guards. That's all for now, back to whatever you were doing, except for you imps, I want a few minutes alone with you in Al's office."

When the eight remaining imps had gathered with Pen and Alastor, their stern expressions were noticed. Penthraig sat behind his second's desk and started with a question, "Ok, what do we know for sure?"

Alastor answered, "Bobi, why don't you start off with what you saw?"

A small woman that looked a lot like Beti, because she was also a Kestrel, offered her report, "I had been assigned to Beti's sector because she had vanished. At daybreak this morning I returned to her last known position, just as Edgi had done yesterday, and found a gravel pit that reeked of brimstone, and I witnessed a wall of scorched pebbles.

"As I climbed above the hills in the area, I noticed a significant warding to the north, a very unusual warding due to its size and strength. It is visible in the light of day. I proceeded to that position and found a human dwelling with an out-building in an upper middle class development that is relatively new.

"The warding encompassed the entire property and rose in a boxy curved-top shape to two hundred feet above the surface. There were no humans that I could detect within the ward and I probably would not have detected them if any were there, such is the ward's power. I reported my findings and was instructed to proceed to the witch's shop to observe.

"I witnessed the arrival of the witch Monica and the human William took up his station at the rear of the shop about that same time, a little before eight o'clock. I noticed when the human Robert arrived at a little after that and I crossed the river to observe his intended entrance of the shop. I saw the ward react to him and watched him return to his vehicle and depart.

"I witnessed the witch Robin's arrival at the rear parking lot a few seconds before the human Robert was shocked. She sat in her car a few minutes before entering the shop from the rear.

"At noon two more witches arrived, a man and a small woman. From then on, I observed no comings or goings other than what seemed to be patrons and nothing out of the ordinary. I returned to base when recalled at three o'clock."

Alastor continued, "When Bobi reported on the warding, I figured it was the new guy, so I dispatched the imp crow Macki and the imp wolf Cali to that position to reconnoiter. Cali was already out there searching for Stoli and Beti so he changed to human form and drove to the address.

"Macki arrived at about the same time, having flown from here. They noticed a lot of disembodied humans moving in that direction and they could see through the ward but noticed nobody inside or on the grounds. I left them on station and positioned myself on the landing pad for better communication. I spoke in real time with both of them and right at eight I heard Cali begin a message and then he just ceased, his life energy was gone.

"Then Macki squawked about an attack with a strange weapon. It was a few seconds later that Macki's energy ceased. It wasn't the same as when they drop the line after a report. It was like their switch was turned off right in the middle.

"I thought of diverting more assets but figured that whatever happened to them could happen again and I didn't want to lose more personnel. And finally, we lost Edji last night. I ordered him to shadow the witch Robin, and he vanished somewhere between the shop and her house."

"So where is this gravel pit that smells like hell and has burn marks all over it?"

"It's about half way between the witch's shop and the boyfriend's place. A little closer to the boyfriend I guess," Alastor replied. "A little place called Miamiville."

"So, this guy brought something new to the party, and they've been practicing down in a gravel pit. Beti told us that the lights and sounds were powerful beyond anything she'd experienced. She made her last report from that same pit and the two we lost this morning were at the boyfriend's place. What do we have on the boyfriend?"

Alastor continued his report, "The first thing Cali did when he arrived on station was a perimeter walk and the mailbox has one of those pierced iron name plates right on top. We cross referenced the last name and address and came up with Jason O'Hara, a veterinarian out in Loveland.

"My next step was going to be a stakeout at his business as well as the witch's shop and the boyfriend's home. The ward on the home is different. Apparently he can see out of that one but we can't see him inside. The imps could see the grounds, but nobody in the home, as I presume he was there and dispatched the imps, so it's a big problem."

"Do we have a picture of this dude?"

"There are lots of them on line, he was a renowned athlete in high school and college, but the vet web site probably has the most recent one."

Penthraig thought for a moment and then said, "Let's get that picture printed out and posted in the cafeteria. Give a copy to all the imps and the humans. Put the humans on the stakeouts. Maybe the witches will be squeamish about killing their own kind. Don't give the guys any details about what happened to the missing imps. We don't want them all nervous about that when they're on station."

"Ok boss, I'll have a picture delivered out to William. He's the one on the witch's shop right now."

"Anything else?" Penthraig directed at the imps.

"I volunteer to deliver the picture to the human William," the demon imp Teri offered. She was a Peregrine Falcon and larger than the other birds in the flock.

"Very well, thank you. Al?"

"Consider it done boss."

Minutes later at Enchanted Notions the cats were in the rear window, to watch their watcher, when all three of them hunched their backs and growled. Pie spit and

Monica moved quickly to their side. She watched the demon imp Teri land behind the row of bushes where the watcher hid.

"Pie," Monica said, and the big black cat jumped down and raced for the back door with her tail up straight, puffed out to the size of a wine bottle. Monica said, "Careful now," and opened the door.

Demon imp Teri had landed just inches from the semi-reclined William, who jumped out of his skin, and into the shrub he'd been hiding behind.

"Shit! You scared the bejeezus out of me."

Teri hopped in front of the wide eyed William and offered the picture from her beak. He took it and said, "What's this?"

Teri shifted to human form to better communicate with the new team member. William's eyes turned to saucers at the sight of the stunning nude woman kneeling in front of him. She was a Peregrine Falcon, the biggest of the falcon family, and she was big as a woman. She stood near six feet tall, and the long muscular legs and large breast of the Peregrine were evident. Jet black short hair framed piercing eyes and a sharp nose. Her breasts and chest were covered with dark, bar-shaped freckles that reflected her bird form. She was a magnificent falcon and an even more striking woman.

"This is a photograph of the warlock Jason O'Hara. You are to memorize his countenance and watch for him with great intent. He is very powerful so do not approach, only report."

"Ok, got it. Memorize, observe, and report. I'm sorry, but the only thing I can observe right now is your boobs. Mind if I cop a feel?"

"Human males! All you can think about is sex and sports. Feel if you must, as if you've never felt a woman's breast."

"I have to admit, I've never handled anything like these babies."

William took full advantage of the permission and said, "You are freaking awesome! Is there any chance we could get together later, after my shift? Or right now if you've got some time?"

"You would be flayed alive if I were to report that you are not attentive to your duty."

"Ok, ok, but what about later?"

"Do you have a large penis? I've heard rumors about black humans."

"What? Jeesh you're the most direct chick I've ever met. But I like it. And I've never taken a survey, but I guess I'm bigger than average but not Mandingo size. Is that ok."

"Come to my quarters when you return. I need to release the tension of the recent losses in our ranks. If you are attentive, selfless, and vigorous, we could be mates for a time. My recent lover was dispatched to the realms this morning and I am already lonesome."

"What? Who was your recent lover?"

"He was the demon imp and temporal wolf, Cali."

"Holy cow, I'm not sure I can measure up to that, but I'll try. Penthraig says he can snap some mojo for me and I'll ask before I come over."

"As you wish," Teri said and changed back to her falcon form to depart, but that's when Pie struck. The big black cat darted from her concealment at the end of the line of shrubbery and lunged for the falcon's neck. Teri sensed the attack a split second before the cat could sink her teeth into the bird's flesh and managed to roll away, but the momentum of the big cat carried her into the falcon and they twisted together in a rolling ball of fur and feathers.

Pie yowled and spit and bit and scratched at the Peregrine, who was losing the fight, but Teri phased to her human form. Pie disengaged before Teri's hands had completely materialized and the big cat darted for cover.

She was in her own back yard so she knew all the nooks to use for escape.

Teri stood with bloody scratches all over her back, neck, arms and chest. She screamed and threatened and fired a plasma ball at the corner where Pie had scurried away. The cat was long gone but the demon fired more plasma balls in anger, and that's when Monica arrived with a shout, "You bitch, leave my cat alone," and she blasted a column of fire from her right hand that took Teri full in her beautiful chest. A split second later there was nothing but a rising ball of dark smoke and the feathers that Pie had torn out.

William stood with his arms raised high, and screamed for Monica to stop when she shifted her attention to him. "Get out of the damn bushes you little prick, and if you even think about tapping a line I'll fry your ass."

"Listen lady, I'm just supposed to watch and report, I'm no threat to you."

"You're spying on me and my shop and reporting back to that skank Penthraig. If that's not a threat I don't know what is."

That's when the rest of the witches and the other cats arrived, all in high dudgeon, ready to act with extreme prejudice. "Where's Piewhacket?" Sara shouted as Callie and Fluffy darted around the corner in pursuit of their friend.

"Come on kitty! Here Pie, come on," Monica called and all three cats poked their heads out from a hole in the floor plate of the old wooden garage attached to the building next door.

"There you are, come on girls," Monica called, and all three trotted from concealment to be picked up by their witches. Monica smoothed Pie's fur and cuddled her to loud purrs and told her what a good kitty she was.

Sara interrupted the homecoming celebration, "So, what are we gonna' do with this dickhead?"

"Jason says we restore the balance," Monica replied.

"Ok, how do we do that?" Susan asked.

"We have a sanction, if you remember. Put your hands down you idiot," Monica instructed William.

"We're certainly not going to kill him. I won't allow it," Robin shouted.

"Shush Robin, between this knucklehead holding his hands up and you shouting murder all over the block, we're gonna' attract the kind of attention we don't want," Monica rejoined.

"Hey, I never signed up for dying over this shit. I just joined up for a good time. I'll leave and never come back, I promise, just let me go."

"Your promise means nothing to us, and we can't do that anyway, not now. It's too big a risk," Monica replied and hesitated with her head down, listening. "Jason says we should put him in the circle and then figure out what to do instead of standing out here in the open. I think that's a good idea, and we can drag some information out of him before we decide what to do."

The witches surrounded William and directed him toward the narrow sidewalk between the buildings that led to Main Street when Susan bent down and picked up the picture of Jason, "What's this?" She stared at it for a moment and then flicked it around for all to see.

"Where did you get this?" Monica asked as she snatched the photo from Susan's hand and pointed it at his face.

"The demon just brought it. She said I was supposed to watch for this cracker and report back, that he was real powerful and that I was not supposed to approach him at all. She said his name was Jason O'Hara."

"Damn it. Ok, let's go," and the ensemble filed up the walk, half in front and half behind William. When they reached the spiritual wellness and healing studio, they placed a chair in the center for their captive and Monica asked for his name. When he said William, she asked for the whole thing and learned that he was William

Henderson, of Indian Hill. Then Monica set the circle silent so he couldn't hear them and he couldn't tap the line. They didn't even want him looking at them so they had turned the chair to face the back of the room. They gave him a bottle of water and told him to sit still and not get up.

"Jason's on the way," Monica reported.

"What's he gonna' do?" Robin asked.

"I don't know, he's not in there anymore," she said with a tap to her temple, "but he mentioned before he broke the connection that we'll find a way to let this guy go without causing problems for ourselves. I don't know what he has in mind. I suspect the line is telling him something and he'll fill us in when he gets here."

Seconds later, the door opened and Amanda stepped in. She moved with a zombie-like shuffle, her head down. The witches all waited and Amanda stopped in front of them, still with her head down for a few seconds of silence. When she looked up her eyes were puffy and red, with dark streaks of mascara run all the way down to her chin.

"I saw it through the window," Amanda said, trembling.

"We know honey," Francine offered. "That's why we ran out the door, you alerted all of us."

"Monica shot fire out of her hand and burned up a naked woman. I saw it. I didn't believe it when I saw it, but it's the truth, isn't it?"

"Yes and no, sweetie," Robin answered. "Monica dispatched a demon to the underworld, back to where it came from. She isn't dead at all, just back where she belongs. Monica destroyed the flesh she used to manifest herself in the real world, and that sent the spirit, the essence of the imp back home. She wasn't supposed to be here in the first place, and she brought this to the watcher," Robin held out the picture of Jason. Amanda took it, and Robin continued, "They want to take Jason's power and use it for evil. That's why they circulated that picture, so they can do harm to all of us. It's what they do, sweetie. So, you believe in magic now, I suppose?"

Amanda nodded and said under her breath, "Now what?"

"Your training begins," Susan finished.

"What are you going to do to that guy," Amanda said, and pointed to William in the chair.

"He's harmless for now. We're waiting for Jason and then we'll ask William some questions, and probably leave him in the circle until we're done with his boss," Monica replied.

"Who's his boss?"

"Listen honey, instead of playing twenty questions why don't I just fill you in?" Monica said, and she did.

William Wakes - 21

Fifteen minutes later, Jason walked in, right at the end of Monica's story that Amanda had gasped her way through. The women all greeted him with a hug, and Jason held on to the downcast Amanda a little longer than necessary, "So, you've had quite the shock this afternoon, I see." Amanda nodded and pressed her forehead into Jason's shoulder. She sobbed and put her hands over her face, forehead still in contact with Jason.

Jason held her away by the upper arms and said, "It'll be alright. You believe me don't you?"

She dropped her hands and looked up, eyes wet and nose beginning to run. Jason placed his hands on each side of her head and wiped the tears off her cheeks with his thumbs, "Don't cry, now you're a part of the team, and we need you, the tough country singer inside there needs to come out for us. Can you do that?"

She nodded and felt a calm strength fill her from the top of her head down to the soles of her feet. A change took place; she was comforted by the power of a seventh son, and reborn as a warrior just from his touch and gentle suggestion.

"Let's roll," she said, and grasped Jason's wrists. She pulled them down and turned to the women, "What's next?"

"That's what he's here for," Monica said with a nod toward Jason.

"Right, let's talk to this guy first," Jason said as he worked his way around the group.

He already knew from the voices in the line that Matthew was tainted, but when he opened his second sight and saw the black tendril of smoke that swirled around in the aura of Penthraig's minion, he gasped, "Wow, look at that will ya?"

The witches opened their sight and saw the same thing, "The only way to get that out is with a cleansing," Francine offered.

"OK, I wasn't sure what the voices meant when they said he should be cleansed. Is that the same thing as an exorcism?"

"No, he's not possessed, he just has a taint; a spell put on him by somebody that wants to control him. Like an ink stain on a shirt. What he needs is a good bleaching, and we can do that right now," Francine replied.

"Will he be more likely to tell us the truth after a cleansing?"

"Yes, we can compel him, but he might not remember the important stuff. That's part of the reason to spell somebody. You want to make sure he doesn't blab on you later, but if we don't cleanse him, he'll just lie, because his mind is not his own, not really, and we can't compel that. If Penthraig is cocky enough, he might not think it's important to block memories, but he's probably the cautious type. He wouldn't have lasted this long if he wasn't."

"Ok Francine, let's do it."

"I need to get some things from the shop first," she said and hurried out.

"You mean she doesn't have one of those cool, everything fits pockets?" Jason asked and turned toward Robin with a smile.

"Oh, she has one, it's just that this is a special kind of cleansing and she needs more than the sage that we'd use for a house. We do that for trapped spirits, but this is a taint from a spell, she needs Ayahuasca for this. And we can't carry everything; the pockets do have a limit."

"I-ah-whatska?" Jason asked.

"Pretty close, but take the 't' out." Susan corrected. "It's pronounced eye-uh-WHA-skuh, and it's a Peruvian climbing vine that shamans make into a thick tea. It's psychotropic in that form, particularly when it's combined with other herbs. Anyway, we use the vine in a dried form the same way we'd use sage for a clearing. It's called 'Spirit Vine' and sometimes 'Vine of the Dead' in the Andes, and Columbia, down 'thataway,'" and she pointed to the north.

Jason pointed back over his shoulder at the south, and Susan turned quickly to point in the correct direction, "Never can figure out where north or south is."

"So this stuff will clean his aura?" Jason asked.

"That plus three, or what you might call the power of three. If it were an exorcism, we'd use a whole coven and keep the dude in the circle," Sara answered.

"Right, if he were demon possessed, we wouldn't want that thing to get loose in here when we drove it out of him," Robin added.

"Oh brother, there's a lot to learn," Amanda offered.

"Don't worry, honey, you'll love it once you get going," Monica comforted. "In fact, let's start with second sight, right now."

Just then Francine returned, but Jason offered, "Let me try," and Monica nodded.

"Turn off the lights while you're there Francine, if you would please. The knucklehead can wait until Amanda gets her sight," Monica said.

"OK, take a seat Amanda. Everybody get situated before I hit the lights," Francine instructed, and they did, then she turned off the lights.

Jason sat facing Amanda and took her hand, "Sit back and relax, but keep your eyes open. First I need to tap the line through you, and the contact at our hands will get really warm, so be aware of that and try to guide your thoughts to the energy flowing through the room."

"The lay line?" Amanda interrupted.

"That's right."

"They think I don't listen, but I do. I hear a lot."

"Ok, Amanda, but keep quiet, don't say anything even when you see something--try to stay quiet. Envision a river of smoky blue-green mist boiling from the wall to your left, passing around us, and through us, and out the wall to our right. Believe it's there and I'll direct the energy through you so that you can begin to perceive."

While Jason talked, the others placed their hands on whatever bare skin they could reach, left hand, face, neck, wherever they could.

"Good idea ladies, we'll all be connected at the end instead of just me and Monica and Amanda.

"Keep your attention focused, Amanda. Envision the line flowing around and through. I can feel it; I can see it developing in your mind. Almost there, give yourself up to it, let go of all control, you must grant the energy access, and don't try too hard to see, that's why it's dark in here, so you don't have to try so hard. Relax your brow and un-focus your eyes and invite the energy in. That's right, almost there, almost there. Don't speak when you see it or you'll break contact."

Amanda gasped because she saw light flicker all around her, like being inside a jar of fireflies.

"Good, good, that's right, hold onto it when it flashes. It's new and scary, but when you feel it you'll love it. It's really warm and inviting, not scary at all once you grasp it. That's it, relax and focus your mind but un-focus your eyes."

She saw lights flash all around and leave, then flash again and stay longer. She concentrated to keep the flashes in sight, and each flash lasted a little longer until she relaxed and invited the light in. Suddenly the flashes consolidated into a coherent light and she couldn't help herself, "Oh my God!" she said, and it was gone. "Crap, I wasn't supposed to say anything. I ruined it."

"It's ok, everybody does the first time, they say, I certainly did. But let's try again."

Amanda struggled again, but this try progressed much faster. In a few seconds she could see the blue-green light flowing through the room like she'd sat down in the middle of a wispy river. She saw everything in the room but all was tinted with the blue-green light. She watched the smoky light flow around the big ball in the middle of the room, and all the women too, but it passed right through Jason, and a lot of it passed through Robin too. Amanda felt static electricity, her hair floated a little, like science class in high school, and she felt warm all over, especially her right hand where Jason held her. That hand was on fire.

"There it is--you've got it. I'll take my hand away now, but you just keep the line for yourself, and don't speak for a while more."

When Jason let go, the light flashed again but held, and everything became brighter. Amanda saw everything in the room as if it were daylight and the blue-green smoke poured through Jason as if he were a sieve. A sense of peace filled her, and her awareness of the natural world around her increased. She felt connected to all of it, and she felt connected to Jason in a way that she'd never been connected to anyone else in her life. She knew he was there in her mind, and she liked it.

"Ok, Amanda, now drop your sight and bring it back up yourself," Jason commanded and she did. She struggled for a moment, but now that she had a taste for it and a little experience, it came back quickly.

"I've got it, it's wonderful," she said.

"Perfect, now I'm going to take your hand again, and tap the line through the others this time, so you can feel how that works. All it takes is a little focus and a polite request."

"Ready," she said, and extended her hand.

Jason took it and she noticed his attention focus on the line. She could feel him reach out with his intent and she heard him down deep in her mind, "Please assist us," and the power of the line surged through the witches, through Jason, and through her back out to the flow of the line. She gasped again and drew a deep breath, then she heard a thousand tiny voices whisper, "Welcome, Amanda, warrioress for peace and protector of the frail, friend of the seventh son, we are happy to serve." Then she heard all of the witches psychic voices, "Blessed be," and "Welcome Amanda," they said in turn.

Amanda heard Jason's psychic voice, "Thank you," and he dropped the line then removed his hand from Amanda's. When he did, the line left Amanda too.

"Oh," she said, "I want it back."

"Go ahead, ask it back," Jason said. When she reached for his hand, he said, "No, you're on your own this time. Focus, and ask."

She concentrated and moved her thoughts outward, toward the core of the line energy, and asked out loud, "Please assist me," and the line snapped to her will. Overwhelmed with the power and emotion of her new connection to the mystical part of the natural world, she said, "Oh, my, thank you," and broke into tears. She cried and laughed in alternating episodes and felt the warmth of the line. She heard the voices rejoice and laude the seventh son. The voices instructed her in her new duty as a member of the team that was tasked to bring balance back to the world, and she was happy to accept her role. She had the impression that if she stayed connected to the line that she'd drown in the information, so she thought,

I'm sorry to go, but feel that I must, I'm overwhelmed. Thank you, and she dropped the line.

The witches, with the exception of Monica, pulled Amanda up from her chair and enveloped her in a circle of hugs and "blessed be's." Monica turned to Jason and said, "Well, wonders never cease! You're better than I ever was, or ever could be."

"Nonsense, I learned from you."

"Two days ago!" she exclaimed and shook her head. "And I guess we've bullied the line all these years. I never asked or thanked the line a single time in all the thousands of times I've tapped it."

"That's because you've never personified it before. You couldn't hear it, because you just hadn't tuned into it like that before. Now you know that it's comprised of intelligences and not just energy. I sensed that from the beginning, it's a seventh son thing, I'm sure. There's nothing that you should feel bad about. And the line knows. Don't worry about it."

"Ok," Monica nodded. "And now we're all connected. I don't mind saying that I felt kind of special being the only one for a while. But it will be safer now, with all of us tuned in." She hitched her thumb in the direction of their prisoner. "What do we do with him?"

Monica and Jason turned to the orb, second sight still active, room lights still out. The line's blue green glow illuminated the space perfectly well to those with their sight up and the mist swirled around the orb where Matthew hammered at the inside of the invisible wall with his chair, obviously screaming as loud as he could, even though those on the outside didn't hear a thing.

"Oh, my," Monica said and covered her mouth with her hand. "I guess he can't see or hear in there. Probably wonders what the hell is going on. Good thing we have a worthy circle now."

Jason chuckled and stepped to the light switch while Monica moved to the circle in front of the flailing

Matthew. When the lights came on, Matthew was stunned to see an angry, pointing Monica right there in front of him. He let go of the chair mid swing and it bounced off the orb, right back into his shins. He hopped around in agony, grabbed each shin in turn and settled hard on his butt.

Monica touched the orb and it fell with a noticeable pop, "I told you to sit still and be quiet," she shouted to stifle the swear words that poured from their prisoner, and all the others gathered at her side. "What the hell's the matter with you? You never had to sit in the dark before?" She finished.

"Why did you turn the lights out anyway? I was scared, that's all."

"We turned out the lights for our own purposes and it had nothing to do with you. Besides, you would do well to remember what happened to your little birdy friend, so shut up and sit still," Monica ordered.

Matthew scowled and rubbed his shins. The chair was unusable, "You're gonna' pay for that you little shit," Sara shouted.

Mathew pointed at Sara and started a directed expletive, "Fu…" formed on Matthew's lips but he never finished, because Jason fired a single silver needle at very low power into the captive's shoulder. It stuck like a dart and fizzed while Matthew screamed and writhed on the floor. He seemed unaware of the injury site, because he didn't grab at the needle or pay any attention at all to the sizzling, smoking wound. On his back, he thrashed and screamed.

Jason hurried to the injured young man, pulled the needle out then laid his hand over the wound to heal it. Matthew lost consciousness.

"Wow, I didn't expect that," Jason said as the ladies gathered around. Jason tore the T-shirt enough to see the wound and it was charred in a circle around bubbled pink skin, like a severe burn.

"Holy cow! Lookit that," Sara pointed. "Is he dead?"

"No, just unconscious," Jason replied as he put his hand back over the wound and concentrated. "Wow, I can feel that thing in him. It wants to block the healing, but I think I can overcome it," and he did. The skin was normal when he removed his hand. "Let's get him up on a table," Jason said as he worked his hands under Matthew's shoulders.

Susan and Robin grabbed a leg each and the three of them hefted their captive onto the Reiki table. Francine said, "It's a blood curse. I've never seen one before, only heard about it."

"What does it mean? Can we do anything for him?" Jason asked.

"It means whoever put the spell on him did more than taint his aura. Just guessin' it was Penthraig, he bound the curse on our young friend here with demon blood. That shows us that this head dragon guy is real bad news, and he's probably got a true demon close at hand. I don't know if we can help him, I think so but I need to call a buddy of mine down in New Orleans. He was possessed by a demon, once upon a time, and escaped, or better said, he was rescued by an old Dominican shaman. That's when my friend became a practitioner. I met him on one of our excursions."

Francine pulled her cell phone out of her special pocket and stepped to the back of the room to make her call. Susan held her hands over William, who hadn't moved a muscle since Jason laid his hands on for healing.

Susan closed her eyes and concentrated, hands hovering over William's eyes only an inch away, "This guy is not at rest," she said in a subdued voice, "his third eye has been blinded, and he's in turmoil all the way down to his soul."

Still not touching, she moved her hands down over the top of his head. With the base of her palms against each other and fingers extended toward his ears she murmured,

"His crown chakra is barely discernable.   I'm going to touch him, if anything weird happens, pull me off."

"Ok hun," Sara said and positioned herself behind Susan, just in case.

Susan paused for more seconds than seemed comfortable to the rest of the onlookers, and then she pressed her hands into the top of William's head. All the others realized that they'd tensed and held their breath with the expectation that something would happen, and when nothing did, they all exhaled at once.

"Oh man, this is stressing me out," Robin admitted and turned her back to the Reiki master at work.

Susan held her position for a very long two minutes with Francine's voice serving as background noise, and then Susan pulled away, "This boy is messed up," was all she could say.

Before Jason could ask for clarification, Francine returned to the group, "Akute tells me that the blood spell is like any other binding, just that it's more powerful. We can do a cleansing with ayahuasca but we have to spot it with his blood before we light it. And I asked him about the damage from the silver needle and he said he wasn't' surprised but that he'd never seen it. He suspected it was the silver that did it. Precious metals and demon blood don't mix, apparently. He said we should use a stone knife, or a thorn, or a rooster spur, to stick him for his blood, just to be safe."

"Huh, so that's why those voodoo guys carry around a chicken foot all the time; who'd-a-guessed?" Jason said.

"Well, we don't have one of those, or a stone knife, but there are plenty of thorns out there. Blackberry bushes are everywhere.   Can't seem to get rid of them," Monica offered.

"I got it," Sara said and headed for the back door. She picked up an athame from a shelf on the way out. Jason figured it was the same one that had been in the circle with him on the day of his affirmation.

"Good thing he suggested a thorn," Francine said as they watched Sara exit. "I would have used that athame to get some blood, and it's silver plated. I might have fried him, but we have Doctor O'Hara with us, and he can heal pretty much anything," she finished with a smile.

"Well, let's not test the limits just yet," Jason diverted, "and tell us more about what your friend in New Orleans said. What's his name again?"

Francine answered, "Akute Laveau, and he's a descendent of a long line of practitioners, but he shunned it all when he was young, sort of like Amanda here, until he was grabbed by a rival group and held captive for blackmail. They got what they wanted and sent him back, but with a demon inside. After his family cleansed him, he jumped into the craft with both feet. He's definitely the guy to call about this. Or I guess we could call on the guardians."

"I thought about that, but we're supposed to ask sparingly, so it's better if we can use other sources when they're available," Jason replied. "What else did he have to say?"

"I told him about Beti and he wasn't surprised about that either. He said the imps have to ally with whoever vanquishes them, just like Beti said. He filled me in on the whole demon thing too. Those birdy demons, like Beti, are classified as imps, but a true demon would have to possess a human to exist on this plane. Akute says a demon has way too much power for an imp manifestation. Their little bird body would spontaneously combust, and he should know, I guess, since he had one."

"Did he mention what to do with a possessed human?" Monica asked.

"Yeah, he said the same thing as what we're gonna' do to William, only it's best to put the true demon in a circle so he can't jump to somebody else when he's driven out. Just like we thought," Francine answered.

"Do we need blood for that one too?" Robin asked.

"Yep, same deal."

"Maybe we should collect a vial, just in case?" Robin offered.

"Good idea," Francine said and produced a small glass vial from her pocket.

"I felt something in this guy when I healed him. Are you sure he isn't possessed?" Jason asked.

"Pretty sure he's just tainted. He still has a human aura, just with a stain on it. Demon blood is real strong, that's what you feel in there, I guess."

Sara returned with a section of bramble cane that she'd prepared with a single half inch barb near the end, a thorn with a handle. "Here ya go," she said, and handed the tool to Francine.

"Perfect. Aren't you the clever ducky?" Francine said as she inspected the shaved stalk. Francine and all the witches brought up their second sight and tapped the line with a request for help.

Jason felt it and did the same while he leaned over to Amanda who stood apart with him for the ceremony, "Did you feel that?" he whispered.

"I felt something. Like a tug on my hair, all my hair at the same time."

"Good, it means they tapped the line, so bring up your second sight and I'll turn off the lights so we can see better," and he waited at the switch for Francine to complete the bloodletting.

Francine used the thorn to puncture William's thumb and milked in into her vial until it was half full, capped it, and then smeared more of his blood on the bundle of dried Ayahuasca vine. She lit the stalk with the long neck lighter that was used on the candles for Jason's circle and blew out the flame to produce a smoldering, pungent, coal.

"Pee yew, is it supposed to smell like that?" Amanda asked.

"It's the blood that makes it smell bad. Normally, it's pleasant, sort of like burning leaves in the fall," Monica answered.

The witches gathered around the prostrate William as the lights went off and Francine waved the smoky vines over him while she stood at the crown of his head and said, "I cleanse this young man of any impurities, particularly the demon blood curse that binds him."

The group, less Jason and Amanda, chanted, "Blessed be."

Francine continued, "I call upon the Goddess to sanctify this cleansing and to help us all make this young man whole and free from the taint of his binding."

"Blessed be."

"As his binding was made for foul purposes, all promises and contracts are null and void and invalid from this time forward, I pray the Goddess so declare."

"Blessed be."

The witches followed Francine widdershins around the prone William as she waved the smoky bundle of Ayahuasca over him and hummed a mystic tune that sounded a lot like Bali Hai from the Rogers and Hammerstein musical, *South Pacific*. The dirty black stain swirled in the blue-green light of William's aura and rose above him, but like smoke in a cave it stayed above him, tumbling and boiling, 'agitated' was what Jason would say to describe it; caught by some invisible roof. Then he had an inspiration and found the athame where Sara had replaced it on the shelf.

Just as the witches finished their seventh revolution, Jason stepped in between Robin and Monica at William's side. The witches were quite concerned about what Jason would do with the knife in his hand, but when he sliced just under the boiling soot, the black taint curled up and away like campfire smoke on a windless day. It simply dissipated when it reached the ceiling and was gone.

"Where am I?   Why is it so dark?" groggy William slurred as he struggled to sit up.

Francine held him down and said, "Don't worry William, you're with friends. Just lie still."

Amanda snapped the lights back on.

"Holy shit, what happened?" William asked again.

"Just lie still for a minute, until you can get your bearings.   We'll explain as best we can when your head clears."

After a few moments of rubbing his eyes with his knuckles, he tried to sit up again, and this time Francine helped him.   In the sitting position on the side of the table he faced Jason head-on.

"Do you remember where you were a few minutes ago?" Jason asked.

"Yeah, I was at this club, with Rachel, and we were having a good time drinkin' and dancin', and then this guy asked me if I wanted to join a game downstairs.   I felt really lucky and went down to play cards.   I was doing really well and drinking something that tasted good, and the next thing I remember is wakin' up here in the dark."

"Shanghaied," Sara said.   "Little brother, you were Shanghaied and we just freed you. What else do you want to know?"

"You mean I was forced to work on a boat, like they used to do to the gold miners in San Francisco?"

"Kinda like that, yeah," Susan answered.   "Only you weren't on a boat and you never left the club. You were enslaved and bound by a demon blood curse. We don't have any idea how long you were under the influence or what you did while you were, except that you were sent here to spy on us and we set you free."

"Holy shit. I thought the slave days were over," he said and rubbed his eyes again.

"Tell us about Rachel, if you remember," Jason suggested.

"Well, she's just this cool chick I met at the club. She was different, like really friendly and not out to skank my wallet away, you know? She's just a nice girl. We danced and hung out. Sometimes she'd go home with me but she was always gone the next morning when I woke up. She was more interested in me as a person than other women I've met. She didn't talk about herself at all, just asked me about my own stuff, and laughed at all my stupid jokes. When I looked into her eyes it was like I was seeing something far away, like a blue lagoon somewhere, and she just made me feel good all the time."

"Was she interested in how independent you are?" Jason asked.

"Yeah, she thought it was really cool that I could come and go as I pleased, that I had my own place and car and money, all that."

"I bet she was glad that you're family left you alone, mostly," Jason offered.

"Yes, she thought that was great."

"Well, I think it's pretty obvious that Rachel recruited you for the Head Dragon. She probably exerted influence over you that was beyond your capacity to see or understand. When she was satisfied that you could be compelled without alerting anybody, she tapped you in."

"Holy shit, so she played me the whole time?"

"Looks like it to me," Jason responded with a shrug.

"Can I use a phone? I want to call my dad. He's used to me taking off, on 'vacations' once in a while. Probably didn't even miss me, I guess."

Francine handed over her cell phone, "You work for your dad?"

"Yeah, he owns a paving company. I supervise a lot of the smaller projects, driveways and stuff like that, and I like to run the paver sometimes. Bosse's kid ya' know-- perks. The guys don't mind 'cause I let 'em slack off when I'm in charge. I buy 'em pizza and beer for lunch. We still get the job done though."

"Ok, you call your dad, and let us know how long you've been gone."

"Ok. Will I ever remember where I've been and what I did?"

"We don't know hon," Monica said.

"Unlikely," Francine said, "and it's probably better that way."

William called his dad and part way through the conversation he held his hand over the phone and asked, "Where am I now, exactly?" and they told him.

At the end of the conversation he informed the witches that he'd been gone three months and his dad had begun to worry since the credit card slips were all local and he hadn't heard a word. His dad had already contacted a private eye but hadn't come to terms yet, so that was good, and a car was on the way.

"Uh, I guess I need to thank you all, and I hate to ask, but have you guys been doin' weed up in here?"

The witches all burst into laughter, "Well, I guess you could say that, but not the way you think," Francine said and held up the still smoldering Ayahuasca. "We don't smoke it, we cleanse with it. And let me give you my card, in case you have flashbacks or any kind of trouble at all. Your chi was out of whack and it will take a while for it to rebalance. I can help with that if you want. For a fee of course. Since you're rich."

"Ok, uh, Francine," William said after looking at her card. "I'm clueless right now but feel great, so I'll see what happens and if there's anything weird, I'll give you a call."

"Ok William, but there's one more thing," Francine added.

"Ok, what's that?"

"Stay away from club Caleo, at all costs. Those are the people who enslaved you."

"Got it. Don't worry. Three months just vaporized like that. I'm not eager to get involved again," and he didn't.

At War - 22

Matthew chatted with the group for a few minutes, until he was picked up by a chauffeur in a limousine. When he was gone, the team discussed plans forward into the evening at Caleo.

"I guess we don't need all the secret stealing away through the tunnels anymore," Sara stated.

"I'm not sure we should abandon those plans," Jason offered.

"Yeah, if I was Penthraig and my birdies kept disappearing, I'd want to know why and I'd surround this place with everything I had," Susan added.

"My thinking exactly," Jason replied. "We should stick with the tunnel escape, and we should be aware that he's probably keeping an eye out, even at the club. Things should look normal around here. Or, I guess as normal as this place gets."

"It's usually pretty normal," Monica responded to the challenge. "It's only since you showed up that all the excitement has started."

"I have to tell ya', it's been a blast the last couple of days," Sara chuckled.

"Jason, how did you know to slice off the taint like that?" Francine asked.

"I don't know. It just came to me that it was the right thing to do. I don't know if the idea came from the line voices in real time or if it was something placed there the other day when I received all that information. I just knew it was the right thing to do."

"Well it's good, because I was just about to get worried when the taint got stuck like that. I didn't have a clue what to do. I probably would have batted at it with the Ayahuasca or something."

"That might have worked, I really couldn't say, but it seems like your buddy should have informed you about something like that when he briefed you."

"Well, he was the one on the table so maybe he didn't get that part of the story afterward. Maybe that's what they did, waved it off with the bundle."

"Or maybe your friend isn't as clean as he thinks?"

"Gosh, I guess that could be true. When we get down that way, we'll have to take a close look and see."

"I'm sure we will, it's part of our task, I'm pretty sure," Jason finished. "Now that's out of the way, we need to get an amulet on Amanda.

Robin and Monica pulled the remaining invoked amulets out of their pockets and placed them on the table, including the fertility goddess, "Oh brother, I need to get that thing back into the case," she said as she slipped it back into her pocket.

"Yeah, I'm not sure I'd wanna' be carrying that thing around in my pocket, might wind up pregnant from a toilet seat," Sara offered to laughs all around.

Jason snapped the light off again and Amada gasped again, "Oh, my, gosh, they glow," she said.

Monica asked, "Do any of them stick out to you sweetie? Does any of them glow brighter or float above the table, anything like that?"

"This one right here does," Amanda replied and picked up a donut shaped amulet that was very similar to the one Jason had selected for his sister. The instant she touched it, Amanda drew in her breath and gasped out, "Oh, it's amazing. I feel strong and powerful, like I've never felt before."

"That's wonderful honey, now put it on and keep it next to your skin all the time; never on the outside, always touching your skin. And whatever you do, don't tap the line to use the weapons. It'll cook your chest like a roast duck."

"Weapons, like the fire you used on the naked woman?"

"Exactly, and a lot more too, and so you can see what it's all about, I'll send you a few mind images from our practice sessions," Monica said as she connected their psyches and showed Amanda what she had been gifted.

The time passed quickly as the witches discussed all that had happened and their rather scant plans for what to do at Caleo. They were going to drink and dance and scout. That was about all they could come up with, probably because they needed a little relaxation and didn't really want to think about the next step in balancing the city. They decided that Sunday morning was the time for action, so their guard would be down a bit.

Downtown, Penthraig was interrupted again, it was after five in the evening and Alastor knocked on the patio windows. Penthraig hit the door unlock button and cleared the darkened glass. He pointed to his right and Al moved laterally a few feet until the sensors picked him up and the door slid open.

"Never can figure where that thing is when the windows are dark," Al said.

"Same here," Penthraig replied. "So what's up now? More bad news I suspect."

"Well, I came up on the roof for better reception because I can't raise the human William or the imp Teri. She took the picture out there and is way overdue. I tried to contact both of them through the line and there's just silence. I can't pick up on their energy at all. I figured you'd want to know."

"Shit! Have they declared war on us Al?"

"No communication at all, so I couldn't say."

"Ok, that's it, we're gonna' visit the witches tomorrow and find out what the hell is going on. They want war, they can have it. It'll take months to replace all those imps, and what about the human? You figure they killed him?"

"Just don't know boss, and I don't feel good about sending another imp over there, or human either. It's just too risky lately."

"Right, ok then. Get me something big, a dog or a goat. I'm gonna' charge the batteries full up so I can go in there with authority. I'm pretty sure they'll invite me in, and once they do, there's gonna be hell to pay, literally."

"Pendi, I'm famished," wafted out from the bedroom, and Marta followed. "Oh, hi Al, I'm sorry, I didn't know you were out here. Sorry for interrupting.

"Hello Marta, you look stunning this evening. And don't worry, I was just leaving."

"How would you like to join us? I was just about to suggest a nice dinner, since I haven't eaten anything but fish eggs and crackers for the last three days."

"Sounds wonderful, thank you for asking, but I have to decline, with regret. Work to do, you know how it is." Alastor bowed and moved to the elevator.

"I do, well then, it's our loss. How about it Pendi? Know a good place for dinner? I looked on line and there's a Palomino not too far away."

"Palomino is great, really good for a chain, but if you want Italiano, I'll take you to Sotto. We call it the Grotto sometimes, because that's what it is. You'll love the short rib cappellaci, and that's just an appetizer. Real family style Italian, in ambiance like you won't find anywhere in the city. The owner runs three good places; Boca and Nada are the other two. I like all of 'em."

"Magnificent, when do we go?"

"How about I make a reservation for six o'clock? I gotta' take care of some things first and then we'll go. It's only about ten blocks from here so we only need five minutes to get there. We'll drive the Ferrari, the valet down there loves it and he treats it like it's his own."

"Italian food, Italian car, what could be better?"

"Ok, then, I'll be back in a few minutes," he said, and left to prepare an assault on the witches for the next afternoon. He also made sure that his own temple was prepared for a sacrifice to increase his power to maximum. He'd never met a witch who could match his power, but the reports of the demise of his own staff worried him a little. He was confident that the life energy of a dog-sized being would put him in position to handle anything the witches could conjure up.

Once through a couple of secret doors in his secret office, Penthraig set out candles and his own athame, but it wasn't just a traditional knife. He used a ko-wakizashi, or Japanese short sword, part of a daisho, or pair of swords that included his katana. These swords were a matched pair and over 600 years old.

The Samurai blades had seen lots of action in ancient feudal Japan and were stolen at the end of the Second World War, brought to America and sold on the black market. The sword's provenance was well documented, having been in the royal house for most of its life, and it was signed by Masamune in the taito signature style. Samurai wore their swords with the maker's signature out for all to see.

Around 1400, the warriors began to wear their swords with the sharp side up, for quick draw-and-strike in a single motion. That new practice caused makers to sign their swords on the other side, to keep their names forward, but Penthaig's sword was signed in the earlier tradition, the real deal, and had tasted blood many times.

There was a story associated with this particular ko-wakizashi that it had been used by its last Samurai owner to take his own life, and so it passed into the emperor's hands. The blood history of such a weapon held great power for a sorcerer of Penthraig's stature, and he would use it to bring the Milford witches to heel. With the power it would yield through animal sacrifice, he'd steal the witches' powers.

Back in Milford, Sharon entered the healing center at about 6:15 to prepare for an astrodice reading at 6:30. She had more than 35 years of experience in Astrology and was well respected in the field. She noticed the scent of ayahuasca the instant she cracked the door, "What have you all been up to in here?"

"Hey Sharon," the group called in unison.

"We had a little clearing to do, that's all," Monica answered.

"Oh no, not another ghost? I heard you moved the last one on a couple days ago."

"We did. This was another matter entirely; a blood curse invoked by our friend Penthraig on an innocent young man."

"Oh my, a blood curse, how awful, did the clearing work? You have to tell me all about it," and they did.

After 20 minutes of rapt discussion Sharon took Jason by the hand in both of hers, "My my, Jason. It's wonderful to meet you. I'd sure like to roll the dice for you one of these days, sometime real soon."

"Sounds great Sharon. It's good to meet you too. We're gonna' be a little busy for the next couple days. How about next week?"

"Ok, we'll set it up. For now, you all have to get out of here because I have a reading in ten minutes."

With time to kill and Jason in the house, they decided to leave Sharon to her reading, Larry and Ida Lee to their shifts, and head down to Padrino's for dinner. Garlic knots, parmesan fries, zucchini, meatball sliders, eggplant parmesan, and three pizzas including the 'Padrino special,' 'Toscano,' and a 'Josie,' were devoured by all seven of them, washed down with wine and beer. Jason picked up the tab and it was almost time to leave for Caleo.

"Should we just leave from here?" Robin asked.

"Let's stick with the plan," Jason replied. "We'll walk back to the shop just in case somebody is watching, and leave through the basements. That will give us a chance to check the area for spies on the walk back to the shop."

"Good idea," Monica replied.

"Everybody open your sight but don't tap the line. The wards aren't strong enough outside of the shop to keep the ripples down," Robin instructed. "Look around but don't be too obvious. We're just walking back to the shop like we normally do."

The group tried to maintain a discrete watch, but any observer would have noticed all those heads on a swivel. They found no spies on duty.

At 8:50 Robin and Jason worked their way through the open basements of the stores on Main and came up through Allen's Coins. Allen had gone home at 6:00 so the shop was dark except for a couple dim security lights. Robin peered through the display windows and found nothing out of order and nobody on the street. She unlatched the bolt and turned the locking button so the door would at least be partially locked after their exit, and all the others had the same instructions. She held the door and Jason slipped out with his keys in hand and led the way to his truck. He didn't open Robin's side for her, because they were supposed to be in view for as short a time as possible.

They noticed nothing out of place, no watchers, and no followers as they left Milford for the city. They took the same path they had taken on the first day when they lunched at Pizelli's, old route 50 onto Columbia Parkway, into the heart of Penthraig's lair.

Caleo - 23

Jason left Columbia Parkway at the sixth street exit, as planned and turned right on Vine.   There was scant parking on the street near Caleo, so they intended to park at a lot across the street and half a block before the club.

"Let's cruise by first and take a look. We'll go around the block and come back to the parking lot," Jason suggested.

"Sounds good to me," Robin confirmed and then both of them opened their second sight.

The glow of red neon from the Caleo sign filled Vine street like a western canyon at sunset, and when they were within shouting distance Robin remembered something, "You know, when that crow was following me last night, I swear when I turned my second sight on him, he could see it somehow."

"Yeah, you mentioned that on the phone when you called me. I don't have a clue, so what do you think?"

"I think we should be careful. Something startled that demon, and if we roll past here with our own neon sign showing, we'll blow our cover," and she closed her sight. Jason did the same.

They drove past and there was a line of college students and young professionals waiting to be carded for entry and Robin said, "I don't remember all those staff people out front when I came here before."

"Really? What's your guess? Do you think they have extra security on duty tonight?"

"Looks like it to me."

"Ok. Let's get to the parking lot and ask the voices of the line if they know anything about your sight, if it tipped that crow somehow."

"We can't tap the line out here, we're too close and if they're paying attention at all, they'll sense it like a church bell."

"Ok, good point. How about we get Monica to do it? She's ten minutes behind, and we can use our psychic connection to reach her, or whatever it is that we share."

"Psychic connection is as good a name as any, I guess, and I think it should be Francine. She can do it from the shop, inside the wards, so there won't be any ripple at all. Too bad I didn't think of it before we left."

"No harm done, it's brand new to all of us, and you did think of it," Jason offered as he pulled into a spot and turned the engine off.

"Ok, how do I do it, I've never tried since we all were included at the clearing earlier today."

"Was that today? Golly, it's moving fast. Ok, you just relax and picture the one you want to connect to in your mind, it's really a lot like opening your second sight, but it's more like opening a window. Francine will hear it and open her own window. It's really kind of a natural thing to do; much easier than you think. In fact, closing the window again is the hard part."

Robin closed her eyes and focused on Francine, and nothing happened. Robin focused again and pictured a sash-weighted window. She slid the bottom half up and reached through to tap on Francine's window, which immediately opened.

Robin? wafted into her thoughts.

Hey Francine!

Wow, this is kind of freaky. It feels like you're right in the middle of my head. I like the window thing. I didn't know what was happening until you rapped on it.

It's way cool. Robin replied. *Listen, I need you to do something. Are you still at the store?"*

A few seconds later, after Robin had instructed Francine and she had complied, Francine tapped on Robin's window and told her through their mind connection that indeed, the crow had seen Robin's second sight as if she had flashlights shining out of her eyes. The line seemed to know everything about it. Now that the seventh son was involved, the team's abilities were a hundred fold, and difficult to hide.

Jason had listened in and then acted like a switchboard to bring the whole group into the conversation. Now they were all informed and they would be cautious while they were close to Caleo.

Right about then, Monica pulled in next to Jason's truck, and Francine walked out the front door of Enchanted Notions, because there was no need to use the tunnels.

"Well, we caught up, so what do we do now?" Monica asked.

"We might as well head up there together. There was a line to get in, so I suspect the rest will be here before we even reach the door."

"The line moves pretty fast," Robin added and struck out toward Caleo with Jason, Monica, and Amanda on her heels.

Half a block north, the internally-lighted sign:

Caleo!

. . . was tilted upward from the 'C' and beckoned to all those who sought entertainment, fun, and refreshment. Underneath, flame-shaped neon lights flashed in layers of red, orange, yellow, and white, to produce a mesmerizing effect, like real flames somehow, and Jason suspected there was more to the sign than just fancy electronics, some kind of mojo, probably. Projection mapping turned the entire façade of the building into a video of beautiful women dancing in heels and short dresses that alternated with rock bands and Champaign being poured and bubbled over a glass. Live music poured out the garage door entry and echoed down the canyon of buildings.

A guard adorned in black fatigues stood at each side of the entry and a podium style desk held a light and another guard that inspected ID's. Some of the patrons who approached the podium looked well under 21, but they were all waved in after a cursory review. The line snaked in at a rate of one every two seconds. Pretty soon, Caleo would burst at the seams, but like a clown car, once they went in, there seemed to be plenty of room for more.

The team stayed on the opposite side of the street until they reached the end of the block and noticed that the line no longer bent around the corner on the Caleo side. They crossed at the light and queued up. Just then, Susan and Mike drove by and waved before they turned the corner to return to parking, the way Jason had done a few minutes earlier.

There had been no additions by the time Susan and Mike joined the line so they were all bunched together, and leaving some space between themselves and other patrons in line.

Monica said, "Well, so much for our plan of a staggered entry."

"Yeah, I don't think it's a problem though. I haven't sensed anything so it seems pretty safe." No sooner than the words had come from Jason, they all felt a tug on the line energy, to which they were all now sharply attuned.

Jason closed his eyes and listened. After a moment he said, "They're tasked for routine sweeps with second sight. It seems the humans under Penthraig's employ have to tap the line to use second sight. The guards have instructions to check every ten minutes."

"Convenient of them to keep to a schedule for us," Monica offered.

"I believe it's so that their handlers can keep track of things. They don't trust their employees to use their own initiative," Jason informed.

"You got all that from ten seconds of listening?" Amanda asked.

"That and a bit more; there are a couple of the guards who have . . . how do I say it? They are sieve-like, intellectually."

"Retards," Amanda offered.

"Amanda!" Robin cajoled. "That's not a polite term these days, you know that."

"Yeah, but it's just us, besides, how would they know?"

"Well, I know, and anybody who has taken care of a mentally challenged child knows, for example. It's very insensitive," Robin accused.

"Ok, Ok, how about Neanderthals?" Amanda said with her hands raised.

"Better," Robin answered.

The group had left ten feet of space to the next in line and two college type couples tried to step into the void.

"Hey, wait a minute you guys. The line begins at the back," Monica urged with a thumb gesture.

"Oh, sorry," a perky brunette co-ed replied. "We didn't know you were even in line, there was so much space. Besides, what is it, senior's night?" she said to chuckles from her companions.

"Ha ha, very funny, just get thee behind me Jezebel," Monica parried. As the four young adults chuckled their way to the back of the line, the group heard, in their heads, Monica threaten; *I wonder how that little bitch would like a brand new crop of zits on her perky little nose?*

Just then, Susan and Mike drove by, and waved.

Good golly, might as well put signs on our backs, 'Jason's Conquering Army' or something, Monica railed in her head, still connected to the group.

Jason responded in thought, *It may be worse than you think. When that man wandered into my house last night, he said I glow like a campfire. I wonder if those guards will see me like that when they tap the line and bring up their second sight?*

Oh, golly, I hope not, and we can't tap in to see without a decent ward out here, Robin reminded.

"Yeah, we need to do something. You guys are witches; can't you do a veil or whatever?" Amanda suggested out loud, still not accustomed to her new role.

Well Amanda, it's time you stopped separating yourself like that, you're one of us now, and you're right, we are witches and we can do a veil, Monica replied. *And only answer in your head please, we can hear you just fine. Robin, you're up.*

Ok, but I'm not sure what I can do without the line.

Sara walked up to them with her husband Dave, and right behind them were Susan and Mike. Dave seemed to have a lead foot and Mike a light one, so by the time Susan and Mike had circled the block, Sara's Dave pulled in right next to them in the parking lot.

The witches were all connected psychically, so Sara jumped into the mental conversation while Susan introduced the men out loud to Jason.

Go ahead honey. None of us is the same as we were a couple days ago. And that amulet between your boobs is just like your own personal line, I'm betting, Sara encouraged.

"Ok," Robin said and closed her eyes, then continued in her mind. *I'm going to try to dim all of us, just in case. I'll picture a haze inside our protection circles and see if that works. I hope we don't look like a bunch of fog bubbles walkin' around.*

"Hey, no cuts," spat the perky brunette at the back of the line.

"Go ahead for cryin' out loud," Monica replied with a wave of her hand to their front.

"Thanks granny," the perky one snapped back.

Zits, Monica fairly shouted in her mind as the young woman passed. With a flick of her wrist the pox was cast. *In about twenty minutes, when she has to visit the powder room, she's gonna' get a real surprise.*

Monica, that is just wicked, I love it, Amanda thought.

Half a dozen couples trickled onto the end of the line over the next few minutes and there was another perimeter check by the guards. One of them had stepped out to the curb and scanned the line. Jason heard him report that all was normal and the whole group felt better that their screens seemed to work.

Francine and Steve had waited for the security check and joined the group right after. There were no complaints about cutting in line because they were all very near the entrance now and the line and ceased to build. Robin veiled Francine as Monica was carded.

"I guess I should be flattered that you'd card me," Monica said to the checker.

"Everybody gets checked mam," he replied. "If my own mom showed up, I'd card her too, it's the law."

"Ok, ok, I get it. But let me give you some advice young man. The next time somebody a little more mature mentions it, you should say something like, 'You look 20 to me miss,' and let it go at that."

He just looked around her and said, "Next."

The group was still laughing when they passed through the doors to look for a few tables to push together. The place was already rocking and dozens of couples were on the central dance floor. Tall tables and chairs were scattered throughout the room and there were cushy sofas here and there. Straight across from the entrance, there was a bandstand but no instruments in view. Above the bandstand was a mixing booth with a DJ spinning platters and playing a mixer like it was a piano and he was Mozart.

The second floor of the building immediately over the club had been removed and large steel beams painted black carried the load across the expanse. Various lights and ductwork crisscrossed the ceiling. To the right of the band stand a nearly full length bar was well stocked with booze and bartenders.

In the caverns beneath, Penthraig prepared for a ritual to drain the life force out of a stray dog that had been supplied by his ruffians. The head dragon was concealed in his secret room behind his secret office.

The place where he performed his sacraments might have been a former beer storage room and still displayed a few wooden kegs for ambiance among the shelves of chemicals, components, and paraphernalia of the practicing sorcerer. One wall was stacked stone, surely the original foundation wall of the building above, and the other three walls were red brick. There was a walk-in sized fireplace that included a wrought iron crane that was used to swing cast iron pots into position above a three foot diameter cauldron. The cauldron rested on a large iron grate with claw feet at the corners and space beneath for a raging wood fire. Long handled ladles and tongs hung from a rack fastened to the fireplace bricks within easy reach for the spell maker.

A fully outfitted commercial stainless steel kitchen suite provided a stark contrast to the ancient utensils of the traditional warlock. There were stacks of wooden bowls for working with potions and brews of all kinds. Stone bowls were there too, and a rather out of place stack of colorful plastic bowls increased the contrast.

In one corner there were chains with manacles attached to the brickwork and a dark drain hole surrounded with ceramic tiles right below, like a macabre shower pan. A hose bib with a short length of coiled garden hose hung on the wall, ready for cleanup duty.

Along one wall was a row of cages with various animals in captivity. Several birds, and a couple cats were there, but most of the cages were empty.

In the very center of the room was a ten foot brass circle inlaid into the wooden floor. This circle was very much like the one at Enchanted Notions. Penthraig stood in the circle with the sedated mongrel lying before him on a wheeled stainless steel table that aficionados of NCIS would recognize as one of Ducky's autopsy workstations.

The Head Dragon called upon the spirits of the line to grant his request to absorb the life force of the dog, and his request was granted, because he threatened, "Give this boon, or the forest will burn." Of course, when the line flowed through the dog into Penthraig there was barely a trickle of energy that returned to the line. After the ritual, the dog was only a shriveled, dried out hint of its former self.

Batteries fully charged, Penthraig returned to his apartment where Marta had refreshed her makeup and had packed her bags for the return trip to Miami.

"Well Pendi, you're fairly glowing. What were you up to while I was packing?"

He answered with a kiss that filled Marta with a magical bliss, the bliss that normally comes only from orgasm, and she was delighted, but confused. Out of breath, she asked, "Wow, how did you do that?"

"Magic, my sweet. Tonight is going to be a good night.

"Mmmm, sounds wonderful, but first, kiss me like that again." And he did. "Let's go down to the club for some drinks and dancing before we say goodbye."

"Let's say goodbye first, then go down for drinks and dancing," Pendi suggested.

"But I'm stuffed from that amazing dinner."

"OK then, how about a nice relaxing hot rock and oil massage?"

"Perfect, I'll probably fall asleep on the table."

Penthraig picked up the phone and dialed an inside number. The service desk in the tunnels answered and Pendi made his request, "Send up two ladies for hot rocks and oil. Yes, my guest and I are in need of some relaxation. Ok, we'll be ready in ten minutes then, thank you."

Battle - 24

Down in the club, the team had spread out rather than clump together, and the spacious dance floor was surrounded by plentiful seating so they had no trouble finding space for everybody. The spin doctor worked two platters plus the digital mixer with magic hands and the music transitioned from popular covers to original beats that inspired all in attendance to move their bodies in rhythm.

Patrons at tall tables and low sofas engaged in conversation while they bobbed their heads and hunched their shoulders in time to the music. The entire room moved as one being, enraptured by the heavy bass lines and sultry voices masterfully overlaid. Somehow the music was loud, but conversation was easy. Jason was sure the entire building was tuned to produce those exact results, all too otherworldly to be real.

One entire wall moved with a lightshow of Projection Mapping similar to the one on the façade of the building only this one was a live feed from the dance floor. The bump and grind of coeds transitioned to views of the DJ rockin' his beats and a shot now and then of the multicolored liquor bottles on the lighted shelves behind the bar.

Remote cameras mounted on the walls and suspended from beams on the ceiling provided the feed and above the DJ a dark window glowed with the fluorescence of monitors that allowed a video director to mix for the projectors.

Suddenly, Amanda and Monica appeared on the wall, moving to the beats and Jason pointed them out to Robin. At the same time, a woman with short red hair in a leather bustier and leather pants, Joni, one of the demon imps, leaned in to a security guard and pointed Monica out as well. Joni had been watching the eastern witches at their shop in Milford for years and knew Monica by sight. The security guard pulled his radio and made a report.

"Wow, they look like they're having fun," Robin said as she leaned in close to Jason's ear. Just then, a nicely dressed middle aged man sidled up between Amanda and Monica and began to dance in a threesome. Amada took the cue and danced off to join Robin and Jason at the table.

"Felt like a third wheel there," Amanda said as she slid onto one of the tall chairs.

"Yeah, looks like Monica scored a lawyer or something," Robin said. "This guy never got out of the 80's with those tassel loafers and chinos. And get a load of the buttoned down collar on that white shirt. I bet the cuffs are monogrammed."

"Not a bet I'd take," Jason offered.

"Me neither," Amanda added and sipped her drink from a straw. "Look, there's Francine and Steve. Lookit' that wouldja,' Steve dances like a white man, hah!"

They all giggled and Amanda challenged Jason, "Aren't you gonna' ask Robin to dance? I wanna' see what kind of moves you have, seventh son. Get out there and shake your booty for me."

Jason stood and with a short bow, offered his hand to Robin who swung out of her chair, took his hand and led him to the center of the dance floor.

About then, Alastor arrived on the elevator that was tucked into the corner behind the bar. Alerted by security, he came up from his office in the tunnels below and stepped over to where Joni was now pointing out the witch Robin to the security guard. He reached for his radio, but Alastor stopped him and said, "Not necessary, I'm right here. Joni, would you accompany me to the video booth please?"

"Of course,"

They walked to the other end of the bar where a wide staircase led down to the tunnels and restrooms, food, gambling, prostitution, drugs, and assorted sordid pleasures to attract hedonists. At the same place, a narrow staircase led upward and was blocked by a chain. Alastor unhooked the chain and followed Joni up to the ring of rooms that surrounded the dance club on what was left of the second level. There was a security control room up there as well as a break room for the second floor employees. Joni knocked on the door marked Video, and stepped in followed by Alastor. Two controllers were busy directing cameras and mixing video for projection on the wall and they didn't even turn around when their visitors entered. Finally, at a break in the action, one of the men turned around and stood to welcome Alastor and Joni.

"We don't get many visitors up here. My name is Mike and this is Jim. What's up boss?" the young man asked. Both of them looked like the stereotypical audio-visual geeks and Jim simply raised a hand to acknowledge the visitors and didn't take his eyes off the monitors. There were six fully articulated cameras in all, and each had a separate monitor. The live monitor was large and located between the two mixing boards.

"Joni here has identified a couple of the witches we talked about at our meeting earlier today," Alastor answered.

"Here, on our dancefloor?"

"Yes, right down there," he said and pointed out the window, a window that the video producers never used and didn't need. It seemed that the original purpose was for a security observation window. There was one on each of the four walls overlooking the club. The security office never used them either, because they had their own monitors and cameras both inside and outside the building, but Alastor knew that the video mixing booth was more flexible for his immediate needs.

"I want you to set up one camera on a cover feed and leave it there for a few minutes while Joni directs the other cameras around the club to see if we have any other enemy visitors. She's really familiar with the witches and should be able to point them out."

The video man sat back down while the other one had already set up a single camera for a cover shot. "Ok, Jimmy, thanks for the cover shot. I'm gonna take the center monitor off live and you can keep track of that through, which one, looks like camera three is the feed right now."

"That's right," Jim answered.

"Ok, you keep track of that and I'll take control of the other five to find our witches. Ok, Joni, up on camera one there," he said and pointed to the monitor.

"Leave that one right where it is, that is the witch Monica with the bob haircut, dancing with the man in the white shirt."

"Is that her husband or the new guy with all the power?"

"Her husband is deceased, but I don't know the man at all."

"Ok, camera two, panning," Mike said.

"There, stop. Back a little, the long haired blond in the black dress. That is the witch Robin. She is not married, and I do not know the man, but he fits the imp Beti's description of the tall blond man at the gravel pit."

"Could be our new guy," Al responded.

"Yes, but I could not say for sure. Now, camera four please."

It took only a few seconds to identify Francine and Steve, then Sara and Dave at a table on camera five. They found Susan and Mike seconds later, on camera six.

Monica and her dance partner began to move out of the frame of camera one so Mike tracked them back to the table where Joni found Amanda. "That one is named Amanda, she has only recently joined the witches shop, but I am fairly certain she is not a witch, but an employee charged with improvement in the design of the shop."

Down in the club, Monica introduced her new friend to Amanda as Mark, a corporate lawyer who specialized in business contracts, and sent him to the bar for drinks. She'd left the dance floor because she felt a distinct buzzing in her chi for a few moments, as if she were being watched, but her trips around the floor revealed nothing out of the ordinary. No watchers at all.

A few seconds later, Robin and Jason joined them with the same concerns. Sara dragged Dave by the hand to Monica's table and said, "We're made."

"I agree," Jason replied as Susan and Mike arrived to fill out the team.

They all studied the crowd, but nobody triggered on any watchers at all.

"What should we do?" Susan asked.

"Well, I don't feel particularly threatened, just that somebody has recognized us. We're well protected and I think we just continue to enjoy ourselves, with one eye out for trouble."

Mark returned with Monica's drink and was surprised to find so many people around the table. Monica introduced them all and they peeled off in couples to return to their own tables.

Monica, Amanda, and Robin left to powder their noses and Jason conversed with Mark about mundane new acquaintance subjects. A few seconds into the conversation, Jason caught the eye of a young woman staring at him from a few tables away. There was no tingling so he didn't think she was the cause of everyone's dismay, so he returned to the conversation with Mark.

Mark excused himself, "I guess it's as good a time as any to visit the men's room, since the ladies are taking their time."

That left Jason alone at the table and he nursed a lite beer while he watched the dancers. A few seconds later, the woman slipped onto the chair next to Jason and extended her hand, "Hi, I'm Rachel, I haven't seen you around here before."

"Hi Rachel, I'm Jason, and it's my first visit. I take it you're a regular?"

"It's my favorite club in the city. I hang out here most weekends, but I usually don't meet anybody like you, so tall and handsome. Are you here alone?"

"As a matter of fact, I'm with somebody, but I think we have a mutual friend."

"Oh really, and who would that be?"

"A young man named William Henderson. He was rescued from a blood curse earlier today. He named you as the last person he remembers, in this very club, from three months ago."

Rachel turned slowly and slinked off the tall chair, "Rachel," Jason called after her, and she hesitated, but didn't turn around. She was listening so Jason continued, "I believe you are part of a conspiracy to abduct and enslave unwitting victims, and I intend for you to pay for your crimes, if you are responsible. If you are enslaved yourself, I intend to rescue you from your curse in the same way that William was rescued. If you knowingly, without being compelled against your own free will, ensnared innocent people and are unrepentant, I have a sanction to destroy you utterly."

She turned with eyes brimming and clenched fists, "You sound exactly like Alastor. I have to do what he says or he will destroy me, and I have to stop or you will destroy me. You might as well get it over with right now and put me out of my misery."

Jason reached out and she took his hand, suddenly she was filled with warmth and understanding. Jason searched her chi for a blood curse and found none, "I see that you've been blackmailed into your roll, through threat of violence and leverage against your daughter. Will you believe me if I tell you that you have nothing to fear from this night forward and that you can leave this place right now with no thought of consequences?"

"I do believe you. There's something about you that makes me feel at peace in a way that I haven't felt since I was a child."

"Leave now and never return to this place. The ones responsible will be dealt with this very night, I swear it by the Goddess Hecate," Jason said, and Rachel retrieved her hand, stared into Jason's eyes for a moment, turned and walked out the front door.

"What the hell?" Robin said as she sat next to Jason.

"What's up with that?" Monica reflected.

Amanda scootched up onto a chair opposite and Jason said, "That, my friends, was the infamous Rachel."

"That's the chick that shanghaied William a few months ago? No, you're kidding," Robin responded.

"The very same, and she attempted to shanghai me just now. And I'm afraid I promised her that she should have no fear of the ones who blackmailed her into doing what she did. In fact, I promised that they'd be dealt with this very evening."

"Well then, it's on now I guess," Monica offered. "And I just met a really nice guy. I really wanted to get laid one more time before the piper called, damn it."

Jason chuckled and said, "Don't worry Monica, you'll have plenty of time with your new boyfriend, right after we handle this guy named Alastor that Rachel mentioned, and the head dragon. Let's gather the team."

Monica connected psychically and everybody came on line at almost the same time, *Oh dear, here comes Mark, what do I tell him? He seems so hopeful.*

Tell Mark that we have to take care of some business. You can trade numbers before we go down. I guess the place to start is in the den of iniquity below. I suppose that's where we'll find Alastor and Penthraig.

In the video room above, Alastor was distraught, "Where the hell did Rachel go? Did she just leave the premises?"

"Looks like it to me boss. We can check with security, they have the outside cameras," Jim answered.

"Look, their flock is gathering," Mike added, and put camera one on the big screen.

"Something's up, I need to inform Penthraig. Joni, you call all the imps and get them on the floor. I want these witches surrounded by our people ASAP."

"Consider it done," Joni replied and she tapped the line to communicate.

On the floor, the team all sensed the ripples, and Monica put Mark's card in her pocket then told him that it would be wise for him to leave.

"Why, we're just getting to know each other?" He fairly whined.

"There are things afoot that you can't possibly understand right now. Just trust me and get out of here, right now. I'll call you tomorrow and we can have a picnic. Right now I have something important to do, and it may involve considerable violence."

"What? Violence? What do you mean?"

Monica didn't answer; she simply touched Mark in the center of his forehead with her index finger and said *leave* with her mind. Mark's eyes glazed a bit before he turned and left.

Sara, Susan, and Francine pushed their husbands onto chairs around Jason's table. "Stay right here, no matter what happens. Protect Amanda, she's staying here too,"

Francine commanded, and the men nodded. They looked bewildered, but they complied because they knew that when the witches spoke in such tones, that they meant what they said.

Up in the apartment, Penthraig was startled out of a doze and warm massage rocks fell from his back to the floor. He was tuned to the imps and heard Joni's rallying call. Marta continued to snore softly while Pen rose and dressed quickly, oil and all. He left the masseurs to tend to Marta while he attended to whatever was going on down in the club. Then Alastor burst into his thoughts, having tapped the line as well to communicate with his boss.

Penthraig, he sent through the line, and all the witches heard it. *I'm sorry to trouble you, but the witches are here, and they have just gathered. One of them, I'm sure it's this Jason fellow because he looks just like his picture, said something to Rachel and she simply walked out the door.*

The damn witches are here? What the hell could they want? Pen replied after he tapped the line as well.

They were just dancing and drinking, but now they have gathered. I called for the imps to gather also, and I'm going down to the floor now.

I'm on my way, meet me at the elevator," and he dropped the line.

"Well, it seems the mountain is coming to Mohammad," Jason said out loud. We'll ask for a parlay down in his office. Everybody on guard, and I think Francine is right, Amanda, you should stay here and tap the line, just in case they have information for us. You can relay anything important from the line to all of us through the mind meld, or whatever it is." *Remember, no weapons when you're tapped in,* Jason finished telepathically.

Suits me just fine, I haven't even tried to use the weapons yet, Amanda replied. She struggled for a few seconds before she could do it, but she successfully tapped in, and every confederate of Penthraig's who was capable, felt the ripples.

"I believe we're going to have company from all flanks in a few seconds, but where we need to be is in front of that elevator," Jason said, so the team moved as one, minus Amanda and the husbands, toward the right end of the bar.

Everybody open their second sight, we want to know who we're dealing with as soon as possible, Monica instructed.

The imps all clambered up the staircase and spilled out into the club just as Alastor and Joni arrived from the video booth. There were eight imps plus Alastor where they congregated just to the left of the bar. They saw immediately that the witches were between them and the elevator where Penthraig would emerge. Just as their panic permeated the air and sizzled in the chi's of the witches, the elevator door opened.

Penthraig's surprise was palpable, but he gathered himself in an instant, and said, "What can I do for you, Monica, and Robin. And am I correct in presuming that this is Jason with you; your new champion."

"It's been a long time Pen," Monica answered. "We need to talk, down in your office, if you don't mind."

"Wonderful, I must confess that I intended to visit your shop tomorrow to do just that, talk I mean. It seems that several members of my staff have gone missing out your way and I wanted to discuss that. Please, join me in the elevator," he said and stepped back. "Alastor, would you join us too, and lead the way to your office, if you please. It's actually more spacious than mine," he said to the witches. "He needs the space to run the business. He's indispensable as my right hand man."

Pen gestured over their heads at the arriving hoard of imps and his right hand man, "The rest of you can return to your evening," he said to the boiling imps, but they all knew that he wanted them back in the tunnels, as backup in case things got out of hand.

The witches looked around as Pen gestured and saw immediately the special auras of the imps and the gurgling black aura of the demon Alastor who was mixed with an unidentified human. Jason had never seen anything like it, and only Monica and Francine had any actual experience with such a being. They sensed Jason's bewilderment and they telepathically pointed out the differences to the team as the elevator descended.

We don't want to kill Alastor outright then, because he possesses a human. All the imps are fair game, and Penthraig just looks like a dirty human. Is that right? Jason asked through their link.

That's right, Monica answered as the door opened onto a surprisingly spacious red brick tunnel with a high curved ceiling. There was a sign on the opposite wall with an arrow pointing to the left that said, "Restrooms and Service Desk." Alastor and Penthraig turned to the right.

The team looked both ways and noticed as the imps all spilled out into the tunnel the length of the bar away. They milled around but everybody knew that they would follow as soon as the team rounded a corner or entered an office.

Back in Milford, at Monica's house, Beti had been alerted too, since she was still tuned to the imp network. Her new friend, and master, as she continued to think of Jason, she knew would be confronted by a true demon, plus the entire cadre of remaining imps, and Penthraig himself. It was too much for her to bear. She tore out the front door and ran a few steps, phased into her sparrow hawk form and took to the moonlit sky while her baggy sweats slumped on the front lawn.

Alastor arrived at his office door and opened it for the entourage. Everybody filed in but Sara, and she said, "I'll just keep an eye out. Call me if you need me." She stayed in the hall while Alastor almost closed the door. He left it open a crack, in preparation for his imps to gain access if needed. Just as they entered, the imps rounded the corner behind them and hesitated a few yards from Sara. On the inside, Penthraig sat on the front edge of Al's desk with one leg dangling.

"Well, it surely has been a long time, Monica. You and Robin have done well. I'm glad to see that. Have a seat and tell me what's on your mind," Pen said as Alastor slipped behind his desk where he stood like a guard at attention.

The team formed a semi-circle in front of Pen, and Monica began, "This is Jason, our team leader and he'll speak for the group."

Jason began without the pleasantries of a normal introduction; no handshake, no small talk, "Penthraig, I have been tasked and sanctified by the Goddess Hecate to bring balance back to the world, beginning here in Cincinnati, with you."

"Oooh, sounds ominous, please, do continue."

"We, as a team, have received sanction to rehabilitate you, or destroy you utterly."

Penthraig laughed, "You intend to murder me, right here, right now, sitting here on this desk? That's absurd. Or maybe it's not so absurd; perhaps you've already killed a few of my employees. Are you already a murderer, Jason?"

"Sanction, is the term we prefer, and it isn't murder at all, we've only returned your imps to the realms where they belong. The Goddess who is in authority to judge you and sentence you for your misdeeds has decided that it's time for action. We are the enforcement arm of Hecate and she has given us a task that we intend to carry out, right now. You have abused the innocent through enslavement, blackmail, and coercion, but still, you are given the opportunity to rehabilitate. We'd rather you give up your life of crime. If you fail to repent of these things, I will destroy you."

"Murder, that's what it is, no matter how you try to justify it, and who are you to think you have the right, from a Goddess or anywhere else to kill me when everyone in my employ is happy to work for me? Their pay and benefits are way better than any other job in the city, they choose to stay here and nobody has been harmed in any way."

"You underestimate the power of the Goddess," Jason answered. "She has informed me that you manipulate your employees with blackmail, extortion, and sorcery, as I've already stated. Those who believe they're happy and acting of their own free will are simply entranced. And I know about the innocent young women, and young men that you spell into lives of prostitution. I also know that after they're diseased and abused and no longer useful to you, they wind up in your furnace. And that's not all, I happen to know that you use torture to glean information about your competitors and all evidence of abuse goes into the fire. Only your demon is privy to these depredations, and we are here to deal with him as well. This is not about gathering evidence of your crimes; we already have a sure knowledge, so there is no need of a trial, because the Goddess sees all. We are not murderers, you are. I and my team are called and sanctified as your executioners, if necessary."

The tension in Pen and Al, the subjects of the wrath of the Goddess, ramped up as Jason laid out the sure knowledge of the truth against them. Their expressions went from mild amusement to serious concern, and the witches were stoked up to welding heat as they learned this new information.

Penthraig stood, and tapped the line, but the witches and Jason simply held their ground, alert, but still as iron.

"So, you think you have the power to come into my place and kill me where I stand? Judge, jury, and executioner all in one, that's you then."

"We don't want to kill you, but we will if we have to. And yes, we do have the power, granted by the Guardians of the Watchtowers and sanctified by the Goddess. All this has been stated, it's time for you to choose."

"Well then," Penthraig answered, "Let's dance," and he fired plasma balls that were an order of magnitude stronger than the ones Beti had fired at the gravel pit. Flame burst into both hands and he flung the plasma straight at Jason's chest and at the witches in rapid succession. Fire that purled with red, blue, green, and black with the smell of sulfur rippled over the witches and set to blazes every piece of furniture on their side of the room.

The speed of the attack and the intensity of the fire forced all the witches and Jason to react out of pure instinct. They ducked and turned their backs and Susan and Francine dove behind chairs in acts of self-preservation from the inferno unleashed at them.

Penthraig saw immediately that his attack had no real effect since the plasma was blocked by their individual protection bubbles.

"Al!" Pen shouted, "together," and they fired in unison, again to no real affect except for the ducking and diving. Furniture blazed, and it looked as if the room would remain a furnace to the destruction of everyone when the sprinklers activated. Susan gathered the water and directed it at the actual flames while Jason called the fire to himself, as its master he pulled it in, consolidated it into a ball and prepared to launch it back at the enemy. What he didn't pull in, Susan and the others extinguished as they followed her lead.

"Out!" Al shouted as they both fired again to keep the witches down. The two men burst through the door and knocked a surprised Sara to the ground. Her protection bubble had activated but the physical force of the door displaced the whole thing with Sara inside it. The imps simply gawked in stunned amazement as their two bosses fired another volley into the room and turned to run down the tunnel. A split second after they vacated the doorway, Jason's fireball exploded into the tunnel, passing over Sara's prone position.

"Hey!" Sara yelled and jumped up prepared to blast a column of her own fire when Alastor reached back in mid stride and shot at her first. She reacted as the others had done, turned her back and ducked away. The imps began to realize a full scale battle was in progress. Two or three of them fired at Sara, who now faced them. The plasma from Al deflected off her protection at the rear and the imp's fireballs deflected off the front. Both sides of her body were under attack and Sara came to her senses. "Damn it, that's it you little pricks," and she fired both barrels of her own into the crowd of imps who were now all shooting at her. The tunnel filled with flames and several imps recoiled from it.

Sara's attack was on target and Kili, the imp coyote, and Ali the hobbie falcon, burst into a billion stars and vaporized leaving nothing but rising smoke and the stench of sulfur mixed with singed dog fur.

As the rest of the soaked team emerged with caution from the office, Sara turned her attention to two other imps who had fired on her. Desi and Laci, two red foxes ceased to exist in the earthly realm. The four remaining imps, two kestrels, a red tail, and a gray hawk, phased to their bird forms and darted back down the tunnel and out into the night.

Sara turned and pointed in the direction of Alastor and Penthraig, "They went that way," and the team sprinted down the tunnel.

Jason was faster and passed the women easily in the first ten yards, rounded the bend and saw the two denizens slowing down from their own sprint that was really more of a jog, since neither of them had paid attention to personal fitness in years. They were headed for Penthraig's secret door to his secret office and the hidden environs beyond, and were almost there when the bricks in front of them opened and Marta stepped into the tunnel, "Pendi, Al, there you are. I've been looking all over for you."

She was in a black leather mini and red leather bustier with fishnets and spiked heels. She carried a little black handbag. Instead of the greeting she expected, Penthraig grabbed her roughly and turned her toward his pursuers.

One arm held her just below the breasts, trapping her arms, and he pulled her back into him in a classic hostage hold with his right hand pressed to the right side of her head. He pulled her so tight that the bustier was overwhelmed and one breast popped out. She struggled in vain and shouted for Pen to let her go, but then the team arrived and Pen shouted above her, "Shut up you stupid bitch," and then to the team, "Stay back or I'll blow her brains all over the tunnel wall, and you know I'll do it." Al slipped into the open office.

Everyone stood still, not knowing what to do, and the team heard Jason contemplate a needle shot to Penthraig's exposed right eye, but the risk was great and the innocent woman shook with fear while she still struggled in his grip. Then something whizzed over their heads in a blur of brown that the team thought was a bat, so they ducked again, out of instinct.

Penthraig was distracted for a second with the hopeful thought that one of the imps had joined him, and in that second Beti flashed by and slashed a talon at the same eye that Jason had targeted. Her aim was true and Penthraig howled with pain and anger at his destroyed eye. He pushed Marta to the ground and turned to shoot a plasma ball at the receding kestrel, but Jason was quicker and blasted Penthraig in the back with the full power and blessing of fire drawn from Nariel, the Guardian of the Southern Watchtower.

The fireball singed the hair on the back of Marta's head and a shockwave knocked everybody but Jason flat. Penthraig was utterly consumed. Not even bones were left, but a ball of smoke rose to the ceiling and spread out in both directions while white ashes fluttered down like snow.

Susan gained her hands and knees and vomited on the floor and Sara said, "Oh Goddess, it smells like burned barbecue in here."

Crying, Marta crawled toward the witches on her scraped hands and knees.

Suddenly a shout blasted through all the team's minds, *Get Alastor!* Amanda screamed, still connected to the line. *He's trying to reach the circle in Penthraig's lab. The line says that if he gets there, he can escape!*

Jason sprang up, bolted for the door and dashed through without a single thought for his own safety. He knew that Alastor's weapons could not penetrate and he wouldn't make the mistake of flinching again.

There was nobody in the room, but Amanda was on it, *Through the door behind the bookcase. There's one more door after that with a keypad and Alastor is putting in the numbers right now.*

The image of the bookcase sliding from left to right flashed into Jason's head and he pulled it out of the way. On the other side of the small room that seemed to hold records of Penthraig's clandestine empire, Alstor had just opened another door. Jason blasted a single needle in his direction but Al had slipped through while the needle impacted and shattered on the steel doorjamb.

Jason clutched the knob a millimeter before the latch would have blocked him out and he flung the door open. Alastor noticed, hesitated, turned and fired a plasma ball at Jason, but this time Jason didn't flinch, and one silver needle stuck in Alastor's left pectoral an instant later.

The demon-possessed human screamed and fell flat on his back, right in the middle of Penthraig's circle. On the way down his shoulders struck the rolling exam table that still held the withered and lifeless dog that had been sacrificed for Penthraig's pleasure. The table rolled out of the circle and bumped into the cages on the wall where several cat's yowled and birds screeched.

Alastor was down, the wound site of the dart fizzed while he screamed and writhed on the floor. Just like

Matthew earlier in the day, Al was unaware of the injury site. He didn't grab at the needle or pay any attention at all to the sizzling, smoking wound. On his back, he thrashed and screamed.

Jason hurried to pull the needle out then laid his hand over the wound to heal it. Al quieted as he lost consciousness.

Robin was the first after Jason to react and she charged into the room ready to battle. She saw Jason on the floor with his hands on Alastor and knew what had happened. Monica arrived next, and out in the hall, Francine helped Marta up off the floor and tried to console her. Susan had recovered and joined Francine, and Sara was moving through the records room when Beti flashed by.

The kestrel landed next to Jason and phased to her naked human form. Robin and Monica started, and almost fired, but Beti ignored them and placed her hand on her new master's shoulder, "Is he dead?"

"No, just unconscious, I didn't want to kill the human he possesses."

"For a full demon, Alastor is a very pleasant sort. He always treated me with respect and fairly. I suspect you will exorcise him and return him to the realms?"

"Yes, that's my intent," Jason replied and turned to face his imp friend. "May I?" he asked and pointed to Beti's forehead.

"Of course."

Jason touched her with his index finger and downloaded the images and information that had been given to him by the Goddess. As he did so, the others were still connected on their psychic net and they all received the same information. The transfer only took a fraction of a second but dozens of images of rape, torture, and murder downloaded for the team to see. Penthraig was involved in most of them, and Alastor all of them, many of them having been committed in that very room.

When it was done, Beti commented, "I had no idea."

"I know," Jason stood and hugged the stunning little blond, in all her glorious nudity. He looked over the top of her head and found Monica and Robin crying, and continued, "Well ladies, we're not done yet. Can we get some clothes for Beti here, and you might want to conjure up some warm wind. You guys look like you're entered into a wet T-shirt contest."

By then, Susan and Francine had joined them with blubbering Marta, who had slumped into a chair. The wet women looked down and gasped at the realization that the cold water from the sprinklers had affected them in a big way. They all spun and pulled their soaked and clingy shirts away from their fronts as Sara laughed, "Hah! How does it feel ladies? Jason's gittin' educated from all of us; me yesterday and y'all today!"

Sara called the wind and blow-dried the red-faced women in a matter of seconds.

"Robin, would you be so kind as to set this circle before the demon wakes up and uses it to escape? Make sure it's got him trapped well and true, please."

Jason held Beti away enough to see her face as she looked up, "And you, missy, were supposed to stay at Monica's."

"But I heard the imp network when they discovered you, so I rushed to help, and my name is not Missy, it's Beti."

Jason chuckled and said, "And I'm so glad you did. Your timing couldn't have been better. You likely saved that hostage woman's life, and possibly many others. We were at a standoff and Pentrhaig might easily have escaped because of his hostage if it were not for your ability to use your own judgment. Who knows what the cost would have been without your intervention. Well done, and thank you."

"I am glad that you are not cross with me. I desire only to serve."

"And I want you to be my friend."

"I am that, certainly, and more," Beti finished as Susan pulled her arm from around Jason's waist and into a shirtsleeve.

On the way through Penthraig's office Susan and Francine had looked for a first aid kit to bandage Marta's bloody knees and ran across a wardrobe full of silk shirts. They picked a nice chartreuse one for Beti and Francine had said, "What are we doing, we don't need a first aid kit, we have a seventh son."

The shirt was adequate cover except for its tendency to cling to Beti's curves, but it would have to do for the moment.   Everybody moved out of the circle and Robin set it, with more than adequate protection from demons, but she didn't think to set it silent since the demon was unconscious.

Marta finally calmed enough to sob, "What the hell is going on? I came down the private elevator to find Pendi and suddenly he grabbed me for a hostage and called me a bitch and then he pushed me on the ground. Who are you people? What just happened? Is Pendi dead? Did you set him on fire? And what's the matter with Al?"

Jason pointed at her forehead and asked, "May I?" just as he had with Beti.

"Be my guest," Marta answered. "If it will get me some answers."

Jason found the connection with Marta a little more difficult than with his team, but in a few seconds he had downloaded the same information and Marta burst back into tears, "I was with a madman and didn't have a clue. He was so nice, and so fun. How could he be such a monster?"

"You sure can't tell by lookin' at 'em honey, I can tell ya' that," Sara offered. "The con men are that way so they can cheat ya,' and use ya,' and dump ya.' If they walked around with a madman sign plastered on 'em, they'd *never* get laid. You have to be careful honey."

Jason kneeled in front of Marta. He pointed at her bloody knees and shredded black fishnets, and asked, "May I?" She nodded.

He placed a hand on each kneecap. Marta gasped and straightened her spine.

"Does it hurt honey?" Francine asked.

"No, it feels wonderful. So warm--and the pain is gone. Can you do my hands too?" she asked when Jason stood. He held a hand in each of his and soon there were no scrapes evident at all.

"He's a seventh son of a seventh son, newly sanctified by the Goddess Hecate," Sara explained.

"I'm not sure what that means, but I believe it, whatever you say. There's not a scratch on me. Even the scars from when I was a little girl are gone from my knees. So you're the good guys?"

"Yes mam," Jason replied.

Just then, Amanda's telepathic warning came to the team, *The line says you're going to have company soon. Humans this time, all of them spelled to protect Penthraig.*

"Ok, what do you want us to do now?" Monica asked.

"I think you and Robin and Francine should stay here with Marta and keep an eye on the demon. Figure out what we need to do to exorcise it. Sara, and I'll take care of the reserves. And one needle only Sara, these are humans and we want to rehabilitate them all."

"A-OK boss, let's go," Sara replied and headed for the door.

"One second honey," Robin called after her. "Jason, next time you rush into the lair of a powerful sorcerer, please make sure you don't run into a ward, you could have fried yourself. It's a good thing Penthraig had more confidence in electronic locks than his ability to cast a ward."

Jason's face turned red and he replied, "Noted. . . I can see that I still have a lot to learn."

"Don't we all," Robin replied and shooed him off with a back handed wave.

Succubus - 25

Jason, Sara, and Beti moved through the records room and peeked into Penthraig's office past the open bookcase.

"Maybe we should stay here and draw them in. When they're all in we can take them by surprise. I bet they don't know much about this office, if anything at all," Jason suggested. He thought about sending Beti back, but relented when he realized that she wouldn't leave his side for the duration, and he also knew that she had extensive knowledge of the workings of Caleo.

They're sneaking down the tunnel in your direction, Amanda sent via their telepathic link.

How many? Jason sent back.

Six, all armed with pistols, all young men. I even have their names if you want 'em.

Ok, but we'll wait on the names, thanks. Do they know where we are?

They only have a general understanding of where the office is. Penthraig kept it as secret as he could. They know that Penthraig and the one they call Alastor are not in touch on their network, as well as several others. Sounds to me like they think their bosses are gone, but they're compelled by their spells to act. The line doesn't know if they'll give up if they know for sure that Penthraig is dead.

Thanks Amanda, and thank the line for me as well please.

Already done, and the husbands are informed of everything. They want to come down and join their wives.

Tell them to stay where they are for the moment. We don't need to worry about them and they have no protection like we do.

OK, standing by.

At that moment, Francine slipped into the group, *I figure you're gonna need help in a minute, Robin's coming too.*

Ok, great, but go back to the other door and when I tell you, slam it real hard. We need to draw as many in as we can, I don't want them to scatter and get back up into the club, Jason instructed.

Fine, but you do know that once I shut that door we can't get back in without the key code or somebody turning the knob on the other side, Francine replied.

No problem, when I healed Alastor, I got the code, and I'm pretty sure you'll guess what it is. Four numbers--and try not to be too creative.

Not 6666? Francine guessed.

You got it, Jason replied and slid the bookcase door to within a couple inches of its jamb, just enough to notice if the bad guy's attentions were drawn in that direction. He also snapped off the overhead lights to throw the records room into darkness.

Sara wiggled in front of Jason so she could see out the crack and Jason was plenty tall enough to look over her head. Robin entered from the other side and Francine turned off the lights to the lab.

Marta shouted, "Now what?"

Monica shushed her. Still connected to the net, Monica knew what was going on and they all had their sight up, so they could see in the dark. Monica moved to Marta and said, "Hush for a minute, they're gonna' get busy out there real soon."

An idea popped into Jason's head so he manipulated a tight horizontal column of wind across Penthraig's office to the light switch and snapped it off. They waited less than a minute before they saw a cautious head peep for a split second through the crack of the open door from the hall. A hand pushed the door open nearly all the way, and then snaked around the door jamb to snap the lights back on.

Well, the best laid plans and all, Jason telepathed.

The same dark-haired head peeked again, longer this time, and then a tall young blond man darted past, through the door to crouch behind a chair. One by one, five of the spelled humans entered the office to take up covered positions behind chairs and the desk, and one of them behind the other end of the bookcase Jason and Sara were peering around.

One of their numbers had obviously been left to cover the exit. They spoke in whispers, so the team had no way to know what their plan was.

It turned out that they didn't really have a plan beyond finding Penthraig and trying to protect him. Jason put his finger up to the crack and took aim at the last figure to enter, the original peeper. Part of the young man's arm was exposed at the corner of Penthraig's desk so Jason focused on that. Just before he fired his needle he telepathed, *Ok, slam it,* and Francine slammed the door.

The sound startled everybody, including Jason, but the jump shifted his target more into the open so he fired a single silver needle into the arm that fully showed around the corner of the desk. The man screamed and fell, the wound site fizzed while he writhed on the floor. Just like the others, he was unaware of the injury site. He thrashed and screamed as the wound sizzled and smoked.

The rest of the humans opened up with their pistols and bullets flew around the room in every direction.

Jason had expected the spelled humans to rush toward the sound of the slammed door, but with their leaders gone and their captain writing on the ground from an unseen attack, self-preservation replaced their resolve. They shot until they were empty and then broke for the door to escape.

Jason pushed the bookcase open and Sara fired at the fleeing men. Two fell screaming with her needles in their backs but two reached the door and escaped, for a step or two. Screams erupted from the tunnel as Sara ran in pursuit. She jumped over the two writhing young men in her path and popped out the door without looking. Jason moved to the first injured man to heal him when *Stop! It's me, Amanda,* filled his mind.

In the tunnel, Sara released the power she had spooled in her hands when she realized that all three of the remaining bodyguards were down and Amanda stood in the tunnel with the three husbands, Steve, Mike, and Dave.

"Dammit, David, you were told to stay up in the club. What part of 'stay' didn't you understand?" Sara shouted.

"It's ok Sara, I brought 'em down. I saw that y'all could use some help and there was no leavin' 'em up there. They were havin' kittens for cryin' out loud."

"Kittens! They're gonna' have more than that when I get through. They're gonna' be shittin' bloody bricks!"

Calm down ladies, we still have work to do, Jason telepathed. *Thanks for the help Amanda. I presume we've contained everything down here for the moment.*

Amanda responded instantly, *Four of the imps flew the coup, but there's something called a succubus in another part of this dungeon. Once we take care of that thing, then we can release the prostitutes. There's an underground brothel down there.*

Ok, perfect. I need to concentrate for a few moments to save these young men. Mike, Dave, and Steve can help get them into the lab so Francine can do a clearing for them. I'll take care of the succubus while the rest of you deal with the clearing.

Careful Jason, the line says that thing is the most dangerous demon down here.

Ok, thanks, I'll get some advice before I go.

Jason pulled needles where he could and healed the young men. Two of the three in the hall were shot through and through, thankfully in non-lethal places, but the last one was burning from the inside out. A needle had lodged in his femur so Jason was forced to draw it out in the same way he had called the metal to him at the gravel pit. The healing was difficult and left Jason sweating and gasping for breath. When he finished and looked up at Amanda, she knew what was coming and diverted it with, "Sorry, I didn't mean to do that. It's the first time I've used any of these new powers and I guess I was on full blast."

"You did better than could be expected, and I'm sure you tried to reduce the power, because full on would have shattered his femur and I don't think I'd have been able to fix that. You knew enough to avoid lethal areas, all three are leg wounds. As it is, I suspect he'll walk with a limp for a couple weeks, but that's all. Well done."

Amanda smiled, she liked this new guy, he was very diplomatic and charming, not to mention handsome. She was used to something quite different in men.

Exhausted, Jason sat where he was as the three husbands carried the last of the unconscious guards to the lab where the witches prepared to do a mass clearing. Jason looked up from his still sitting position to find Amanda and Beti observing.

"What happened? Are you ok?" Amanda asked.

"I just needed to catch my breath is all."

The women took a hand each and helped him up. He ran his hands through his hair and asked, "Ok, where's this succubus?"

Beti answered, "Not far from here, at the end of the hall of pleasure, as Penthraig used to call it."

"Ok, I guess you should stay here and help with the clearing, Amanda. I'm gonna' scout a little and see what I can find out. When the guards are cleansed and released, we'll tackle the succubus as a team."

"You got it boss," Amanda said and entered Penthraig's office.

"Ok Beti, you can show me where this thing is and on the way there you can tell me what you know about it."

Beti started back in the direction of the elevator and informed Jason about the next trial they would face as they walked, "We all avoided Nahmdatter because she is ravenous and indiscriminate. She feeds upon foe or friend without concern. Only a true demon can control her and now that Alastor is imprisoned and soon to be exorcised, the succubus is easily the most dangerous being left to encounter. Like a siren she sings to her prey and drains their power like a vampire drinks blood. She exudes wellbeing and the hope of pleasure and so lures her victim. She once sang to me, and I thought it was my friend Stoli. She mimicked his voice and I was about to touch her door when Stoli pulled me away."

"Why did she call to you?"

"She was hungry. I was nearby, that is all."

"Wow, pretty interesting. What would she have done to you once she lured you in?"

"She would have drained my life force, probably. She can enslave, to cause young women to submit to prostitution, and young men to become lackeys, such as those who you recently vanquished, guards and human spies."

"Like William Henderson, I guess."

"Yes, like him, but William and the others were not enslaved by the succubus. They were entrapped by the women shills in the club, and Alastor enslaved them with a blood curse. Nahmdatter is capable of all of that, but it's not what Alastor used her for; he could do all that himself, as a true demon. He used the succubus to draw power from witches and the gifted. He would have used her on you, and the result would have been a great wealth of power to share with Penthraig."

"If she's so powerful, how did Alastor control her?"

"The underworld is a caste system, where every being has its place and every ascending level increases in power over the lower levels. It is designed so that one being has power and authority over all other beings, like a king has power over his subjects. A succubus is one level below a true demon, and so must obey or be destroyed. The caste is irrefutable and irrevocable."

They entered the tunnel lobby and passed by the reception desk where two female employees scheduled 'dates' for the lascivious, poker for the gamblers, and drugs for the addicts. The women were familiar with all the imps and greeted Beti with surprise.

"Wow, haven't seen you in a couple days, Beti. Looks like you've been busy," the dark haired one said with a giggle. "You're lookin' pretty snappy in that silk shirt, girlfriend," the black one said.

Beti nodded in their direction and continued past, which would have been her usual practice anyway. There were two guards on duty, one at the entrance to the cafeteria, and one to the entrance to the rest of the tunnels including the hall of pleasure. Under second sight, the guards were normal humans, rental security, mostly for show, so they barely noticed as Beti and Jason strode past them into the next maze of tunnels.

There were people coming and going, mostly men, but the occasional woman. All of whom were interested in various vices that could be had for a price in the tunnels.

At the first branch to the right, Beti stopped. "This is the prostitution wing, and the succubus is in the room at the very end. She never comes out, and whoever goes in never comes out either."

"Ok, I presume you still have clothes and other possessions somewhere on the premises?"

"Yes, in the quarters section of the tunnels down this hall," she said and nodded toward her room.

"Why don't you get dressed and meet me back here. I need a little more rest and I'll just hang out on this bench. We'll wait for the others here as well."

"As you wish," she said and turned away from the branch that held the succubus.

Jason sat down to relax and watched her tight body, mostly hidden by Penthraig's silk shirt, but not entirely. It clung in places and shifted in others as she walked, quite the sight for a horny bachelor, and as she disappeared around a bend, Jason leaned back against the cool bricks and closed his eyes. He shut down his second sight and disconnected from the psychic network after informing the team that he needed some quiet time.

Jason drifted off to sleep for a moment when suddenly he heard Beti call from behind. He was sure of it, but how could it be possible, there was a solid wall of bricks behind him.

He listened. And there it was again, Beti's voice calling to him. *It's some acoustic anomaly of the tunnels*, he thought as he stood and turned about.

A strong urge to discover this anomaly pulled him in the direction of her voice, now down the Hall of Pleasure, "Jason, come to me," was all she said, but it lilted and pierced at the same time, only a few feet away.

"*What do you want Beti?*" Jason thought on the net.

Silence. . .

"*Beti? Just get dressed and meet me back here.*"

"Come to me Jason, I need you," the quiet but penetrating voice of the cute little imp drew his attention to the sound. His absent minded steps carried him toward the voice; he must find it and learn the magic of the tunnels. He shuffled forward, intent on discovery, and passed what seemed like a hundred doors on each side of the Hall of Pleasures. His impatience made the trek last an eternity although it was only eight doors on each side before he came to one on the very end that was unlike the others he'd passed. This one displayed an ironwork façade with scrolls and sigils the likes of which he'd never seen. Something medieval he suspected, but he didn't know and didn't care. The voice of the cute little tight-body imp called to him again.

"Come in Jason, and welcome."

He pushed down on an iron lever and expected to see Beti inside, but he found a raven haired beauty instead.

Tall, buxom, in flowing silks, she stood straight, statuesque, like living marble, a Michelangelo rendered effigy of a Goddess.

She spoke with Beti's voice and that comforted Jason, "Welcome my friend," she said, but he knew she was not Beti. It didn't matter; he was smitten, and moved to her arms. She embraced him and kissed him on the cheek. "Welcome, powerful one," she whispered into his ear.

Jason looked into her eyes and saw swirling red and black ink deep in her pupils. He wondered about that, *How can it be that her pupils are so alive*, he was mesmerized even more.

She spoke in a different voice now, one that dripped with honey, deep and sultry, "Welcome my friend, one who has power from a Goddess, a seventh son, so handsome, so strong, so intelligent, and so talented. You are as a God yourself, you wield the strength of hundreds and there is none who compares. You are the fulfillment of my dreams and I want you as I have never wanted any man. Come, lie with me, you are weary and in need of rest and relaxation. You deserve to be pampered and served. I would give you all that you need, come and lie with me," she said and began to sing.

She sang a lullaby so sweet and pure that it could have been an angel, and somewhere deep in the recesses of his mind, Jason heard warnings, but they were muffled by the beautiful song and far away. They reclined on her canopied bed and now he lay with the most beautiful woman he'd ever seen so he didn't care about warnings. She licked him on the neck and stroked his bulging manhood through his jeans, and all he wanted was to spend the rest of his life in her embrace. Then she straddled him, kissed him deeply, the grind of her hips stoked a flame in his loins. But there was something different about the kiss, something more intimate than he'd ever felt. It was as if she had kissed his very soul, and he longed to share with her, to give to her his essence.

And that was exactly what was happening when the door burst in.

The beautiful woman became a hag still astride him when she broke the kiss. She sat up, snapped her gaze to the door, and hissed like a cat. Jason saw now that her face was covered with sagging wrinkled skin and warts and patches of black cancerous lesions. He watched with detached amazement as she was knocked off of him by a volley of silver needles fired at full power. The succubus flew against the wall at the edge of the bed as if she'd been hit by an invisible bus, and then she vaporized to nothing but ashes and black smoke that rose into the bed's canopy and dissipated.

Now someone familiar but very far away called to him, and something sharp impacted his cheek but he didn't really understand that she had slapped him. Slowly he came around, and recognized the very stern face of Robin that hovered over him. She slapped him again, and he was fully awake.

"Holy cow, what happened," he said, still lying back.

Robin grasped his chin and turned his head left and right. She watched his eyes follow as the pupils returned from their dilated state, "The succubus nearly drained you, that's what happened."

"And you saved me," he said and reached both arms around Robin's neck, pulled her down and kissed her hard on the lips.

She pushed him back on the bed, "Ok, Romeo, I can see there are some residuals, so you just lie there and rest a minute. When this goes back down we can talk some more," she said and flicked his bulging jeans with the back of her middle finger.

She stood up and Jason saw the members of his team, minus Monica, Francine and the three husbands. "Where's Monica," he asked.

"She's still in the lab, the demon is awake."

$\mathcal{D}$emon - 26

Beti darted in and phased from kestrel to naked human then rushed to Jason's side, where she shouldered Robin away, and Robin reacted, "For crying out loud Beti, will you please stop that! The party's over in here--and you're nekked again."

Beti kneeled next to the bed and stroked Jason's forehead while she ignored all else. Robin yanked a sheer from the canopy and draped it over Beti's shoulders in an attempt to preserve at least a hint of propriety.

Jason recuperated and while he did, Robin, Susan and Sara moved through the Hall of Pleasure and tossed patrons out.

"Ask for your money back," Sara shouted as she shoved a half dressed man down the hall. The objects of the lustful patrons were 14 women and two men, boys really, and the witches gathered them together to herd them to the lab where Francine still progressed through clearings of the six guards who were taken down in the last stages of the fight.

"Good thing Francine collected that vial of blood from William earlier today. Every one of those guards had the same taint," Susan said as she prevented one of their charge from turning the wrong way.

"This is sorta like herdin' sheep," Sara offered. "Hey, we're sheep-herders, no, whore-herders," she chuckled. "The good thing is that these whores smell a whole lot better than sheep."

"Sara, they're sex slaves who don't even know what they're doing, not whores," Susan tossed at her.

"I know it, but 'whores' is funnier."

"You know, it kinda' is. You have to admit," Amanda offered.

When they arrived at the lobby the guards and receptionists reacted, but thought again when Sara produced a ball of flame in each hand and shouted, "Back off! Y'all's shift is over. Go on home now, this place is under new management," she shouted, and the workers left.

Robin knocked on Jason's mental window. He answered, *Hey Robin, I'm feeling better now.*

That's good, because I think we're gonna' need ya' pretty soon. Francine is finished with all the guards but one. She needs more tainted blood. A lot more if we're gonna' take care of the demon, and we don't have anything to poke the guy with. She didn't put the thorn in her pocket so all we have is metal. The guards were dumbfounded and they don't remember a thing, just like William. They've all left for home already. She started on the prostitutes because they don't have blood curses, just some kind of hypnotic suggestion. She had a time figuring it out but now she has the method and she's moving through them pretty fast. We still have a few minutes though, so why don't you take Beti down to her room and get her dressed. Don't leave her or she'll fly back to you again, and get naked again.

A-ok, got it. Good thinking. I'll be there soon.

Francine had moved the guards to the outer office and commandeered Penthraig's desk as an operating table. Now she was at work with the prostitutes. She cleared them by reaching into their crown chi with her new skills at melding, found Pen's powerful suggestion, removed it and replaced it with her own suggestion that no memory of their experience at Caleo would remain to plague them.

When she had finished with the fourth patient, Sara asked, "Why did you bring those guys back out here?"

"Because that demon is pissed, let me tell ya.' I never heard language like that and all his rants were too distracting. The boys are still in there, looking for something to poke this last guard so we can get more blood."

"Huh, sounds interesting. I think I'll go in and have a chat with the demon," Sara suggested.

"Well, be careful."

Sara hurried through the records room and had barely entered the lab when Alastor, or the demon named Alastor inside an unknown human, blasted her with a voice that was a full register below the lowest baritone Sara had ever heard, "Ah, the little troll-witch comes to torment me," he growled.

"Wow, is that your real voice peckerwood?" she said and strode up close to the circle that roiled with black and red clouds of smoke-like ether.

"I am Alastor, the executioner, the consort of Nemesis. I am he who visits the iniquity of the fathers upon the children and the children's children to the third and fourth generation. When I escape this infernal bubble I shall show you who I am. I shall cut off your eyelids so that you must witness the depredations committed to your own body and those of your friends. I will sever your breasts from your chest and disembowel you. I will roast your limbs in place and then dine on your flesh. Your screams will not drown the pain and you will remain conscious for all because I shall will it upon you so that your pain will be exquisite and lasting."

"Peckerwood is an expression, dipshit. And before you feel the need to tell me your real names again, dipshit is an expression too, and it describes you to a 'T.' And you're not gonna' disembowel anybody because Jason's gonna' ship your sorry ass back to where you belong."

"You ignorant, sodden, sack of meat; you couldn't possibly understand that I belong here. It is my duty to bring pain to the generations of humanity who anger the Gods and Goddesses. I'll enjoy gnawing on your bones as you scream and beg for death."

"You dumb jackass, you're the one who's ignorant. No, I take it back, you're insane. If you were the real Alastor, why would you be hangin' out in a dance club and playin' second fiddle to a third-rate magician?"

Alastor lunged at the spherical wall of black and red, and howled with the rage of seven banshees. Sparks and electric bolts flashed and thundered at the confluence of the wall and demon as he pounded it with his fists, but Sara didn't flinch. She was through with flinches, and she knew that to call a sorcerer a magician was about as wicked a thing as she could say about Pentrhaig, and to call Alastor a lackey to a magician was close to the most insulting thing that a demon would ever hear.

"Sara, hon, I think you've got that thing riled enough," Dave, her husband, called from a few feet behind. "Come on back to the other room now. We found a stone knife."

The demon ceased his howls, and looked deep into Sara's eyes, attempted to probe and search her mind, but she blocked him. She noticed his concern but turned to join Dave.

"What do you think you can do with the stone knife?" Alastor asked.

"What did you say? 'THE' stone knife, huh? I imagine pretty much what you used to do with it, or Penthraig more likely. We're gonna' get some tainted blood from the last of the guards, your blood, I expect, and we're gonna' use it to burn your ass."

"So, you actually believe that you can enter the circle with me, little troll-witch. By sunrise, you shall be in my power, and no one will hear your screams as I devour you alive."

"Not me, butt-plug, you must have brain damage. Jason is gonna' do fer' you. And I'm pretty sure you'll be unconscious when he puts you down for good, just like that dog over there on the gurney. In fact, we'll probably put you in that furnace you love so much, with the dead dog on top of you," Sara said, and left the demon to howl and swear blue streaks like nothing she'd ever heard.

As they passed through the records room, Dave offered, "Oh boy--that sure got his goat. Hope all that stuff you said about putting him down is true. Can Jason do it?"

"Well, let's put it this way, in a few minutes we're gonna' bet our lives that he can."

In the office Francine inspected the stone knife found by the husbands, "Whoa, this thing is awesome. Are you sure this is stone with all this color; pink, green, blue, yellow, it's more like stained glass or something."

"That's Flint Ridge chert," Jason said from behind her as he and fully dressed Beti entered the office. "It's my favorite material to knap. "It comes from only one place on Earth, right here in Ohio, about 30 miles east of Columbus, near Zanesville," Jason informed.

"Knap?" Robin asked.

"It means to chip, it's how you make arrowheads out of flint and obsidian and all sorts of rock."

"You make arrowheads out of this same stuff?"

"Yes, and spear points, and knife blades. It's a hobby, and I give most of it away for Christmas presents or whatever."

"Of course you do. Seventh son, maker," Sara replied.

"Did Penthraig make this?" Francine asked.

"Let me see it," Jason said. After turning it in his hands for a few seconds he pointed at a spot near the antler haft, "This is signed with the symbol for Roy Miller. Roy is the most renowned knapper in Ohio, one of the best in the world probably. He has his own quarry at Flint Ridge and works the high color chert almost exclusively. A blade like this one is a masterpiece and worth a couple thousand dollars."

"Wow, a rock and a piece of antler, who knew? Sure is pretty, and it's just what we need," Francine said. "I'm gonna' do a clearing on it first though. No tellin' what's on here from before."

"Penthraig cooties for sure," Sara added.

"So, where is the woman Penthraig held hostage? Jason asked.

"Her name is Marta," Susan answered. "She said her plane had arrived, she had received a text, and she took that little elevator over there to Penthraig's apartment to freshen up and gather her things. She's probably on the way to Miami by now. She left her card for you," Susan finished and handed the business card to Jason who looked at it briefly and slipped it into his pocket.

"Did she leave before Alastor awoke?"

"Yes, she said she couldn't stand seeing him unconscious in that bubble and didn't want to be around when we did whatever we're going to do. She said she just wanted to go home."

Francine proceeded with the sex slaves and sent them on their way one by one. Then she cleared the knife with the diminished nub of ayahuasca that she had left. After burning the vine of the dead for so long, the room smelled like a Seattle Hempfest.

"Will that be enough to deal with the demon?" Susan asked.

"I think so, it doesn't take much, but I never did a demon before so I can't be sure. When we draw him out, exorcise him, the banishment language should control him at least a little. Plus, we have seven, and that's a good number."

"We have eleven with Beti and the boys," Susan pointed out.

"Even better," Monica agreed.

"I don't understand," Jason said.

Monica answered, "It's all about strength in numbers, coven is the traditional word, but we prefer a circle. It's really just a like-minded group of people who gather for a common purpose. In the old days, there were hierarchical organizations, Penthraig was for that kind of coven. He's the one that started ours, as a matter of fact."

"Ah, so that's how you and Robin were familiar to him."

"Yep, he was our leader back in the day, but that kind of organization is full of issues. Power struggles, ego battles, all kinds of problems that are the opposite of the kind of spirituality we want to practice. And Penthraig was too interested in sorcery, or dark arts. Back then he killed worms without remorse, for personal gain, and when he began to talk about the power potential of bigger living things, like dogs and cats, we broke away. He moved downtown and built his empire, right where we're standing, on the backs of living things of all kinds. We didn't know how bad it really was."

"Ok, so what do we do with the circle, in respect to the demon?" Jason asked as Francine used the stone knife to stab the finger of the last tainted guard. She milked a small stream of blood into her vial and Jason absentmindedly reached over to heal the tiny wound as Monica answered his question.

"We hold hands in a ring, around the orb if we can reach that far. Holding hands helps us bind our intent to our purpose, in this case to call out the demon and banish it to the realms. The energy flows around the ring and we can focus it into the center, at the demon."

"Ok then," Jason said. "I guess we better get busy. Let's see, how big is the brass circle in there?"

"Looks like about ten feet," Robin replied.

"And you set it high, so the bubble is sitting on top of the ring. The bisect line is up by three feet or so?"

"That sounds about right."

"So that gives us about a fourteen foot diameter bubble at the widest point. We need to add a couple feet for clearance so that gives us a diameter of sixteen feet. Let's see, sixteen times pi. We can use ten and that would give us thirty one point four, call it thirty two. Six times pi gives us about nineteen, call it twenty and add that to thirty two, that's fifty two. There are eleven of us, all over five feet, and since our arms are about the same as our height when we stretch them out, that gives us more than fifty five feet of circumference. All the guys are six feet or better, so add four to that, plus another three for the ladies who are five-six or over, and that gives us somewhere around sixty three feet of circumference fingertip to fingertip. We should be able to hold hands all the way around without any trouble."

"Whew, I'll take your word for it," Robin said.

"Is there a chant or something? And do we need to be able to touch him?" Jason asked.

"The chant is whatever the Goddess inspires, and it's possible that we'll need to touch him, but we can't take the circle down until we're sure we can contain him," Francine replied as she finished healing the chi of the last guard and sent him on his way.

"Getting in that circle with him could be very dangerous," Monica added. If we find that we need to touch the human body, even if he's unconscious, when we call the demon out, the demon won't be unconscious. He'll still be trapped in the circle if it's up, but he might have enough power to harm the human that he once possessed, and anybody else that's in there with him. The faster we can banish him, the less chance he'll have to harm anyone."

"Ok, so we have to knock him out again, just to get in there for the clearing of the human?" Jason asked.

"All we need to do is get the ayahuasca in there, until we see if that works. If we need to lay on hands, that will be a different kettle of fish," Francine replied. "We'll try the clearing from the outside first and see what happens, but we need the burning herbs in there to begin with."

"How about if Robin cuts a small hole with the little Japanese sword we saw in there?" Steve suggested. "I'm sure it's what Penthraig used as an athame, that thing is dripping with experience. It has an evil aura, I didn't even want to touch it, but Robin can use it to cut a window to toss the herbs in."

"I don't think so," Robin replied. "Even a small hole will be enough for a full demon to do something bad. He could even leave the human and escape through the hole if he was quick enough. What do you think Beti? You know more about demons than any of us."

"I agree that the demon is very dangerous, but he is limited in a physical body, and once liberated from a body, he would not be able to persist on this plane for a very long time. A matter of hours probably, but once he is free of the human, he can become a mist and slip through any crack. He can wield incredible power, more than what you experienced before, but I don't know if it is enough to overpower your defenses. There is nothing comparable to your shields in my experience. If he escapes, he will inhabit the first compatible host that he finds and will melt into the populace. Then he will strike you from concealment, en ambuscade. It is advisable to destroy him utterly. He will be back if you don't."

Francine hesitated for a moment while the group processed Beti's advice, and then offered, "Ok, we need to get the parameters established, so we should start the chant, and then on a key word Robin can take the bubble down. Whoever is behind him at the time can hit him with a needle to knock him out again. The demon seemed to be locked into the unconscious human when that happened the first time."

"Sounds good to me," Robin said. "I'm guessing that he'll face you while you offer the chant. We'll be on the other side of the circle so he can't see when I take the bubble down. And Jason, you can shoot him again."

"Ok, so what's the key word?" Francine wondered.

"You'll be the one chanting, so you can pick it yourself," Robin replied.

"Huh, let me see, something that wouldn't come out in the normal course of things, something nonsensical . . . how about abracadabra?"

"Works for me," Robin said."

"Abracadabra then," Jason agreed. "When you say it, Robin will drop the bubble, and I'll shoot him in the ass. Robin can reset the circle once he's down."

"OK, I should call upon the Goddess to get things ready, just in case. When that's done we'll have some protection and some time. That's when I'll say the key word. Monica, you can lead us in, widdershins around the circle, Robin and Jason need to be in the middle and I'll be on the end. That way when Monica gets all the way around, she'll meet up with me and you guys will be opposite."

"I mighta' made a little mistake," Sara demurred.

"What?" Monica asked, deadpan.

"I told the demon that Jason would be the one to fry his ass, so he'll probably be focused on him the whole time. Maybe he'll face Francine when she starts the chant, maybe not."

"Ok then, Robin and I will split to thirds and whoever is behind him when the bubble drops will be the one to shoot. Not you Amanda, not until you have some practice. I'm not sure what will happen if a needle passes through that thing and hits one of us."

"Got it, no problem," Amanda answered.

"I'm gonna' pop the bubble so maybe it should be me," Robin offered.

"Sounds good, there will be less hesitation because you'll know exactly when the bubble will fall. The rest of us will use up a split second between the drop and the shot. He who hesitates is lost, and all that," Jason agreed.

"Ok then. I'll drop the circle on abracadabra, Francine will make sure he faces away when she says it, and I'll shoot him at the same time. Then I'll reset the circle to make sure he's still trapped. Let's do it. I'll go third, and Jason will go seventh, of course," Robin summarized.

"Hold on a second," Jason said. "Beti, I've been thinking about your advice, and I'm not sure I'd know how to destroy the demon utterly. I had the impression that he would just return to the realms, like the imps, if we blasted him. How, exactly, would I destroy him?"

"The imps are lesser demons, and we can manifest a body, animal or human, but greater demons, like Alastor, cannot be contained in such a manifestation. They require a full flesh and blood host. If you destroy the human host, as you did Penthraig, the human spirit would go on to the next place, but the demon would simply be released into this plane. Your banishment by authority of the Goddess will send him back to the realms, but as I mentioned, he would be back eventually. To destroy him utterly, you need to wield the power of the gods, which I believe you already possess, and include the intent of his destruction in your strike. That will take the demon's spirit to the next place, from whence he cannot return."

"The next place?" Jason asked.

"The next place is that hidden realm from which none return. It is said that the gods and goddesses do not even know the details of the next place," Beti replied. "Humans share a concept of such a realm that they call heaven."

"Or hell, in that demon's case," Sara injected.

"The next place could be hell for some, I do not know, and not even the gods know such things. All is rumor and obscurity."

"Ok, then, let's get going. It's time to finish the job. Everybody open your second sight, just in case," Monica said and led the conga line. Robin stepped into the third spot and Jason the seventh, as was fitting. Francine followed and as soon as Monica opened the door, the demon began his tirade in a voice that sounded like raspy thunder.

"What the hell is this? It must be mother and her ducklings. Where is your famous champion? Oh, there he is; the one who thinks he has the power to slay dragons. I'll show you who has power little boy. You truly believe that your thirty years on this puny world can trump my millennia of experience?"

Jason did not respond, because he suspected that the demon's intent was to sow doubt. Jason stared and smiled as he followed Sara around the circle, with Beti barely a step behind, all of them hand in hand.

The demon saw the smile, and followed Jason around his third of the circle, "You're a cock-sure little prick aren't you? And I see you have a traitor in your midst, the imp Beti. What makes you believe that she won't throw you over the same way she did us; at the very instant things don't go her way? She will sell you out for her own pathetic surface existence, won't you Beti?" he asked, but she didn't respond.

"It's alright Beti, I understand that you must look out for yourself. That's what I would do, and that's what I want you to do. Help me, and when I am free, you will be rewarded most handsomely. If you don't, you'll eventually return to the realms, as all imps do, and I will make sure you are tortured for eons."

Beti simply stared at the demon while the circle closed hands around the bubble and Francine began, "Mother Hecate, Goddess of magic and the crossroads between temporal and spiritual realms, attend us as mediator and advocate of the righteous, holder of the keys of the gateway, and protector of the worthy. We beseech thee, blessed be."

Most of the members of the circle parroted the blessing, and the rest realized that they should do likewise.

Francine continued, "Mother Enodia, attend us, stand in the way, protect us at the entrance and the exit, we beseech thee. Blessed be." This time everybody, including Beti, followed in unison, "Blessed be."

The demon did not stand still; he stalked around the circle and examined each face in turn. Then he stopped close to the wall in front of Francine, "So, you think you can banish me before I slit your throat? Pathetic human, you will writhe in pain before the night is through. Even if it were possible for you to banish me before I can rip your heart from your chest, I will be back. I'll find another Penthraig, and I will sell my services to him as I have done countless times over a period that spans eons, and he will end the banishment. I will include in the pact that I shall have power to seek you out to destroy you. It is only a matter of time, and in the realms, time is meaningless."

"Big talk means little penis, that's what I think," Sara injected. "Why don't you shut your trap for a minute? We're gonna' fry your sorry ass either way, so just take a break for your last breaths in a human body."

When he turned to Sara, Francine said "Abracadabra," and the bubble popped. The demon hesitated as the pressure differential equalized and the swirling black and red ether boiled away. Alastor understood that the circle had been taken down, but his hesitance was long enough for Robin to fire a single needle into the center of his back.

The demon screamed and turned toward Robin, who re-set the circle in the time it took for him to spin. In all cases previous, when the demon or anyone tainted by his blood had been hit with a needle, they simply fell to the ground and writhed, but this time, the demon did not go down, he screamed and wrenched his torso so far that the group thought the human would snap in half. He tried to reach the needle in the sizzling wound, and while he screamed and twisted something odd happened. His demon spirit began to phase away from the human. The group gasped as the demon's upper body twisted away from the human's upper body, as if there were two beings branching off of one leggy tree trunk, and that's exactly what was happening.

The demon used his earlier experience to produce an opportunity to escape before the control of the silver needle overcame him, and before a banishment could be pronounced by the witches. He resisted the effects of the silver and was very near to success when Jason yelled, "Robin, take it down, shoot him again!"

Robin dropped the bubble and fired again. She hit the human body and it dropped, but too late, the demon separated in that same instant and manifested as an eight foot tall red skinned musclebound bull of a two legged beast with massive black-lacquered horns that pointed forward, the fangs of a saber toothed cat, talons for hands, and cloven hooves for feet.

Jason screamed "Wait," as Robin fired another needle that passed through the ethereal body of the demon without effect, and hit David in the shoulder. David screamed and went down while the demon laughed and gathered power in his hands. He fired searing flames at his attacker.

Robin spun away and dove to the ground in reflex but the plasma reflected off her personal bubble and set the sofa ablaze. Jason yelled for the wives to protect their husbands, who had no shields. The demon blazed plasma at random around the circle and everybody hit the deck, except for Sara, who stepped in front of her husband and stood ramrod straight while the waves of plasma broke around her as if she were the bow of a ship.

Susan and Francine dove on top of their husbands, Dave was already down. In the midst of all that, Beti phased to her bird form and took to the air, un-noticed by the demon.

"Robin! Reset the circle," Jason screamed and darted in to pull the human out. From somewhere in the back of his brain an idea formed and flew to the surface, he began a shamanic chant in the pure Adamic language, the first language of man, the language of the Gods and Goddesses before it was corrupted by scattered nations. He shouted at the demon to stay back and called upon the goddess to protect them, all in a language that he did not understand, a language that none of them had ever experienced.

The demon reacted with surprise and in fear of its power, having not heard the pure language for eternities, but he saw his chance for escape and leapt toward the door. He bounded out of the circle and over the head of Monica and Francine crouched prostrate on the floor on top of Steve.

At that moment Beti attacked, her talons raked the back of the demon's neck and left gaping, smoking wounds that caused the demon to stop and howl. He turned and fired more plasma but Beti was faster and she darted in an angular path that the demon could not track. The exit seemed his best option and he went for it, but what he did not see was the goddess Enodia herself standing sentinel at her post.

The demon approached the door at a run and Enodia stepped from the shadow of the frame in a back spin with her flaming Excalibur-like sword in a baseball swing at waist height on the demon. Her tresses and robe twirled out to produce the effect of a beautiful tornado. The blue flame sword arced scythe-like and sliced the demon in half. The ethereal blade pulled the ethereal body of the demon into wisps as if he had become a pillar of smoke, and he simply dissipated. Enodia curtsied to the group still lying on the floor around the circle and then she backed in reverence to her post at the door frame.

"Holy shit, did you see that?" Monica said to no one in particular. Exclamations rose with the group while Jason attended the injured human.

Dave held his left arm like a sling and said, "What about this?" He nodded toward the silver needle sticking in his shoulder, but Sara gave him no love for it.

"Pull it out and suck it up ya' big wuss," She said, and he did.

"Huh, barely even feel it now," Dave said. "But it hurt like hell when it went in. Felt like I got shot."

"Sorry sweetie," Robin offered.

"No problem Robin. I'm A-OK and this has been one helluva party. It's totally worth a sore shoulder."

Beti landed and phased to her naked human form next to Jason who continued to minister to the victim, but the group barely noticed as they moved cautiously toward the door.

When they gathered before the Goddess, Robin bowed her head, "Mother Enodia, we thank you for interceding on our behalf in our hour of need."

"No enemy of the seventh son shall pass when I am called to duty, and it is my honor to serve. Fear not for the demon is destroyed. He is now in the hands of the judges," Enodia offered.

"Blessed be," the group responded and then Enodia was gone.

The group returned to the circle where the human was sitting up. Jason and Beti kneeled at his side.

"He'll need a clearing, I'm afraid," Jason said to Francine.

"You boys quit staring at Beti and get that shriveled up dog in the furnace, and put mister demon host on the gurney for me," Francine directed. "Is your shoulder ok Dave?"

"Good to go, kinda feels like I got a tetanus booster or something."

Susan offered Beti's clothes to her and she pulled them on where she stood.

"Anybody got a lighter?" Francine asked as she picked up the bundle of herb from the concrete floor. "The ayahausca has gone out in all the excitement."

Jason walked over and lighted the stub of the remaining herb with a tiny column of fire from his index finger. Francine fanned the smoldering ayahuasca and said, "I guess you didn't use that during the battle for a reason."

"Yes, I knew somehow that the weapons we have are only effective in the physical realm. The demon wasn't physical once he left the human body, so there was no point in shooting. You saw what happened to Dave. Filling the place with fire would have been a very bad thing for the husbands and Beti. I guess we need to add something that will work on demons in spirit form."

"That flaming sword Enodia used looked pretty good," Amanda offered.

"Yeah, but I'd prefer a flaming machine gun or something that you don't need to get up so close to use," Sara added.

Jason stepped past Francine and doused the smoking sofa with water from his fingertips, apparently from the moisture in the very air. "Thank the goddess for flame retardant furniture," he added.

"You are welcome, Jason Patrick O'Hara, seventh son of seventh son," a disembodied female voice echoed through the chamber.

"Blessed be," the group said in unison.

Bill Awakes - 27

"Three days ago we were readin' tarot and rollin' dice, and now we're savin' the word and workin' with Goddesses. All I got from it was a bruise on my ass from that dough-head Penthraig when he knocked me down. Whaddaya-think-a-that, plain ol' Jason the vet?"

"I think you've got the makings of an interesting T-shirt, 'I vanquished a demon and all I got for it was this T-shirt and a bruise on my ass.'"

When the chuckles died down, Jason answered the question, "I think I'm amazed and exhausted."

Francine finished the clearing of the man who used to be known as Alastor.

"Where am I?" the man asked.

"More importantly, who are you?" Francine rejoined.

The man tried to sit up but Francine prevented him with a hand on his sternum, "Just lie back for a little while, until you get your bearings, and tell us who you are."

"My name is Bill Schmidt and I live in Evondale."

"Any family?"

"No, my wife passed away a couple years ago, cancer, and I've been alone since then, no kids. I have a brother in California but we barely speak anymore, nothing in common. He's a big time real estate developer and I'm just an inventory clerk at G.E. So where are we, and how did I get here?"

"Well, you're in the bowels of the night club Caleo, but how you got here is a good question. This is gonna' be a shock for you, but you've been possessed by a demon for at least the last couple of years," Francine replied. "Probably more like five or six."

"A demon! Oh god no, what did I do?" Bill covered his face with his hands and murmered, "No, no, no-no-no, what did I do?"

Beti stepped up to the gurney, pulled Bill's hands away from his face and asked, "Do you remember me?"

"You look kind of familiar, but I'd have to say no, I can't seem to place you at all."

"I suspect that you grieved your wife and dabbled in mysticism. Is that right?"

"Yes, I wanted to contact her. I read books, old books, and I tried to summon help from beyond with a séance. And I made contact with an ancient soul who said his name was Alastor. I was thrilled and amazed, and he said he could bring my wife, Barbara, but that he needed permission to meld our chi's, you know, like the old spiritualists. He would be my spirit guide. So I gave him permission, and that's the last thing I remember."

"Permission is a powerful thing, my friend, and he took advantage of you. He was my boss and has been running this place and doing all kinds of evil for years while you were dormant in your own body," Beti explained.

Bill burst into tears and recovered his face. The group left him for the moment and gathered around Jason.

"I wonder if he even has a home to go back to?" Francine whispered.

"It takes seven years to declare a death for a missing person; maybe he's been gone that long. It's been nine or ten years since we were with Penthraig. He didn't have the knowledge to make a deal with a demon back then, that's for sure," Monica said under the sobbing a few feet away.

"No, but once he was on his own, it probably didn't take too long to learn. I'm guessing he started using higher animals right away and probably grew his power exponentially," Susan added under her breath. "If Mr. Schmidt hasn't paid his mortgage in all that time, I'm sure his house and his stuff are gone. His brother probably had to get involved in all that, as next of kin, I guess."

"Well, what are we gonna' do with him?" Francine asked quietly. "We can't turn him loose like we did all the others. They all had places to go in the local area."

"The way I see it," Sara murmured and pointed to the door, "as far as anybody out there knows, he's still Alastor, and he still runs this place. I guess he has an apartment here and everything. He should just stay."

"Brilliant, Sara," Robin said and offered a fist bump, which Sara thumped with enthusiasm.

"Sounds like a perfect solution. Bill can run this place legit from now on, and the balance will be restored. No more demons, drugs or hookers, no more gambling. Just dancing and a little drinking, the kind of club anyone would like," Amanda summarized.

"Yeah, maybe they can go back to making beer down here, one of those micro-breweries," Steve added. "That would be a good use of the space. I could help with that."

"We could do a clearing on this whole building, and use the circle to jump the lines between here and our circle at the store," Francine interjected.

"Sounds great, but I'm exhausted. You guys do whatever you want, I'm going home to sleep for a week," Jason said and moved toward the door.

Robin hesitated but Jason waved her on, "Come on Robin, I have enough energy to take you home."

The rest of the team convinced Beti to take Bill to Alastor's apartment, since she knew where he lived, and Monica convinced her to ride home with her and Amanda instead of following Jason, as she wanted to do. Then the team filtered out past the dance floor above that still gyrated to the music as if nothing had happened below.

When Jason pulled into her driveway, Robin suggested that his lighthouse-to-the-passed home would be full of ghosts by now, and if he didn't want to deal with it that he could spend the night, and he did.

END

Turn the page for a preview of

Enchanted Emotions

book two of the Enchanted series.

Preview

Enchanted Emotions

Book Two of the Enchanted Series
By Barry Bonnell

Group Sex - 1

Jason O'Hara woke in dungeon-dark, unfamiliar surroundings and stumbled out of bed in need of the facilities. He bumped into what he would find out later was the dresser, and then stubbed his toe on the armoire. His muffled curse seemed to turn on a light, and then he remembered where he was, Robin's house.

"Out the door and across the hall," she said from her side of the bed. "No master suite with bath in this part of town," which was one of the older, late 40's ranch style developments of Milford, Ohio.

"Right, thanks," Jason said and hurried across the hall.

When he came back, he found Robin propped up on a couple pillows with the bedding pulled to her neck, her blond hair framed her face, and he tried to remember, *Did we do anything last night?*

He was still fully clothed, except for shoes, and figured that there was probably not a lot that had happened in that state of dress. Then the fog cleared. They had talked for a while in the driveway where Jason was supposed to drop her off, but he couldn't keep his eyes open. She suggested that he spend the night and he agreed through semi-consciousness. Robin had basically carried him into the house, because he was just too exhausted from the fight with the dark wizard Penthraig, and his minions, the succubus, and the demon, and from all the healings he'd performed down at the evil wizard's club, *Caleo*. Robin had pushed Jason into the bed and she swung his feet up, that's where she pulled off his shoes, and it's the last thing he remembered.

She had tucked him in, and then showered, night-gowned up, and slipped in beside him. He didn't know, but she kissed him on the cheek and fell asleep on his shoulder.

Now it was 4am on Sunday morning and he stood at the foot of the bed where Robin addressed his hesitation, "Why don't I turn off the light and you can get out of your pants and shirt and get back into bed. I promise to keep my hands to myself," she said and snapped the light off.

The sound of pants hitting the floor made her smile and when he scootched close, she put her head on his shoulder. He wrapped his arm around her and they listened to each other breath for a few moments, then he said, "You know, I was pretty much happy with my life three days ago, before I stumbled into your shop. I'd fallen into a routine, and I was comfortable with it, with life in general. I felt safe and content with things; worked with the pets at the office; and bangin' around in my workshop at home felt like the life of Riley. I did whatever I wanted and answered to nobody. I'd hang out with the guys once in a while, and I've been on a date or two, but the boat was on calm waters and I was happy to float along.

"Now I realize that I was just a passenger, not really alive, just drifting along with the routine. Then, something really odd happened to me when I walked into your shop, for the first time since my divorce, I was lonely. Before I walked into your store on Thursday I was content, and now I can't sit for ten minutes without thinking about you. I pine for you when we're apart, and can't wait to see you again. There's nothing calm about my life anymore and not because of the magic, well, partly because of that I guess, but it's mostly you."

Robin said nothing but tears ran down onto Jason's T-shirt so he pulled her in a little tighter, and continued, "I don't know how else to define it, I'm falling in love with you, Robin. Fell, is better. I'm suddenly completely unhappy and terribly lonely. I want to be with you all the time."

Robin sobbed and snuffled, "But there's something you need to know about me. . ."

"Oh God, I was afraid of that, you've bewitched me. It's all a spell, isn't it?"

Robin giggled through her sobs, "No Jason, I haven't spelled you. I do admit that when I wear my top-hat, it's got a little mojo on it, just to smooth out the wrinkles and boost things up here and there. It's nothing really. I wouldn't do such a thing as love-spell you."

"Whew, that's good to know. So what's the problem?"

Robin sobbed harder, "I'm just really unlucky at love, that's all."

"Unlucky, you're kidding. I'm feelin' a little insulted right now; you have a seventh son in your bed and you think that's unlucky."

"Well, I've been right here all night and you haven't even tried to touch me. I'd say that was pretty unlucky."

"So, you want to get lucky, huh? I'm thinkin' that's kind of guy's line, isn't it?"

"Oh shut up and kiss me," she said, so he did, and soon Jason was touching her all over the place.

They were just about to get even more personal when a voice broke into their heads, "*Ok guys, I've had enough,*" Monica shouted into their minds, and both of them nearly jumped out of their skin. "*You've got to get control of this psychic network thing before you sex-educate all of us. We're all on line now. I'm sorry, but there's nothing we can do about it until Jason teaches us how to block the passion vibes. It comes across like ya'll pushed a panic button and sirens are going off in my head. Not to mention the obvious. Hate to tell you, but we're all about to get laid at the same time. Not that I'd mind, but that kind of thing should be more private."*

"*Hi Rob, hi Jase,*" Sara called into their heads.

"*Hey guys, Steve says hello and he wishes he could hear too,*" Francine added.

"Oh no!" Robin shouted and ran from the bed with the sheets wrapped around her like a cocoon.

Jason laughed and shouted after her, "Now I get it, unlucky in love. I believe you now."

"Shut up knucklehead," she yelled back from the liquor cabinet where she poured a shot of Jack.

END

for now. . .

ABOUT THE AUTHOR

With a background in Journalism at Ohio State University, and careers in baseball, flying, healthcare, and his own import company, Barry Bonnell enjoys a very broad base of experience. As a writer he has found his skills useful in many disciplines both in business and for pleasure.

And he says, "I've found that in writing, business and pleasure is pretty much the same thing."

Miamiville and Milford, Ohio are home. Barry and Stefnie, his wife of 42 years and counting, have raised their family in the Seattle area...

...and they're still there.

MESSAGE FROM BARRY

Thanks dear readers, I hope you enjoyed Enchanted Notions. Book two of the Enchanted series is well on its way. Follow me on Facebook and Twitter, and visit BarryBonnell.com for updates...